P9-BZF-019

A. ALVAREZ

HUNT

SIMON AND SCHUSTER · NEW YORK

PUBLISHED BY SIMON & SCHUSTER

A DIVISION OF GULF & WESTERN CORPORATION

SIMON & SCHUSTER BUILDING

ROCKEFELLER CENTER

1230 AVENUE OF THE AMERICAS

NEW YORK, NEW YORK 10020

DESIGNED BY EVE METZ

MANUFACTURED IN THE UNITED STATES OF AMERICA

1 2 3 4 5 6 7 8 9 10

LIBRARY OF CONGRESS CATALOGING IN PUBLICATION DATA

ALVAREZ, ALFRED.

HUNT.

I. TITLE.

PZ4.A469HU   [PR6051.L9]   823'.9'14   78–16201

ISBN 0-671-24421-3

To Mo and Jacky Anthoine
and my sister Sally

The names and personal details of tens of thousands of people scrutinized by the Special Branch for reasons of national security are to be fed into a new criminal intelligence computer bought by Scotland Yard and shrouded in mystery.

When plans for the computer were drawn up two years ago it is understood that the Special Branch was allocated space on it for up to 600,000 names out of the system's total capacity of 1,300,000 names by 1985. The work would begin with the transfer of a much smaller number of records as a pilot project.

Yesterday a police source said that the Special Branch had yet to decide how many names would be placed on the computer and denied that anything like 600,000 names would eventually be filed.

The Times, 9 September 1977

He who desires but acts not breeds pestilence.
William Blake, *Proverbs of Hell*

1 CONRAD JESSUP, foxy mustache, sly melancholy eyes, sat over his beer and brooded: "Loves me, loves me not, loves me, loves me not." He sipped his beer, puffed his cigarette, and stared at his newspaper but did not take it in. Did not even take in the daily horoscope he usually paid so much attention to.

A rather high complexion and in the foxy brush of hair, russet and black, the first streaks of gray. Something heavy about him: about the paunch, about the mind. Heavy and uneasy. The beginnings of middle age.

At that time his dossier read: "Born 8 September 1940. Height 5 ft. 11 in. Weight 180 lbs. . . . Married Elizabeth (Betsy), *née* Armitage. Two sons . . ." Etcetera.

However.

However. Conrad also painted. Not passionately perhaps, but at least not prettily. With a certain clumsy conviction. He kept at it, too. Every Sunday, rain or shine, indoors or out.

The dossier mentioned that, but briefly, as if to imply he was merely a Sunday painter, just like all the rest.

It was a misjudgment on their part, one of many. They were invariably stronger on facts than on judgment. But because they seemed to know all the facts he thought they were invincible. And that was his misjudgment.

For example, he was like all the rest but more so. For

Conrad also painted four nights a week after dinner, shutting himself away in the attic while his wife watched television. There she sat, glued to the tube like a postage stamp, while he labored away under the roof with brushes and palette knife, shaping a life for himself, or trying to.

A year before, and for years before that, he had been home less and running harder in an altogether different direction. These details, too, were in the dossier: the names of the bookmakers, the sums involved, even the name of the collection agency which put the fear of God into him so effectively. But all that, apparently, was in the past, so his wife did not complain when he hid himself away after work and disappeared on Sundays. Anyway, she preferred the television, although she tried not to show this on Friday evenings and Saturdays when he grimly devoted himself to her and the kids. Buying himself peace, he called it, buying himself time.

The attic was low and cramped, with a single grimy skylight. But he had put up neon strips, boarded over the joists, and could pull up the aluminum ladder after him once he was through the trapdoor. Untouchable. The smooth, penetrating smell of oil paint worked on him like a drug. It seemed to reach far back into his head and turn off all the noise: office noise, marriage noise, the noise of the television.

Yet he had only married for a quiet life. A friend at work had said, "Take the plunge. She's a good girl, solid. She'll look after you. Marry her and put her behind you, then you'll have a base. It's what you need, it's what we all need." The friend, whose name was Horace, had married unsatisfactorily and too young, had a wife and three small children whom he scarcely saw, and at that time was methodically working his way through the girls in the typing pool. Solemnly almost, as though it were a life's work. Conrad appreciated the irony and recognized the salesman's pitch. But that's what they all were in those days. Hard sell or soft sell; it didn't matter which as long as it worked. So he took Horace's advice, as if there were a commission depending on it. Which may have been the case since, shortly after, Horace was promoted to the head of the sales department, whereas Conrad remained where he was, at the bottom of the heap.

But it was true, she was a good girl, devoted to him in her passive way and flaring up only occasionally when she thought he was taking her too much for granted. "What do you take me for? A piece of wallpaper?" Anger brought a brief shine to her cheeks, which in turn made her briefly attractive, since at heart he wasn't a bully. In the end, they both resigned themselves. It wasn't a bad marriage, as marriages go. She had even, in her vague fashion, stuck by him during his earlier troubles.

Even now the dossier on Betsy Belling, *née* Armitage, former wife of Conrad Jessup (*q.v.*), contains very little of interest.

So he sat drinking. The beer tasted sour and the froth tickled his foxy mustache. Yet there he sat, sipping, wiping, sipping, brooding. Not a bad marriage when all's said and done. Not too bad.

He doodled with a thick pencil down the edge of his newspaper, heavy confident physical lines: the curve of a hip, the curve of a breast, the curve of a cheek. Over and over. He began raptly to fill in the forms: groin, nipple, the delicate planes of the haunch and inside thigh. But he left the face blank. "Loves me, loves me not," went the voice in his head. There was no answer because there was nobody there to answer. He paused, his pencil poised above the paper, thinking: Fill in the face, anyway. Any face.

Instead, he drew a heavy mane of hair, loose over one shoulder, blotting out a breast. "Thy breasts are like two young roes that are twins. Thy neck is a tower of ivory; thine eyes are like the fishpools of Heshbon, by the gate of Bathrabbin." Christ, he thought, they did go on in those

11

days. He wondered what Heshbon was like now. A suburb, probably, patrolled by militia. Not that he would ever know.

He put down his pencil and took another swig of beer. The murky afternoon light of the pub, blurred with tobacco smoke, suited his mood. His skin seemed to ooze a little from the beer he had drunk. He felt fuddled and vaguely unquiet, consumed with idleness. He pictured his wife bustling around the house tidying things, slicing bread, slicing cake, making all ready, dreadfully ready, for the children's arrival from school. This filled him with obscure rage. He clenched his left fist so tightly that the nails left little half-moons in his palm. How she would love to get her hands on his studio and reduce it to paltry order. The thought of the chaos of squeezed paint tubes and clogged brushes, tins with no lids and filthy tattered rags gave him pleasure. So did the thought of the bulky padlock which dangled from the trapdoor. He wondered if it tantalized her as much as he hoped, as much as he intended. For a brief moment his idleness flared into something else: an intense desire to smash things—the padlock, his wife, the inept canvases scattered around the attic, even his un-demanding children. Undemanding because uninterested, unaware of his existence. Lay them all waste. His fist clenched tighter, then suddenly relaxed. Ho hum. He finished his beer.

But he was no longer tranquil. The humid, flickering light of his imaginings had come between him and the almost empty pub, spoiling his mood. He felt restless. He turned to the racing page of his newspaper and skimmed dis-consolately through the lists of runners. The margins were already black with squiggles and numbers, for Conrad still studied form and had his own private system of runes. But that day none of them looked right. Nothing had been going for him at the racetrack and he had been losing steadily for weeks. Steadily but discreetly. His wife was

12

convinced he had given up the horses, just as he had given up poker. Now the sight of his predictions depressed him. He had lost his touch, his magic. He was adrift. What he wanted was an outsider.

He wanted his luck back.

Form and reason had got him nowhere. It was time he tried instinct. Instinct and chance. Which was what the real artists he envied called inspiration.

So he skimmed the lists, looking for a name. Xanadu, Charlie's Girl, Sea Breeze, Tomtom, Thunderbird, Red Duster, Blue Chip. What names, what a world. Blue Chip by Gilt Edge out of Treasury Bond. Nothing for him, he thought, nothing at all.

Silver Arrow, Bendino, Young Hopeful, Artist's Moll, Rosamunda, Sarabande. He paused. Artist's Moll? Running in the 3:30, no history to speak of and not mentioned by any of the paper's three racing correspondents.

Artist's Moll. Fifty to one.

He thought of his wife mesmerized in front of the flickering, crashing television, and of the face whose details he could not fill in.

Why not?

A few doors up from the pub was a betting shop. The usual Irishmen lounged despondently, staring at the blackboards and the printed lists of runners. Conrad took a betting slip and opened his wallet. He had twenty-two pounds to last him until the end of the week and fifteen of that he owed to his wife. Fuck it, fuck her. He filled in the form and slid it under the grille, along with four five-pound notes. The cashier glanced up at him beadily, vaguely surprised, then his eyes went blank again and he handed back a receipt.

Conrad lingered in front of the blackboards, listening to the voice of the commentator trying to work up enthusiasm for the 2:30 at Newbury. "Rainbow Girl goes in front at the two furlong marker. Gray Streak is dropping back . . .

Rainbow Girl is lengthening her lead . . . Rainbow Girl blah blah . . . At the post it's Rainbow Girl by five lengths." Conrad looked at his paper. His own hunch, Blue Peter, had not even been mentioned. Rainbow Girl was seven to five on. It was a day for favorites. Mother of God, he thought, and I've just put twenty quid on a fifty-to-one long shot.

Back on the street he was filled with panic. Two pounds between him and Friday and nothing to speak of in the bank. I can't even buy paints, he thought. A week ruined for a gesture, for a passing dissatisfaction. After all, she's a good woman. What am I bitching about? The idea of having been so careless with himself filled him with gloom. A good woman. Good enough. Artist's Moll, for Christ's sake. There was no moll and he was no artist. Even if there were and he was, he was too old to bet on outsiders.

The day was sunny and windy, the air luminous. Birds were thrown about the sky under the flecks of hurrying cloud. A palette of silver, that's what he'd need. Like painting with light. And this added to his gloom because it reminded him of the thick, muddy canvases stacked in his attic. From up there in the clean bright sky he too would have looked like that: thick with resentment, muddy with self-pity, clumping heavily back to the office and the job which didn't pay him enough, a job he should have graduated from years before.

He said to himself: Concentrate, gather yourself together, lose weight, begin again. Then maybe you'll get your luck back.

The great glass doors of the office block swished together behind him like an indrawn breath.

2 SHE SAT ON THE EDGE of the bed, her hair hanging forward around her face. "It's getting me down," she announced.

Elizabeth sat at the dressing table with her back to her, watching her in the mirror. She shifted the bottles of perfume about like chessmen, selected one, unstoppered it, then put it back. "Just once more, darling. Just for me."

"Something's up." The girl shook her head fretfully. "They're getting terribly edgy."

"Of course they're edgy." Elizabeth leaned closer to the mirror and began to make up her eyes. "That sort of person always is. Being edgy is how they get their kicks."

"That's no reason why I should sit still for it."

Elizabeth put down her eye brush and turned to the girl, smiling. "No reason? Come now, love. You and your expensive tastes, Tim and his."

The girl flicked back her hair irritably. "Why do you take their side?"

"Not taking sides, darling. Just counseling patience. I have my responsibilities, too. A bargain is a bargain."

"That man Miller. Do something about him. Put him in his place. I don't have to eat the sort of crap he hands out."

Elizabeth smiled at her like a proud parent. "Quite frankly, convent girls aren't supposed to talk like that."

"Quite frankly, don't worry about how I talk. Worry about Miller."

"Maybe he fancies you."

"That's not part of the deal."

"As long as you remember there is a deal and you're part of it."

"It doesn't include taking his insolence."

"What did you expect, darling? Virginia Woolf? A little impertinence is a small enough price to pay."

"I'm the one who has to pay it, not you."

Elizabeth surveyed the girl bleakly in the mirror. "Pay? What do you know about paying? You're a taker, darling, one of God's little spenders. But sometimes the cash flow dries up. Mysteriously of course, just like it starts again mysteriously. Then you toss your pretty head and complain about the injustice of things and demand that your friends help you."

She paused and ran her tongue briefly over her lips. The girl on the bed began to fidget.

"Well, we do, don't we?" Elizabeth went on. "Only this time you're being asked to perform a small service in return. All in all, it's not much."

The girl stared at her in the silence that followed, then shook her head quickly as though trying to wake up. She went and stood behind the older woman and began to stroke her cheek tentatively with the tips of her fingers. "You know I'm grateful. Haven't I proved it?" Her voice rose slightly, then steadied. "But you don't understand: I'm frightened. Those awful men frighten me."

Elizabeth went on painting her eyes. She seemed to be having trouble extending the line from one corner and clicked her tongue irritably. Finally she said, "I don't know which I find more unattractive, your fear or your constant whining."

"*Please.*" The girl kissed the top of her head gently.

Elizabeth shrugged. "I'll do what I can. But it won't be much. Naturally, I have to be discreet."

"Naturally." The girl rubbed her cheek against Elizabeth's immaculate hair and smiled at their image in the mirror. "We make a fine pair," she said.

"Pair?" Elizabeth answered. "I suppose that's one way of putting it."

3 "SHE FOUGHT LIKE A TIGER," Duval was boasting, "all the way to the bedroom. Protesting her innocence. 'I'm not that sort of girl,' she kept saying. I kid you not. Stuff you just don't hear these days. It was like one of those old-fashioned blue movies. If I'd had a mustache, I'd have twirled it." He was small, wiry, and dark, with a hungry face.

"Makes a change," said Conrad.

"That's all very well, but you don't know what the result was."

"Don't tell us. Let us guess." Horace peered down over the top of his pint glass, smiling and fatherly. He had a powerful beer belly and a complexion like a stormy sunrise, red and purple; he ran the department like a dynamo. "She got pregnant?"

"Nothing so simple."

"She fell in love with you?" suggested Conrad. "Isn't that what they all do?"

Duval shook his head, paused, then announced in a hollow voice, "Crabs. She gave me crabs. 'I'm not that sort of girl,' she said, then gave me crabs. Try explaining that to your wife. Or to your family doctor."

"You should have used the company man," said Horace protectively. "That's what we pay him for."

"I'll know next time. If there is a next time. Which God forbid."

"You should have come to me." Horace sounded genuinely worried.

"What could you have done? Got me the powder wholesale or something?"

"Something."

"What's she called?" asked Conrad. "For future reference."

"Don't worry. She's left. And I've forgotten the name. Suppressed it, I suppose. It was one of those foreign handles. You know, Quasimodo. Something like that."

"I remember her," said Horace. "Pretty little girl."

"Pity about her back," said Conrad.

They finished their drinks. Duval said, "My round," and took the glasses.

Conrad watched him thoughtfully as he shouldered his way to the bar. "All that woman trouble. It makes me feel old. God knows how he keeps it up. Or why."

"Some people just like it that way," said Horace. "What about you?"

"What about me?"

"You seem preoccupied."

"Meaning my work's gone off?"

"Your work's fine. Meaning you seem preoccupied."

"Must be my age. The middle thirties are a preoccupying time. Or can't you remember?"

"Oh, I can remember. Just." He lit a cigarette and watched Conrad stealthily through the smoke. "You're not playing the horses again, are you?" His voice was concerned, faintly cajoling.

Conrad smiled deprecatingly. "Of course not. I've given them up. As you know perfectly well. Enough is enough."

"Just asking. You never can tell, can you?"

"No, you never can tell. But don't worry. It's the truth."

"I wouldn't like to see you in trouble again."

"That's nice. But I'm not in trouble, just preoccupied. It's age, not horses."

"I was only asking, you know."

"I know."

Duval came back with the drinks. Although the bar had begun to empty, the noise had increased, as though to ward off the hours of work and torpor which were to come. As usual on his third pint, Horace began to boom: "Did you hear the one about the milkman? He rings the bell at this house just before Christmas . . ."

It shows, Conrad was thinking. I have a secret and it shows.

"The lady of the house answers and says, 'Just the man I want to see. Come upstairs . . .'"

What is it, then, this thing that has happened to me?

"So she takes him up to her room and into bed. When they're finished he's putting his clothes back on and she . . ."

An instrument. An instrument for changing my life. Like a gun would be an instrument for changing someone else's.

". . . gives him a pound note. 'What's this for?' he asks . . ."

Then what am I waiting for? Christmas? The Second Coming?

"And she says, 'It's my husband's idea. I wanted to give you a fiver for Christmas . . .'"

Nude after nude, and all of them faceless. Sketch books, memo pads, the margins of business brochures and circulars. An endless wealth of women's bodies and not a face among them.

"'. . . but he said, "Fuck him, give him a quid."'"

The three men laughed. Horace loudest of all. He always applauded his own jokes. They drank more beer.

A face, Conrad thought. That's what I want. That's all I want. The rest is neither here nor there. Just the means to a face.

Aloud he said, "What do you think about the Second Coming?" His voice was slightly fuddled.

"Never heard it," said Horace. "Tell us the one about the second coming. Who was the lucky man?"

"I mean seriously. What do you think's the idea?"

"For God's sake"—Duval shrugged ostentatiously for Horace's benefit—"everyone knows what the idea is."

"But doesn't it strike you as a bit odd? I mean, people talk about it like . . ."

"Who talks about it?" Duval asked.

". . . like a second marriage. You know, 'We blew it once but maybe it will be better second time around.' "

"That's for sure, anyway," said Horace. "It may not be good, but at least it's bound to be better."

"That's not what I mean."

"What do you mean, then?" Duval asked.

"I'm not sure. But I just don't see why everyone has to think they'd do better if they got a second chance."

"They have to," said Horace. "It keeps them going."

"Who the hell cares, anyway?" asked Duval.

Conrad realized that he had lost the thread. "Well," he said lamely, "I just think it sounds funny, that's all."

"Ha, ha," said Duval.

"Use an ashtray," Horace told him sternly. "Don't grind your cigarettes into the goddamn Axminster."

The barman was huge and blue-jawed, but he wore a flowered shirt, tight black trousers, and a belt buckle the size of a dinnerplate. He began tinkling a little bell and intoning, "Time, gentlemen, please," in a pale, chirpy voice.

Conrad looked at him sourly. "Not lovable," he said. "We should use another pub."

Horace put a paternal arm around each man's shoulders. "Come on, Rembrandt. Come on, Kafka. Time to go back to work."

"Who's this Kafka?" Duval was petulant and slightly tipsy. "I always thought I looked like Dustin Hoffman."

"Ignorant bastard," said Horace affectionately. "Ignorant and vain."

4 THE FLOOR under the little rock overhang was level and sandy. He crawled in as usual with his dustpan and brush and sat up. At the back of the tiny cave was a brick wall darkened with soot like the back of a fireplace. The row of bricks below the rock roof was missing. That, he supposed, was where the smoke went, although there was no trace of a fire on the clean sand floor. He knelt in front of the wall, poked his brush up into the gap, and began to sweep away busily. Soot poured down, piling up on the floor in front of him. He brushed harder. Then the spiders began, small at first, but black as pitch and very active. He watched them scrabbling up the mound of soot, black on black, and brushed no more. Larger and larger spiders slithered out of the rift. He backed away until the tip of the overhang was pressing against his shoulders and waited for what he knew was coming.

But as usual, its arrival was swifter and more brutal than he was prepared for. It squeezed through the narrow gap and landed heavily but silently on the floor of the cave. King spider, the size of a young dog. Its many-faceted eyes took in everything at once, including Conrad pressed against the dipping rock roof. It too began to clamber up the mound of soot. He knew it was biding its time, waiting to attack, yet he did not move. To get out from under the overhang he would have had to bend his head and shoulders toward it and twist his legs beneath him. In doing this, he might lose his balance and lurch toward it, or at least make a sudden movement which would draw attention to himself. So he remained crouched on his knees, staring and stock-still, the soles of his feet pointing toward freedom.

He awoke shivering, staring with wide eyes at the black space between the wardrobe and the chest of drawers. Betsy lay with her back to him, her knees drawn up like a baby. She breathed slowly and deeply, as though she were breathing underwater, slow motion even in sleep. But re-assuring. He put his hand on the long swell of her hip and stroked the blanket gratefully. Nothing moved in the dark-ness. There were no spiders. He settled back against the pillows and studied the blue ink of the window. He felt vaguely ashamed that, at his age, the springs of terror still ran so pure.

Quietly, so as not to disturb his wife, he got out of bed, pulled jeans and sweater over his pajamas, and went out on to the landing, closing the door softly. He paused in the darkness, listening. Only the faint hum of the refrigerator downstairs and the creak of the dog's basket as the creature lifted its head to attend.

He switched on the landing light, climbed the aluminum ladder, unlocked the trapdoor, and clambered into the attic, pulling the ladder up behind him. Softly, he lowered the trapdoor again and switched on the lights. His pictures stared at him from around the room, muddy ominous shapes. Like the dream spiders, he thought, but without the power of dreams. Blackness without terror. Mere gloom.

Along one side of the room ran a battered, paint-daubed carpenter's bench, strewn with mess. He tugged at its single drawer, which opened part way, then jammed. He hit it with the heel of his hand, first one way, then the other, until something gave inside and he could open it all the way. From under an old sketch pad at the back he took a fat manila envelope. He pulled a stool up to the bench, cleared a space in the rubble, and as he had done every evening for a week, opened the envelope and began to count the twenty-pound notes.

There were still forty-five left and the sight of them filled him with awe. Artist's Moll at fifty to one. Twenty quid on the nose producing, after tax, nine hundred and thirty-three beautiful pounds and thirty-three pence. Threes and a multiple of three. Maybe there was magic in that. He understood that what had happened to him happens once in a lifetime. His solemnity increased.

He also understood why Horace was worrying about him again. Yet he had done nothing since the win. Neither blown the lot nor built it up while he was hot. Which was his usual recipe for disaster. Instead, the money seemed in some curious way to have killed off his desire to gamble. It was too big, too improbable. It was beyond luck. A sign. Something was about to happen in his life and he didn't know what.

Artist's Moll. He began to study his wife carefully over the dinner table: comfortable breasts, strong wrists, and distracted smile. Artist's Moll? At least she had a body he wanted to paint—rounded and assured, weighing plumb to the center of things. A body to rely on. It was her eyes that bothered him: hazel brown and friendly, they no longer quite seemed to see him. All those years of television had given them a high, impenetrable glaze, as though they had been simonized. When she looked at him, even on those rare occasions when she looked at him fondly, she never quite took him in; his image bounced off like raindrops.

So he didn't tell her about the win. Or, rather, he told her only enough to satisfy his conscience.

"Let's go out to dinner on Friday."

"You know we can't afford it."

"I didn't mean the Savoy. Just something local. To cheer us up."

"Then there's the baby-sitter."

"It's O.K. I won a little money on a horse."

She raised her hand defensively to the side of her face and winced as though he had slapped her. "Not again. I thought all that was over." Her voice lifted plaintively. "You promised."

"Don't worry. Just a one-off bet. Half a quid on a long shot. I fancied the name: Artist's Moll. All for you." He squeezed her waist fondly.

"Promise it was just half a quid?"

"How could I afford more?"

"How much did you win?"

"Twenty-five pounds. Less a bit of tax, of course."

"Oh," she said, her blank eyes round with surprise. "Those *are* long odds."

"All for you," he repeated. "A new dress and a meal. How about it?" He tried to kiss her but she turned her head aside.

"You shouldn't do it. Remember where it got us last time."

"I'm not *doing it*. What's wrong with a little flutter once in a blue moon?"

He wondered what brilliant intuition had stopped him telling her the truth. She wasn't ready for luck, still less for grace. Her life wasn't adapted to it.

"As long as it's only once in a blue moon," she said grudgingly.

So she took the money and bought herself a shapeless Indian dress in the summer sales. With what was left they ate Italian, then went home and made tipsy, garlicky love. And she appeared to forget all about it. Sex always made her forget things. Sex and television.

Yet afterwards she seemed unusually wary of him, watching him truculently at table and keeping away from him in bed. He took no notice and told himself she would get over it. The money seemed to have set a space between him and his old life. Or maybe it had simply made him indifferent. He wasn't sure which and didn't much care.

He ran his thumb speculatively across the edge of the bundle of notes as if it were a pack of cards. Waiting, waiting. He wanted a sign and all he got was spiders.

5 "TIM."

He grunted and opened his eyes reluctantly. Her eyes, inches from his, were wide and cold.

"Come with me, Tim."

He managed a ghoulish grin. "That, my sweet, is what I intend to do. Any moment now."

She shook her head to and fro on the pillow. "That's not what I mean."

Timothy went on smiling. "Later," he said, and closed his eyes again.

Later he said, "Where this time?"

"Hampstead Heath."

"God." Timothy grimaced. "The places they choose. I wouldn't even know how to get there."

"You know how to call a taxi. Surely you acquired that skill at Eton?"

"Among others."

"There's a party first at the Lazlos'."

"Those awful people. The truth is, I've never understood your taste for Hampstead Jews."

"Another truth is, you get on my nerves. You should try the awful people I'll have to meet later."

"I can't. As you know perfectly well. It just isn't on."

"Please." She pressed her side to his, took his hand, and squeezed it. "I'm scared."

"Why now, all of a sudden?"

"I think they know something."

"That's not possible."

"Anything's possible."

"What makes you think so?"

"Miller. He looks at me like I was"—she hesitated—"dead meat or something."

"Maybe that's how he looks at all women. What about the other one?"

"He does what Miller tells him."

Timothy sat up. Under the lamplight his bleak body was as pale as a fish's. "There can't be any trouble. They wouldn't risk it. They need you more than you need them."

"It doesn't feel that way."

When he did not answer she flicked her fingers imperiously and said, "At least you can roll me a joint."

He groped about for the tin, opened it, and said, "No papers."

She gestured toward the other side of the room. "On the mantelpiece."

He got up irritably. "You smoke too much."

"And spare me your advice. If you have my bloody welfare so much at heart, come with me tomorrow."

"Don't be absurd. Anyway, they're sending me to Brussels."

"How convenient. Every time it happens they send you to Brussels. Why Brussels of all places?"

"That's where it's all happening these days."

"I hate the lot of you."

He handed her the neatly rolled joint. "Quite right too," he said.

6 DUVAL WAS SAYING, "The only bird who ever made me come too fast turned out to be a lesbian." The *me* was heavily stressed, challenging.

"You Tarzan, me dike," said Conrad. "I always thought any girl could make that happen if she disliked you enough. But I suppose it's changed since my day."

"Boys, boys. It's not worth arguing about," said Horace. "My motto is: There's no such thing as an impotent man, only an incompetent woman."

"Which makes everyone happy, right?"

"Why so bitter?" asked Duval. "Surely happily married men like you don't have these problems?"

"Not having those problems doesn't mean we don't have problems. Right, Horace?"

"Right, sunshine."

Nevertheless Horace watched him beadily, trying to size up the next cloud on his horizon and wondering how it would affect his work.

Which was what Duval had intended.

It occurred to Conrad that they both thought he was gambling again. Perhaps the whole office thought the same and they were all watching him.

"I'm getting old," he said placatingly. "Sex talk has begun to bore me."

"So it should," said Horace. "In these secular times marriage is the only way of taking a vow of chastity." And he laughed his booming laugh.

Back in the office Conrad shuffled through the pile of papers on his desk and brooded. Betsy too thought he was gambling again. Which meant television and more sloppy recrimination if he stayed downstairs, or an empty canvas waiting to be filled in his studio.

Why not, he thought, since that's what they all think?

He picked up the telephone and dialed Herb's number.

"I thought you'd given up." Herb spoke urgently and fast, as if every moment might be his last. As usual, he made Conrad feel slow-witted.

"I did for a bit. I . . ."

"Wife trouble or money trouble?"

"Just trying to kick the habit."

"Poor thinking. There isn't enough pleasure around as it is. So if you like it, do it. Eat, drink, be merry, and play cards. That's my advice."

"What about women?"

"Them too. I'm a happy man."

"Funny, you don't sound happy."

"Be that as it may. You didn't phone to discuss my problems."

"I phoned to see if there's room for me at the game tonight."

"For you, any time."

When he called Betsy to say there was a client in town her voice was unsteady, as if she was on the verge of tears. He told her he would be late and rang off quickly.

But on his way to the game he remembered he had no money, so he turned and drove home, hurrying in with a great show of urgency. The television was blaring as usual. "Just got ten minutes to change," he called. The boys took no notice and Betsy glanced at him briefly and resentfully, gray-faced. Her eyes were puffy.

He changed his suit quickly, then went out on to the landing and stood listening. Tinny voices and tinnier applause from the television. He pulled down the ladder quietly, undid the padlock, and climbed into his studio. He tiptoed across to the bench, counted fifteen twenty-pound notes from the manila envelope, stuffed them into his wallet, then went back downstairs, padlocking the trap-door behind him again. When he kissed his wife's cheek she neither moved nor spoke. All the way to the game he kept touching the fat wallet in his breast pocket to remind himself of his luck.

It was as if he had never been away. The same faces around the same table under the shaded light, the same cigar smoke and the same ritualized language. Edgy, graying men, mostly overweight, with blue jaws and pouches under their eyes, trying to do each other down while preserving the illusion of bonhomie. A friendly game. Conrad took an empty seat and touched the wallet in his breast pocket superstitiously.

Maybe he would receive the sign here. Tonight. It was a better place than most for signs.

There was a new player at the table, an excessively large man whose name was Abe.

"Our New York connection," said Herb.

"I'm the token Yank," said Abe, "the proof that they're liberal."

He had the shoulders of an athlete, but his body was now encased in fat, like an insulated boiler. Conrad wondered from what heights he had fallen to land slumped in a seat at this particular poker table. But he handled the pack like a professional, precisely, economically.

The cards went around. Conrad felt his tensions slowly dissolve in the rhythm of the game, the concentration, the little stir of excitement at each new deal. Even the monotony of waiting was pleasure of a kind. Here, at least, he knew what he was waiting for.

I'm still a gambler, he thought. What else is there?

After a while he said, "It's nice to be back."

"Didn't I tell you?" Herb passed him the pack. "Your deal."

"You told me." He shuffled and passed the cards to Abe to cut. "What's nice is, nothing's changed. You're still saying the same old things deal after deal."

"So?" said Abe.

"So it's comforting. Like mass to a Catholic."

"Jewish mass," said Herb.

Abe said, "The difference is, you don't know what the cards are going to say. Deal 'em."

Conrad dealt. "Mine says ace. Must bet a pound. Never disgrace an ace, as the prayerbook says."

He picked up his hole card, leaned back, and looked at it. Another ace. He leaned forward again carefully and glanced around the table. Next to him George folded a seven, Pat called with a king, Herb folded a three, Paul called with an eight.

Abe was showing a ten. "Make it two pounds," he said.

Conrad pretended to hesitate, stroked his mustache, and looked hard at the cards around the table. Then he called the bet, trying to seem nervous. Pat went through the same performance. Paul folded.

Conrad dealt again: four to Pat, seven to Abe, ten to himself.

"Your ten," he said to Abe, according to the ritual.

"Check."

"Check," said Pat.

"Five pounds," said Abe.

Feigning hesitation again, Conrad pushed in a five-pound chip.

Pat leaned on the table and shifted his large buttocks in his chair as though preparing to stand. "Let's separate the men from the boys," he said. "Your five with another ten." He leaned back again, looking pleased with himself.

Abe pondered, eyed each player in turn, meditatively, as though measuring them for something, then turned his cards over. "You two tigers fight it out without me."

"Whatever you say," said Conrad. "Your ten and raise you twenty." He watched the smile freeze on Pat's blunt, grayish face.

There was a long silence while Pat studied the cards and the pile of chips in front of Conrad. Finally he said, "Hell, why not?" and threw in two red chips.

"*Meshuggah*," said Herb.

"Dumb Irish," said George.

"Just proves they're not ready for self-government," said Paul.

Conrad dealt again: a seven to Pat, a four to himself. "Your four," he said, and pushed the rest of his chips forward. "All in."

"How much is there?" asked Pat.

"Twenty-eight pounds." Conrad fixed his eyes on a spot on the baize halfway between his cards and the loose pile of chips in the center of the table.

"Well," said Pat, "it lays me odds, doesn't it? Twenty-eight to win a hundred and something. Nearly four to one."

"You have to win it first," said Herb.

Conrad kept his eyes down and said nothing.

Pat brooded, picking up a handful of his chips and letting them fall again. A clock ticked. "Cli-cli-cli-cli-click" went the chips. Finally he said, "You need the case ten. I need the case seven, we both need a four. It's worth a little wager."

Abe rolled his eyes to heaven, Herb shrugged, George lit a cigarette and said, "Easy come, easy go."

"What the hell," said Pat at last. "It's only money."

"Plastic," said Paul. "It's only plastic."

"That's right, fella. Only plastic." Pat pushed in the chips, then turned over his hole card to show his second king. "Hit me," he said.

"You're losing so far," said Conrad, and turned over his ace in the hole.

He dealt the cards: he gave the last seven in the pack to Pat, a deuce to himself.

"Luck of the Irish," said Pat contentedly.

Conrad stared at the fourth seven. With luck like that there was nothing to say.

Abe was the first to speak. "You shouldn't have been in the hand." He sounded indignant, as if he had been the loser.

"That's what they always say." Pat stacked his chips smugly, color by color.

Herb took up the attack. "Crazy. You knew he had aces wired."

"Not crazy." Now it was Pat who was indignant. "I'm a gambler, for Christ's sake."

"That's not what the game's about."

"I won, didn't I? *That's* what the game's about." He went on piling his chips neatly, but his bluff Irish eye was truculent and his voice aggrieved. It was about winning, but it was also about bonhomie, about being one of the boys, about being one with the boys. "God knows," he muttered, "I've paid enough for my luck in the past."

"Don't complain," said Herb. "Not that I could deny that."

"What?"

"That you've paid in the past."

"Thanks," said Pat. "The last of the humanists."

Abe addressed the shaded lamp over the table, as though there were answers up there in the smoke: "How do you play with such *meshuggenahs?*"

"By the book," said Conrad. They all knew what the real grievance was: not winning—that, as the Irishman said, is what the game's about—but winning unaesthetically, spoiling the symmetry of the occasion.

He took out his wallet. "Give me another hundred."

Herb counted out the chips and said, "Better luck with that lot."

"Luck? Who said poker's about luck?"

"Pat did."

Conrad cut the pack George handed him and said, "Let's play cards."

A couple of deals later he folded early and went out to the bathroom. His hands were unsteady and little pins of anxiety were prickling in his stomach. He lowered the cover of the lavatory and sat for a while with his head bowed, his hands under his thighs, staring at the tiled floor. The tiles were Spanish, with ornamental loops and brackets and a little flourish in the center, like a nose. His wife's accusing face emerged briefly at his feet, then vanished.

He shook his head and stood up. "Right," he said out loud.

He rinsed his face in cold water, rubbed it vigorously with a towel, and looked at himself in the mirror. Self-control, he told his image. Forget about luck. He combed his hair and went back to the game.

But the cards were not running for him. For two hours he sat, head bowed, watching, waiting, folding hand after hand. Middle cards—sevens, eights, nines—nothing pairing, nothing flushing, nothing straightening, and the wild cards —when they played them—never hit him. He dribbled a little money away in antes and an occasional compulsory bet, and stayed in once all the way on a high-low deal only to be outdrawn on the last card. After a couple of hours he had lost twenty of his second hundred pounds.

He told himself it could be worse, he told himself that at least he hadn't lost his discipline after all these months away, he told himself that, anyway, it was a pleasure to be playing again, that the rhythm and concentration were their own rewards and he was still controlled enough not to be seduced by them. He tried not to think about his wife or the empty canvas in his attic, nor about the office and the plots that were hatching there. Yet somehow, at the back of his mind, the troubles waiting for him outside seemed obscurely connected with his bad cards. Maybe the gods really had left him. He could think of no good reason why they shouldn't. So he concentrated on the cards, feeling that if he relaxed and let his mind wander he would drop into the black hole at his feet and never surface again.

The game droned on, the money moved around the table. The American was winning discreetly but only the Irishman was hot, following his streak, drawing miracle card after card and bucking the odds. He drank and talked encouragingly to the other players and smiled a great deal, his waxy face damp with pleasure. He took money off Paul, who let himself be charmed by the smile, the loose boozy manner, and his own uncertain cards. The others waited out the storm and took only what they were sure of.

Then slowly Conrad's luck began to turn. In seven-card stud he played kings-up nervously to the end and they were good. A few hands later he was dealt a pair of deuces in the hole and a deuce up. He raised early to make it expensive, not wanting to be outdrawn, and everyone saw him. But after two more cards his hand had not improved while Herb showed three clubs and Abe a nine, ten, jack. When Herb bet only Abe and Conrad saw him.

Paul flipped out the cards: "Four clubs, queen to the straight, a pair of sevens. The pair bets."

Conrad looked anxiously at the other hands and checked. Herb bet ten pounds and Abe, after a long pause, saw him. Conrad also took his time and finally threw in his chips, grumbling, "You boys can't have them all the time."

Paul dealt the last card facedown. Conrad checked again without looking at it and Herb immediately bet twenty pounds.

Abe stared mournfully at the four-flush, then at the pair

of sevens, his large soft body perfectly still. At last he said, "I've gotta believe you," and turned over his cards.

Conrad shuffled his three hole cards together, then drummed his fingers on the table irritably. "I don't," he said loudly. "See the twenty and set myself in."

Herb smiled. "How much is that?"

"Another forty," said Conrad belligerently. "Is that too much for you?"

"Pity you don't have more." Herb counted out the chips into the center.

Conrad smiled, not in triumph but with the pleasure of feeling the tensions dissolve in his stomach. "Too true." He turned over his two hidden deuces. "Full house, deuces over."

Herb swore obscurely in Yiddish.

"I was lucky," Conrad lied, "I caught it on the last card."

He counted his chips as he piled them: one hundred and ninety-five pounds. A fiver for an evening's entertainment. Cheaper than the cinema and a pizza.

He relaxed in his chair. His blood seemed to be flowing more easily, the ache behind his eyes had gone. Careful, he told himself, it can go away again as quickly as it came.

He lost a little on the next pot, then won again twice, small amounts, with everyone except Pat folding early.

The clock struck two.

"Last round," said Herb. "Comes the dawn and duty calls. Or rather, comes seven forty-five."

"Now you tell us," said Abe. He took the cards and began to shuffle them quickly and delicately in his hairy hands. "Five-card stud," he announced. "A little classical poker to round off the evening."

Conrad sat back in his chair, watching the cards go around. He was ahead now and had proved what he had come to prove: that his luck hadn't altogether vanished and that he could control his depression when things went

37

sour. All in all, it had been a good evening. The deal circulated without even tempting him to play.

As Abe shuffled the pack for the final deal, he glanced at Conrad and something seemed to flicker in his dark mournful eyes. Amusement? Malice?

Now you see it, now you don't.

The big man set the pack on the table for Pat to cut, then dealt swiftly.

Conrad's up card was a four. He lifted the corner of his hole card, expecting the usual rubbish, and saw another four. He straightened his back and looked around the table. Deuce, jack, queen, ace, another deuce. When Pat bet his ace, Abe and George folded their deuces and the others came in warily.

Abe dealt again, intoning, "A four to the four, seven to the jack, ten to the queen, another four to the ace. Pair of fours bets."

When Pat received his four Conrad looked at it hard and checked, trying to seem nervous. Herb and Paul checked after him. The Irishman bet ten pounds vigorously.

Conrad studied his hand a long time, then saw the bet reluctantly. The other two did the same. Again Abe flipped out the cards: "King to the fours, nine to the jack, trey to the queen, deuce to the ace-four."

Conrad picked up his chips, hesitated, then said, "Check."

"Check."

"Check."

"Twenty-five pounds," said Pat.

Conrad fiddled with his chips again, hesitated again, then saw the bet cautiously. The other two folded.

"Just the two tigers left," said Abe, according to the ritual, and dealt for the last time. "Eight to the pair of fours with the king, pair of deuces to the ace-four."

"Check," said Conrad immediately.

Pat settled contentedly in his chair and twinkled his bluff blue eyes at him. "So you were trying to do a Pat

O'Gorman, Con, me boy? Didn't you know it only works for the Irish?"

Conrad said nothing. He didn't trust his voice.

Pat was enjoying himself. "Let's have a little wager, shall we? What do you say to fifty quid?"

Conrad smiled at him at last. "All right, see your fifty . . ."

"So you did pair your king?" Pat was also smiling.

". . . and set myself in," Conrad finished and pushed the rest of his chips into the center.

The table went silent.

"Bugger me," said Pat.

He looked at Conrad's cards carefully, then appealed to the other players. "It's kings-up. It must be kings-up and he's trying to buy the pot. I've got one of his fours. And if he'd had three of them he'd have raised earlier, right?" He brooded again over the cards, talking to himself. "He doesn't believe me. The stupid sod doesn't believe me. Aren't I right?"

Nobody answered.

Pat went on, "Well, aces-up beats kings-up any day of the week. How much is the bet?"

"A hundred and thirty pounds." In his excitement Conrad's voice cracked slightly, so he sounded nervous.

Pat took this as a sign. Immediately, he picked up his chips and began counting them into the center. When he had finished he flipped over his ace in the hole and said aggressively, "Beat that."

Conrad smiled sympathetically. "Sorry," he said, and turned over his third four.

Pat stared at the card as though he had never seen one before. "Jesus, Mary, and Joseph. You had 'em all along."

"That's how it is. You win a few, you lose a few. You do it to me, I do it to you."

"But more expensively." Suddenly Pat laughed and spread out his hands. "Well, I said I was a gambler. This time I lost."

39

"Right," said Abe. "This time you lost." He and Herb nodded to each other sagely. Honor had been restored to the game, aesthetics vindicated.

They wandered out into the silent suburban street. The night sky was vaguely orange against the roofs, with puffy clouds hurrying over.

"Poor old Pat," Abe opened his car door. "You really sneaked up on him in that last hand."

"Just lucky," said Conrad carefully, thinking: What's in it for you?

"Who are you trying to kid?"

They both laughed uneasily.

"Look," Conrad began, "did you . . ." Then he stopped.

"Did I what?"

"Win?"

"I made out O.K." Abe climbed into his car and lowered the window. "You play a neat game of cards," he said. "Maybe you and I can do some business together."

"I don't know what kind of business you're in."

"Business. Making money. That sort of thing. You seem like a guy with a certain temperament. Perhaps we could be useful to each other."

Conrad was glad it was too dark to see the other man's face. He was blushing with pleasure. Just like a small boy.

"I'll call you sometime," said Abe, then drove away.

7 THE DOG WAS WAITING in the hall as usual, pleading with adoring eyes for a final stroll down the road. Conrad opened the door of the sitting room and stood sniffing. The air was heavy with a staling, pungent, unfamiliar smell and the cushions on the sofa were rumpled. One of them hung halfway to the floor.

"What the hell?"

His wife didn't smoke Gauloises. He picked up the fallen cushion and stood with it in his hand, staring at one of his muddy paintings over the fireplace. Then he went out into the kitchen. There were two whiskey glasses among the plates and cups on the drying rack.

She can't have a lover, she's got the television. Then he realized that he knew nothing at all of her daytime life and was simply assuming that because he was faithful, she must be too. That was the way the Irishman's mind had worked on the last deal: he had two pairs, therefore Conrad had the same. Look where it had got him.

"Bugger me," said Conrad, just as Pat had done.

When he opened the front door Kim shot out into the darkness, wagging its tail with delight, and peed three times on the weary privet hedge. Conrad sauntered after it. The night seemed darker and colder, gathering itself together before dawn. He looked at his watch: three o'clock and a new date. It seemed unthinkable that another day should already be stretching before him when the old one was still not done.

Betsy with a lover? That also was unthinkable.

The dog bounced ostentatiously in front of him, forelegs down, hindlegs up, as if penning a sheep the size of a dinosaur.

"What are you getting so worked up about?" he muttered. At this dead void hour its enthusiasm seemed offensive. The animal caught his sour eye and immediately ran on ahead, pretending to have remembered something urgent.

At the end of the road it paused and waited for Conrad to catch up. He stopped, about to turn for home, then looked at the creature's adoring, hopeful face, shrugged, and walked on. His mind was still churning confusedly away, replaying the evening's hands, thinking about his wife.

The streets were empty and there was no sign of the dawn.

If she was on to his gambling, she would want her revenge. But how could she have acted so fast? Where could she have found the initiative? The energy? The desire? Their mutual friends were all married, the husbands had office jobs. Who did she know? Who had the time?

He stopped short.

Of course.

It had been a woman, not a man. She had complained, she had wept, she had drunk too much whiskey and been sympathized with. Then she had gone to bed, tearful, tipsy and consoled.

Of course.

At the poker table he had to think the worst of everyone in order to survive. With Betsy it didn't apply.

He felt suddenly grateful to her. Grateful and fond.

He walked on slowly, enjoying the stillness and silence and darkness, feeling his mind unclench.

The dog was lying flat, its jaw pressed to the ground, waiting for a sign. Across the main road the lights faded into blackness and the air was suddenly chill. The Heath opened like a great cold mouth. It seemed to be waiting for him.

The dog was in a trance of expectation, nose quivering, already smelling the grass and leaves and patches of rank mud.

Why not? he thought. A pleasure for Kim, peace and quiet for me. It's years since I've seen the dawn come up.

He bent down and slipped the lead through the dog's collar. Immediately, the creature was up and straining forward. Conrad cuffed him and said, "Walk properly."

They crossed the road and paused under the last of the streetlights while he let the dog go. It shot off in a wide arc, sniffing the ground ecstatically, tail going like a fan, came bouncing back to Conrad hoping for a stick, then shot off again into the darkness.

After fifty yards the faint glow from the streetlamps vanished and the gloom was impenetrable. The only sound was the crunch of Conrad's feet on the gravel and the dog rustling somewhere ahead. The details of the night's game faded in his head and he began to feel tired.

At the bottom of the hill the air was damp and cold as the gullet of a shark. He shivered violently and stopped. At once, Kim came bouncing up to him and waited, looking up at him with emotional eyes. He stooped and patted the dog's head.

"I was like you once," he told it. "But you won't get over it."

He shivered again and walked on. It was unnatural that a summer night should be so cold. Even the dog seemed subdued at last and trotted docilely in front of him, tail down, nose sharp, wolfish.

He thought he heard a faint sound in the darkness ahead. He paused and the dog paused with him. A breeze moved briefly through the leaves, disturbing the stillness. Dawn, apparently, had been mysteriously delayed.

"Too bad," he said aloud and turned for home.

"Bastard." The voice was thin and came from a distance. Then: "Stop." Higher, ragged, tailing off.

Then a faint cry.

Kim barked and Conrad turned back in the direction of the sound. They both stood listening. The dog's head was cocked, its ears up and nose twitching.

Nothing.

The breeze moved again in the trees, the cold tightened its grip.

Off to the right a vague dark stain of gray was spreading upward into the night sky. Conrad realized that dawn was finally coming and this made him obscurely satisfied, as though he had completed an important task. He walked hesitantly in the direction of the sound. He felt curious and also faintly irritated that he hadn't, after all, had the park to himself. The dog moved attentively in front of him, then barked and dashed forward excitedly, disappearing into the darkness. Conrad heard steps running on the gravel path ahead, going right toward the trees above which the sky was beginning, with infinite slowness, to pale. Then there was silence again. Whoever it was must have taken to the grass.

The dog reappeared, wagging its tail and pleased with its daring.

When Conrad reached the point where the main paths crossed he stopped again and stood listening.

Silence.

He turned left toward where the sound had come from. Kim moved busily ahead, sniffing the ground. Suddenly, it disappeared into the bushes on the right of the path. Conrad followed it.

The long grass was soft under his feet and a bramble caught his trouser leg. He jerked it free and stumbled over the dog. The animal was sniffing at a long pale shape on the ground. Conrad bent down, reached out, and touched it tentatively with the tips of his fingers.

Warm.

His hand pulled back of its own accord, as if burned.

He squatted down, holding his breath, listening.

Only the sound of the dog panting beside him and the blood hammering in his ears.

He began to sweat heavily. Kim went on sniffing in a puzzled way.

He fumbled for his lighter, clicked it three times, then shook it angrily and blew into it. He clicked it again and this time it lit. In the small, flickering light he saw a pair of summer shoes in soft leather and long, elegant legs.

He clicked the lighter off and stood up quickly. He felt guilty, as if he had been caught prying. Then he flicked the lighter on and bent down again. The body was lying as it had fallen, head in the bushes, legs sticking out into the grass. There had been no attempt at concealment.

I must have disturbed him, he thought. Then he remembered the whiskey glasses in the kitchen and added, for luck: Or her.

The girl's dress was rumpled up, exposing her thighs. Her shawl had slipped down her back and spread out on either side of her like wings. She wore a silk scarf loosely knotted around her neck. The scarf and one shoulder of her dress were sticky with blood which oozed slowly from the side of her head. Conrad looked at her in the unsteady light. She was young and fine-boned, with long eyes which curved unexpectedly up at the corners and a soft, slightly goatish mouth. Despite the mess in her blond hair, her face was peaceful and faintly quizzical. An expensive young lady, not easily surprised and not of his world. The kind seen from a distance going into smart restaurants or somewhere fashionable in the sun with men always a bit too old for her. She seemed absurdly out of place on Hampstead Heath at this dead hour. Also absurdly overdressed.

He touched the wound on her head and felt the blood moving sluggishly. He couldn't hear her breathing. When he put his hand on her dress to feel her heart he registered only that her breasts were firm and full. He pulled his hand away quickly, shocked by his triviality, flicked off his lighter, and squatted down again in the dark, wondering if he was hallucinating.

He reached out carefully and touched her side. The smooth, silky material of her dress felt faintly electric to his fingers. Sweat trickled down from behind his ears into his collar.

He snapped on his lighter for a last look. Her open handbag was lying off to one side, but he was afraid to touch it. On one corner of her shawl was a gold label: "Olivia's. Knightsbridge."

His fingers were sticky from where he had touched her head. He wiped them on the grass, then began to run cumbersomely toward home. Kim dashed ahead, barking idiotically with delight. As he lumbered vengefully after it, he tried to shout "Shut up," but his breath rasped in his throat and only a twisted noise came out. On the uphill slope back to the main road he slowed gradually to a walk. His legs ached, his throat felt like sandpaper. "I smoke too much," he muttered, then remembered he had other troubles now.

Ahead of him, the streetlamps were still bright in the graying air. Twenty yards short of the road he saw headlights sweeping around the curve of the hill. Without thinking, he moved behind a tree. A refrigerated lorry racketed past, bound for one of the markets. Billingsgate. Nine Elms. Smithfield.

Her attacker must be off the heath now, walking under the sodium glare beyond South End Green. Or perhaps he had circled around toward the ponds on the edge of Highgate. Or doubled back the way they had come to a car parked near the Whitestone Pond. Unlikely. They were deep into the heath, too deep for a stroll. They must have been walking across. Going somewhere. Anyway, who takes a stroll at this hour?

I do.

He crossed the main road on to the side streets that led toward home, Kim trotting quietly by his side. A single bird cheeped drowsily, then was silent. He walked slowly, trying to look casual and nonchalant, a respectable insomniac enjoying the dawn air with his dog. But the sweat poured down his face and his breath still hurt. It seemed a long way yet to the security of his front door locked behind him on an unstable world. He walked faster. The thought of Betsy and the children quietly sleeping made him suddenly affectionate and yearning.

Why me?

But when he saw the telephone kiosk shedding its dull light in the gloom he remembered there was a girl out there on the Heath with blood in her hair. Someone should be told. But if he telephoned from home they might be able to trace the call.

He looked carefully up and down the street. Nothing moved. A bird cheeped again and another answered uncertainly. He pulled open the heavy door and dialed 999. The dog sat outside the kiosk watching him, head cocked, tongue lolling from the side of its mouth.

The operator answered immediately, but when he asked for the local police the station phone rang several times.

Hang up while you've got the chance.

Go.

Then he heard, "Hampstead police." The voice at the other end was bored and heavy.

Hang up.

Let it be.

Go.

Instead, he said, "Someone's been hurt on the Heath. A girl." He gave the details, trying to sound cool and factual.

47

But his voice kept running out of control. He tripped over words and had to repeat himself. He was trembling and the receiver was so slippery with sweat he was afraid he would drop it. He stumbled finally to a close, feeling he had been talking for hours.

"May I have your name and address, sir?" The voice was alert now and guarded.

Conrad hung up.

As he pushed open the kiosk door the dog gave a short welcoming bark. Conrad swore at it and saw a postman cycling past on his way to work. The man was looking at him. He seemed surprised.

Conrad turned and walked quickly away.

"That's torn it," he muttered.

He felt cold and tired. His damp shirt was chill against his back and he could smell his own sweat.

"Unclean," he said.

It occurred to him that he had never really been in trouble before.

Not real trouble.

Whatever Betsy believed.

8 THE MEN WERE TAKING the furniture away again. She stood in the hall and wept, but they took no notice of her. As they pushed past with the television set, she saw that one of them had her doll under his arm. It was a large doll which closed its eyes and cried when you tilted it. It was crying now.

She tried to grab it from them but her arms were too heavy to move. When she spoke her voice came out like a child's.

"My daddy gave me that."

The men glanced at her contemptuously and slammed the door in her face.

She woke to find Conrad standing by the bed, staring down at her. She was so relieved to see him that she started to smile. Then she remembered she had a grudge against him. She moved her head irritably on the pillow, the smile faded.

There was something scary about the way he loomed over her. Her first thought was that he was going to attack her, then that he wanted to fuck her. Which frightened her even more. But when he did not move or speak she looked at him more calmly. He was sweating and his clothes were askew. Behind him the window was already pale.

She rolled over and peered at the alarm clock. Past four.

"What sort of a time is this to come home?"

"Listen, darling. I've just . . ."

"Where've you been, anyway? Who've you been with?"

He turned his back and began to undress. "Forget it," he said.

Immediately she was sorry. She watched him move dully about the room in the gray light, hanging up his suit in the wardrobe, dumping his clothes one by one in the laundry basket. Shirt, socks, underpants: a separate journey across the room for each.

Something odd about him. The room was filled with the sharp smell of his sweat.

When he went out to the bathroom she lay wondering how she could say "Sorry" without appearing to apologize. She was still trying to work this out when he came back in, climbed into bed, turned his back on her, and almost instantly began to snore.

She listened to the sparrows chirping in the trees outside. Something odd about him.

Something wrong.

Again.

She knew she should be sorry for him, but all she felt was impatience which suddenly turned, as she remembered her dream, to blazing anger.

This was not an emotion she was used to and she contemplated it with surprise, almost with wonder.

Then she drifted slowly back to sleep while the outraged voices in her head mingled with the birdsong and the first faint sounds of the wakening city.

9 CONRAD WOKE RELUCTANTLY and left without speaking to her. As usual, the news on the car radio was all bad. Another bombing in central London, another splinter group from another obscure revolutionary party holding another group of hostages in a bank, another multiple pileup on the M1, another shutdown at British Leyland. In short, the mixture as before. There was no mention of the girl on the Heath.

Conrad switched to the music program and thought about nothing while Mozart filled the car and spilled out into the fuming traffic. At least it was a beautiful day, cloudless and calm, the air silvery, promising heat.

"You don't look well," said Margy. She was a good secretary, cheerful and efficient, but she ate recklessly and suffered in the heat.

He patted her damp, dimpled shoulder. "Bad night."

Her eyes widened with concern and she dabbed at herself with a tiny lace handkerchief. Even the freckles on her face seemed to be sweating. "You're not gambling again?"

He took away his hand at once. "For God's sake, don't *you* start." He marched, tight-mouthed, to his office door, but when he glanced back he saw she was blushing. "There are other ways of having a bad time," he said.

She mumbled apologetically and followed him in with a cup of coffee, fussing around his desk and making placating noises.

His hands were unsteady, his head buzzed with fatigue, but work, at least, took his mind off the mess he was in. Everything depended on whether or not the postman had recognized him. The light from the kiosk had been dull and yellowish, but probably enough in the surrounding gloom. Probably more than enough. Anyway, there had been the dog. He must know the dog. Postmen always do. There is a whole library of cartoons on that subject.

When he closed his eyes he could hear a faint whirring noise. Somewhere under the building engines were laboring to circulate a little fresh air. It would have been easier and cheaper to open the windows and let the world in. The designers, however, had thought otherwise. They must have had their reasons.

He went over to the window and looked out. Far below, the traffic jostled, the crowds moved purposefully: girls with bare arms and hair bouncing on their shoulders, men in shirtsleeves carrying their jackets. The heat beat through the double glass.

He watched from his aerie and thought about the girl on the Heath. Her blond hair in the darkness, her expensive clothes, made her seem in his imagination somehow silvery. Silvery and rare, like a lynx. Like a dead lynx.

Something about her closed, curving eyes.

He pressed his forehead against the hot glass, then leaned back and watched the little patch of dampness evaporate, leaving a faint smudge.

Maybe she wasn't dead. He could easily have missed some vital tremor, some vague flicker of life. He had no experience in these matters. Besides, he had been frightened.

He went back to his desk and began to check through a sales program. He worked efficiently, calculating probabilities and alternatives as precisely as he had at the poker table. But at the end of each section he paused and let his mind wander.

Perhaps she had been walking home from a party with

her chap. Perhaps they had some tipsy idea of swimming in one of the ponds or making love on the damp grass. Perhaps they had fought because they had made love already.

A lovers' tiff: her head bashed with something heavy, her handbag lying open as though ransacked.

She must have been walking on her own and someone had jumped her. The Heath is crawling with loonies. In broad daylight men flash their rigid cocks at mothers pushing prams, at small children.

But at three A.M.?

Even loonies have to sleep.

Yet the girl hadn't been sleeping.

Neither had Conrad.

The engines labored but the air smelled stale. Maybe the architects had a deal with the air-conditioning people.

One thing he was sure of: she didn't belong there, even in daylight. She wasn't a Hampstead girl. Even the rich ones maintain a certain tattiness, an air of dressing down to the image of a serious intellectual suburb. This one was too silvery, too expensive, too quizzical. Then he remembered the Knightsbridge tag on her shawl.

Poor little bitch. She had been a long way from home.

At lunchtime Duval put his head around the door and said, "Coming to the Crown?"

"Maybe. When I finish."

Duval raised his eyebrows and smirked. "You're kidding, of course. Or could it be our aging whiz kid is after promotion at last?" When Conrad did not answer or look up he added, "Next week at your local Odeon: *The Resurrection,* starring Conrad Jessup. Or should it be *The Second Coming,* old boy?" He closed the door behind him with exaggerated care.

Conrad sat on, listening to the tired air whining through the vents in the wall. Then he looked up "Olivia's" in the telephone directory and jotted the address in his diary.

The typing pool was empty except for a group of girls

gossiping in one corner. When he smiled at them they looked away and began giggling together. It seemed to him they were sharing a private joke at his expense. Did they know something about him he didn't know? Was the word out on him already?

He left his car in the office park, bought an *Evening Standard,* and took the tube to Knightsbridge. The front page was full of the latest disasters. He peered without much interest at the smeared, grayish photographs. In one, a paunchy man sat on a curb holding his head. There was rubble all around, his face and shirt were splattered with blood. In another, there were blurred, tangled shapes of what had presumably been cars. In front of them stood an elderly woman and a policeman. They both looked surprised.

Buried on an inner page among items about pools winners and pop stars he found a brief paragraph saying that a girl had been assaulted on Hampstead Heath and was now in hospital "in a serious condition." So at least she wasn't dead. He read the paragraph several times, pondering on the word "assaulted." It suggested all sorts of enormities and more troubles than he was willing to contemplate. He had a sharp, brief image of her exposed thighs and soft mouth, then turned back quickly to the front page and other people's outrages.

As he did so, he realized that the young man sitting opposite was staring at him. His face was long and pale under a helmet of polished black hair, his mouth unnaturally red. He seemed to be playing a tune on himself. His bony fingers moved from forehead to hip and back, touching invisible notes. He was watching Conrad carefully.

The moment Conrad caught his eye, the young man leaned forward and whispered, "Why won't you leave me alone?"

The wheels roared on the track, the carriage swayed. Conrad found that it was not possible to look away.

"I know you." The young man raised his voice. "Don't think I don't."

Conrad mumbled, "There must be some mistake," and made an attempt to smile.

The young man's fingers played a complicated passage on the side of his face from jawbone to nose. "Don't try it, mate. I'm warning you." He paused, then blinked his baby-blue eyes as if trying to hold back tears. His voice filled with sorrow. "O.K. I know it's no use going to the police. You're in this together, aren't you? You can't fool me."

He blinked again, then his eyes narrowed and became cunning. Conrad stared in amazement. It was like watching a quick-change artist: the shifts of mood were baffling, unreal, more intimidating than the words.

The young man leaned even farther forward. "I'm not alone. I have my friends. Powerful friends."

"I'm sure you have," Conrad muttered.

"You'd better believe it."

"I do. I do believe it."

The man's cunning stare shifted abruptly into grief. "Then let me be. I can't take any more. I'm having dreams."

The noise of the train intensified, then relented as the brakes came on. "I'm going now," said the young man. "If you follow me, you know what'll happen. I won't be responsible."

Conrad shook his head.

"Think about it," said the young man. "There's not a court in the country would convict me."

The train stopped and the young man went to the doors. When they opened he waited, watching Conrad, then stepped out quickly as they began to close. He stood on the platform staring after the train as it pulled out. His hand was playing tunes on his neck.

Conrad leaned back in his seat. His whole body was trembling and he could feel the sweat seeping down from his armpits. He wiped his face with his handkerchief, then blew his nose decorously. There were only half a dozen people in the carriage and none of them seemed to have noticed.

At Knightsbridge he plunged into the stream of lunchtime shoppers gratefully, as into cool water. Avoid dark places, he told himself. The Underground. The Heath at night. Close your ears to the malicious voices. Play safe.

He walked slowly past Harrods, admiring the window display and wondering how much it took to end up like that young man, feeling himself watched from every chink of darkness and touching himself to make sure he was still there.

It took more than he wished to give. More than he had to give.

Not that that was the question.

They gave. You took.

The shop was in a side street. In the window two dresses lay indolently against silk cushions. Their materials were full of colors and so fine that they seemed to float. The sign over the window said, "Olivia's. Decorations." He supposed the cushions were also for sale.

Inside, oriental lamps made dim patterns on the ceiling. Along one wall was a deep illuminated embrasure, full of diaphanous, shimmering dresses, color upon color. The air was vaguely fragrant.

Conrad stood in the doorway, blinking his eyes against the sudden gloom. The opulence of the place made him aware of how shabby his office suit was, how stale and fatigued his lumbering body.

A slim girl with loose dark hair and thin arms came toward him from the shadows at the back of the shop. She smiled encouragingly and said, "Can I help you, sir?" She seemed glad to have something to do.

"I'm looking for a little present. Nothing too elaborate. More of a gesture, you understand."

"Of course, sir. Had you anything in particular in mind?"

"A scarf maybe. Or a shawl. Something like that."

"Exactly."

The girl went to a cabinet and pulled out a drawer crammed with bright silks. She poured them onto the table in the middle of the shop with a grand, magnanimous gesture, like someone opening the door to a sanctuary. Conrad stood admiringly above them, lifting them up and letting them slip through his fingers. They felt subtle and faintly electric, as exciting as a girl's hair.

"Beautiful."

"Hand-printed," said the salesgirl. "To our own design, of course."

"Of course." He smiled at the girl and she smiled back carefully and professionally, sizing him up.

"And how much are they? Roughly, of course."

"Roughly twenty-five to forty pounds, sir, according to the size."

"I see." He did indeed. "And the shawls? I suppose they are a little more expensive."

"A little." The girl began to fold the scarves into a pile. "They start at about seventy-five pounds. Can I show you some, sir?"

Conrad shook his head. "That's rather more than I intended."

Almost as much as those two aces had cost him.

He began to pick through the scarves again, letting them whisper through his fingers, while the salesgirl stood patiently by his side, saying nothing. Now he knew their price they seemed even more erotic.

A walking treasure chest, he thought. He began to calculate swiftly, as though adding up the pot before seeing a bet. The scarf, the shawl, the no doubt astronomical silk dress, the Italian handbag and shoes. Three, four hundred pounds at least. Not to mention rings and necklaces which he hadn't noticed. And she was dressed lightly for a summer night.

What sweat, what manipulation goes into adorning these creatures? Where does money like that come from? Not that it mattered to her any longer, lying in her hospital bed "in a serious condition."

A door opened behind him and a heavy male voice said, "We understand, ma'am, but you appreciate the seriousness of the inquiry."

Conrad lifted one of the scarves and turned slowly as if examining it in the different lights. A woman was standing with two men at the doorway of the inner office. She had silver hair and a taut face, the skin drawn back and tucked in tight, like a hospital bed. Her cheekbones were high and Slavic, her mouth precise. She wore a dress of dark, shifting greens.

The men were burly and soberly suited, one grizzled, the other fair, like father and son. The elder of them shook the woman's hand and said formally, "Thank you, anyway, for your cooperation. It is much appreciated."

The woman murmured something Conrad could not hear and closed the office door on them firmly.

As the two men crossed the shop, they looked at Conrad carefully but automatically, as if they were trained to look hard at everyone. The younger man had bright, curly hair and a baby's pouting mouth. He held the door open for the other man and stood back respectfully.

Conrad watched them go. They glanced into the shop window as they passed, then walked off in a businesslike way.

He turned to the girl and looked at her in dismay. "What shall I do?" he asked.

Her face was thin and nervous. She wore curling false lashes which made her eyes seem unnaturally large. "Pardon?" She wrinkled her forehead and moved back a little.

"I mean, there's so much to choose from, how do I make up my mind? Perhaps I should take another look at my wife's dresses." He was sweating again so profusely that

58

he was afraid he would leave marks on the delicate silks.

"Perhaps you should, sir." She moved farther around the table, pretending to tidy the scattered scarves.

Conrad edged toward the door. "I'm sorry to have taken up so much of your time."

"No trouble at all, sir. That's what I'm here for." But her nervous face said: Please go. Please keep me out of it.

Conrad closed the shop door behind him. He looked down the street and saw the younger of the two men open the door of a car parked on the double yellow lines at the corner. The older man got in and the younger doubled around to the driver's seat. He moved briskly, with a military air.

Conrad turned and walked off quickly in the opposite direction.

Now you've done it, he told himself. Now you've really blown it.

He felt curiously elated.

10

"SOMEONE CALLED," said Margy, "while you were drinking your lunch. But he wouldn't leave his name."

"Any clues?"

"American, I think."

"We don't have any Americans in our lives at this moment, do we?"

"Canadian, then. Maybe it was the buyer from Eaton's again."

"Let joy be unconfined," said Conrad, and forgot all about it.

Late in the afternoon the sky began to fill with heavy-bellied clouds. Each time Conrad looked up from his desk the day was darker and more lights were coming on in the offices opposite. Dimly, through the double skin of glass, he heard the thunder rolling closer. The air thickened, blackened, became soupy. Finally, the storm broke immediately overhead, like a mountain of tin plates falling off the roof. The buzz and click of the office stilled for a moment as everyone paused to look. The rain was bouncing off the pavements in a gray haze and cars moved like speedboats, sending up plumes of spray.

Margy came in with a pile of papers. She put them on Conrad's desk, then crossed to the window. "Just like the tropics," she said.

He went and stood beside her, peering out. She smelled of sweat and peppermints. "On that," he said, "you and I are great experts."

"I've been around. I've been to Spain. Anyway, you know what I mean. It's a bit strong for here."

"Anything's a bit strong for here, but I know what you mean. More like a happening than weather."

"It makes a nice change."

"At this moment in my life, I don't need any more nice changes." He patted her large bottom. "Work," he said.

"Work?" she echoed. "What's come over you all of a sudden?"

By the time he left, the storm was drifting away. He drove with the window down, sniffing the cool air, listening to the hiss of the tires on the wet roads. But at home Betsy was sitting with the children in front of the television as usual, a glass of whiskey in her hand, a new bottle beside her on the floor already a quarter empty. She glanced at him irritably when he came in, but did not speak.

He spent the evening in his attic, staring blankly at a canvas he had begun but could no longer remember why. Every time he looked away he saw out of the corner of his eye the face of the girl on the Heath lit by the small flame of his lighter. Curving eyes. Cheeks full of shadows. Sensual, peaceful mouth.

But he was too tired to cope. So he went back downstairs and was asleep even before the television finished.

At some dim point of the night he woke from his usual uneasy dreams. It was the indeterminate hour when the world seems in abeyance. The traffic had ceased, the birds had not yet begun, the streetlights were out. Betsy slept tranquilly beside him, making no sound. The summer gale had blown itself out.

He had been dreaming of a jungle, a greenish darkness in which something stirred. In his sleep he thought about it quite rationally. He knew it was nothing to worry about, nothing threatening, nothing to set the alarm bells ringing. Just a vague presence demanding to be recognized. Nevertheless, it made him uneasy.

He got out of bed, pulled on a sweater, and climbed up to the attic. The canvas on his easel was jungle green, as in his dream. A flat uninhabited background of dark greens and black, waiting to be brought to life.

Quickly, so as not to lose the disturbance of the dream, he began to dab in the eyes of the girl on the Heath. But open and cold. Blue, white, gray, and in the shining black at their center a square of brightness. A source of light from elsewhere reflecting the source of light within the painting.

The pale clear colors seemed to fuse together without effort and the surrounding darkness began to cohere.

So that's how it's done, he thought, as though he were watching someone else at work.

He squeezed a worm of orange and a worm of red onto his palette, stirred them together, picked up a brush, changed his mind, dipped his palette knife into the paint, and smeared on a thin outline of the face: jawbone and mouth, the swell of a cheek, a faint straight line along the ridge of the nose. He worked deftly and with assurance, knowing he could always handle line.

He stopped, peered, used his fingernail to scrape away the paint where it seemed too thick. He wanted the bare fragile bones, with the darkness shining through. A dream face staring from the dream and still part of it.

Well, he thought at last, that'll do. That'll do for the moment.

He could still feel the disturbance of the dream working obscurely inside him, as though he were not yet fully awake.

When he went back downstairs the sun was already up in a clear sky and the birds were busy. He fell asleep immediately and his wife had trouble waking him. He left for the office without going back up to the attic to see what he had done.

When he got home that evening Betsy was sitting at the kitchen table, supervising the children's supper. But he could smell the whiskey on her even before he bent dutifully to kiss her cheek. Under the staring fluorescent light her skin had an unhealthy grayish shimmer, like a television screen.

"You O.K.?" he asked.

"Just a sniffle, that's all. A sniffle and a bit of a headache." She glanced up at him, surprised, almost grateful. "Say good evening to your father, boys."

The children muttered "Hi" without looking up. Their faces were smeared with tomato soup, their fingers inky, their nails black with dirt. Conrad wondered where the ink came from in this age of ball-point pens. Their filth was somehow touching, reminding him of his own battered and confused childhood. He felt sorry for them. But as usual they took no notice of him, so he shrugged and went upstairs.

He changed his clothes slowly, puttering aimlessly about the bedroom, listening to the children playing on the street outside and the traffic mumbling home. Finally, he stretched, yawned, as though to persuade himself he didn't care, and climbed up to the attic. He took elaborate care to keep his back to the easel while he switched on the lights and bolted the trapdoor. Then he took out a cigarette, turned, fiddled with his lighter, and glanced up casually.

The painting looked at him and he looked back at it astonished.

The real thing. The genuine article.

His eyes prickled, his throat felt vulnerable. He prowled about the studio, squinting at it from all angles. He walked away, then swung suddenly around, trying to catch it off guard. In the mess of pots and tubes, old brushes and bits of rag, it remained inviolable. Full of light, full of life.

63

Got it, he thought. This time I've painted the light, not the darkness. The light endures, only the objects change.

He perched on a stool in front of the painting and wondered why he felt disappointed.

Finally, he carried the canvas down to the sitting room and propped it in the fireplace. Betsy was watching a man with dominating teeth who was explaining the virtues of margarine. She smiled with the housewives who mistook it for butter.

"What do you think?" asked Conrad.

She glanced at the painting absentmindedly. "Very nice." Then her eyes wandered back to the television.

"Thank you, Mr. Ruskin. And for your next impersonation."

Betsy looked at him wearily. "What do you expect? In the circumstances. You want me to phone the BBC and tell them to send a camera crew straight over?"

"Screw you too. In the circumstances."

She shrugged. "You know me, Conrad. I never could tell Stork from butter. Console yourself with that."

Her face was gray and smeared. Just like a television screen.

"Why are you drunk?" he asked, quite pleasantly.

"Why are you holding back on me?"

"Holding back? Holding back what?"

"Search me. You've got something going and you're not telling. A little secret from the little woman." She giggled, then looked him truculently in the eye and finished her drink.

"Either you're having a paranoid breakdown or you're even drunker than you look."

"Either you're gambling again or you've got a girlfriend stashed away somewhere."

He studied her wiry curls and pallid, indoor complexion. For better or for worse, he thought.

"One bet on a horse and suddenly I'm Nick the Greek. It was half a quid, for Christ's sake. Fifty lousy pence."

"One drink and suddenly I'm an alcoholic."

"One?"

"O.K., Nick, maybe a couple. Now pour me another." She handed him her glass and he took it without arguing. "Not that I'm altogether discounting the idea of Womance. Got it, Conrad? With a Capital W. All gingham and bows and pert bitable backsides."

Conrad divided what was left in the bottle between them, thinking: Maybe it'll take her mind off gambling. Her mind.

"A little Womance to get you over the hump of middle age."

Conrad dropped the empty bottle into the wastepaper basket. "That kills it," he said.

"Even so, better a little Womance than a little wager."

"O.K.," he said brusquely. "Enough's enough."

She emptied her glass again. "Enough for you or enough for me?" She rose abruptly from the sofa and squared off in front of him like a boxer. "I want another drink."

"The bottle's dead."

"Then let's go to the pub. Plenty of living bottles there." She marched to the front door and stood, swaying slightly, against the evening light of the street.

"You've had enough."

"Don't come the moralist with me. In the circumstances."

Conrad shrugged. He turned to the closed door of the kitchen and shouted, "We're going to the pub. Do your homework before you watch any TV."

There was no reply.

The bar was full of rather heavy young people set on enjoying themselves and the jukebox was playing Andy Williams. For some reason, this seemed to cheer Betsy up. Nevertheless, she knocked back her first whiskey in one

65

gulp, belligerently, as though issuing a challenge. Conrad refused to be provoked. He swallowed his too, and re-ordered.

When the next drinks came he smiled at her and asked, "What about your secret?"

She nodded appreciatively. "Once a poker player always a poker player, eh, Conrad? Since when were we discussing my secret?"

"Stands to reason."

"Reason?" She studied the fresh whiskey in her glass for a moment, then shrugged. "Thirty-four years old. There's one reason for you. And married to a gambling man. There's another."

"A reformed gambling man."

"Who's to say? I mean, it may sound all right in the folk songs, but I'm a bit old for that, aren't I?" She sipped her drink and began to sing quietly:

I'm a rambler, I'm a gambler,
I'm a long way from home,
And if people don't like me
They can leave me alone.

Conrad looked at her with distaste. Her creased dress hung from her wearily. The skin on her breastbone seemed weary too, and he could see the beginnings of wrinkles in her neck. He wondered why it was always the neck that went first.

"Joan Baez can keep it," said Betsy.

Conrad said nothing.

"Thirty-four's not very old when you come to think about it."

"So think about it. Or don't. As the case may be."

"Buy me another drink, then."

"Come on, sweetheart, that's enough for one evening."

He put his hand on her arm and bent toward her. "Let's go home and make love."

Her eyes widened in mock surprise. "So that's what you call it. All right, be my guest. It makes a change, anyway."

"A change from what?"

"From fucking," she said loudly.

The faces in the bar turned to them hopefully.

Betsy raised her voice. "I thought you always called it fucking. Plain old simple fucking."

"You're drunk."

"Does that turn you off, Conrad dear? Have I suddenly become not so lovable? Or even fuckable?"

The other people in the bar had stopped talking and waited with expectant faces. The two barmen dourly polished glasses.

Betsy began to croon: "Oo-oo-oo, what a lot a little whiskey can do-oo-oo."

Conrad dug his fingers into her arm and pushed her in front of him to the pub door. The crowd of portly young people drew back grinning. One of them called out, "Make way for the lovers," and bowed ceremoniously as they passed. Another said, "The golden oldies are having a night out." His girl stretched her bright red mouth and giggled.

"All right, officer"—Betsy smiled regally on all sides— "I'll come quietly." Then she began to sing again, loud and clear, "Can't help fuckin' dat man ob mine." But when Conrad tightened his grip on her arm she struggled and hissed into his face, "Let go, you bastard. You're hurting me."

He dropped his hand at once and strode angrily off down the street where the lime trees spread their summery, faintly acrid scent on the darkening air. Just short of their gate he stopped and waited for her to catch up. She walked unsteadily, brandishing a paper handkerchief and sniffing loudly. Her makeup was smeared and the light from the streetlamps made her face seem yellowish and full of shadows. The curls on her head looked wiry and damp to the touch. Poor sad bitch, he thought. The games people play in the name of marriage. When she came up to him he put out his hand tentatively and touched the bare, vulnerable nape of her neck.

"You look a real mess."

"You're a prig, Conrad, a boring bloody prig. What do you care what a gang of creeps in a bar think?"

"I don't like to see you making a fool of yourself."

"You mean in public. What else have I been doing for the last dozen years?"

"My," he mocked, "you are sorry for yourself tonight."

She shrugged his hand away. "No more than seems appropriate."

"That's your story."

"And I'm sticking to it."

Finally they smiled at each other without malice. Then, hand in hand, they climbed the steps of their dingy terraced house to chase the children to bed, eat slabs of bread and New Zealand cheddar, walk the dog down the road, put out the cat, bolt the front door, then the back, lock the downstairs windows, turn out the downstairs lights, fill the Russell Hobbs automatic bedside teamaker, brush their teeth, set the alarm, and then, only then, make love on their interior-sprung Slumberland mattress between patterned fitted sheets from Marks & Spencer.

Making love or fucking: what's in a name? But that night they were kind to each other, and careful.

He fell asleep with Betsy curled along his back, her hands clasped across his stomach. Like two spoons in a drawer, he thought.

During the night the dog began to bark furiously. Conrad woke abruptly, convinced that someone was lurking just outside in the street. He waited, his heart pounding unreasonably. Then two cats began yowling to each other in ecstasy. He lay listening to them and to Betsy's deep slow breathing and to the dog growling to himself as he settled back into his basket.

Betsy began to snore gently. He stared at the window and wondered why she had chosen this moment to provoke a crisis. If "provoke" and "crisis" were the right words, considering her bleary condition.

"Don't push me," he whispered into the darkness. "I might just settle for the dog."

He lay watching the shadows of the trees gesticulate against the window and drifted slowly back to sleep.

11 THE POLICE ARRIVED the next morning while Conrad was still shaving. Betsy came and whispered to him in a gray, urgent voice. But he took his time, dousing himself in cologne and dressing carefully for the office.

They were waiting for him in the sitting room. A redfaced sergeant in uniform and the young plainclothes detective with blond curls whom Conrad had seen in the boutique. They were staring disapprovingly at the painting propped in the fireplace, but when the detective saw Conrad his shallow eyes widened, then narrowed knowingly. Conrad looked at him blankly with his poker-player's face.

"Conrad Jessup?"

"Yes."

"We have reason to believe you can help us in our inquiries about an incident three nights ago on Hampstead Heath."

Conrad turned to Betsy, who was hovering at the door. "Get me a cup of coffee, will you?" When she did not move he added, "Please." Then, "*Darling.*" She looked at him in bewilderment.

He turned back to the policemen. "What incident? What reason?"

"We are not obliged to answer those questions, *sir.*"

"Don't be absurd. I'm a solid citizen. I hold a responsible

job with an international company. This isn't a police state. At least, not yet it isn't, Heinrich."

"Evans," said the fair-haired detective. "Detective-Sergeant Evans, CID."

"Of course you're obliged, Detective-Sergeant Evans." The policemen said nothing.

"Do you have a warrant?"

"We have a warrant."

"I see." Conrad looked at the two men, but the red-faced sergeant went on staring at the painting. The young detective seemed to be enjoying himself. "Perhaps you would be kind enough to explain," said Conrad in his most managerial voice.

The detective shrugged. "A young woman was assaulted on Hampstead Heath at around three A.M. on the morning of the twelfth. Less than an hour later you were seen, in a disheveled condition, coming out of a telephone kiosk not far from this house." He intoned the facts solemnly and with relish, like a litany, and was having difficulty in concealing his pleasure.

"Sorry to butt in, but I don't see how those two facts are related."

"It was about that time, shortly before four A.M., that the incident was reported to the police."

"So?"

"If it was you in the kiosk, sir, isn't that an unusual time to be making a telephone call?"

Betsy came in with the coffee. When she handed him the cup the spoon rattled on the saucer.

"Think of it this way," said Conrad brightly. "It's only eleven P.M. in New York. Eight in Los Angeles."

"Are you suggesting, *sir*," again the detective put a heavy emphasis on the *sir*, "that you were phoning New York from a public telephone box at four in the morning?"

"I'm not suggesting anything. But, as I said, I work for an international company. We have offices everywhere."

"You have your own telephone in this house?"

"You're missing the point. Isn't that right, Betsy? He doesn't get it."

Betsy was staring at him. "Stop it," she said harshly.

"The note of command," Conrad said to the policemen. "In case you didn't recognize it." He took a mouthful of coffee, then another. It tasted miraculous. "No more games," he said. "Yes, I found the girl. Yes, I telephoned to report it."

"Why didn't you leave your name, sir? A great deal of time and trouble has been wasted."

"For obvious reasons. I mean, put yourself in my place. I found this girl lying in the bushes with blood all over her head. Or, rather, the dog found her. And I was scared stiff. I heard someone running off in the direction of South End Green. But he might have doubled back and been lurking about, watching me. How could I tell? And I didn't know if the girl was alive or dead. I suppose I panicked. It's not unnatural. So I ran for it. Then I thought, someone's got to be told, she needs help. And I dialed nine-nine-nine."

"Why didn't you tell me?" Betsy was squeezed against his left side, though whether protectively or for protection he couldn't tell. When he turned to her, her face was very close to his. There were whitish marks at the corners of her eyes and the stiff curls stood up from her head in alarm. He could smell her thick morning smell of sleep and unhappiness.

"You weren't listening," he said. "Remember? You didn't want to know."

"You haven't answered my question," the detective repeated. "Why didn't you leave your name?"

"Because I was frightened. Because I was confused. Because I didn't want to get involved." Conrad shrugged. "All the worst reasons."

Neither of the policemen was amused.

"I would be grateful," said Evans, "if you would accompany me to the station, sir, to make a proper statement and answer some further questions."

Conrad kissed Betsy at the door. "That's what I like about England. They may arrest you for nothing at all, but they call you 'sir' while they're doing it."

At the bottom of the steps he turned and called, "Phone Horace and tell him I'm ill. I'll see you later. Don't worry, I won't be long."

Betsy put her hand to her mouth and began to chew her forefinger. "You should have told me," she said. "It's not fair." Her eyes filled with tears and he wondered for a moment how he could fix that effect in paint.

The sergeant stayed behind in the house with Betsy. As Conrad climbed into the police car, two of his neighbors passed on their way to the tube. He nodded to them jovially but they stared stonily ahead, pretending not to notice.

At the station they sat him on a wooden chair in front of a wooden table in a windowless room, then went out and left him to contemplate the painted brick walls and the three other chairs. The room was lit by a single bulb behind wire mesh on the ceiling. On the wall was a small darkish mirror through which, Conrad assumed, they were watching him.

He sat quietly for a while, then pulled out his diary to see what appointments he was missing. He felt pleasantly calm. He heard booted feet moving up and down the passage outside, doors banging, voices. A distant telephone rang incessantly and once, from somewhere far off in the building, a dog barked. It was all very peaceful.

He shifted his buttocks on the chair and tried to remember details about finding the girl. Useful details. But all he could come up with were a few isolated images: the shape of her closed eyes, the stickiness of the blood in her hair, the first shock when he stretched out his hand in the dark and touched her leg.

73

Frivolity.

Fecklessness.

He tried to think about the footsteps he had heard. One person or two? He had no idea. He couldn't even remember being frightened, but he could remember the shape of her mouth.

His head buzzed a little. He yawned.

The room was chilly and the only air vent seemed to be the gap under the locked door. No deals here with the air-conditioning people.

He must have been frightened; it was part of his story. But he wasn't frightened now.

Reassured and sitting bolt upright, he drifted off to sleep.

He woke with a full bladder. When he knocked on the door a constable opened it at once, led him to a lavatory smelling equally of urine and disinfectant, watched impassively while he relieved himself, then took him back to the room and locked the door. Almost immediately, Conrad dozed off again, carrying with him into unconsciousness a vague feeling of surprise at his appetite for sleep.

He was woken by the sound of the door being unlocked. The other detective he had seen in Knightsbridge came in, followed by Evans and a young constable carrying a notebook. Thick-shouldered, grizzled, a pipe clamped in his long jaws, the older detective was wearing a tweed jacket and gray flannels, like an old-fashioned schoolmaster.

The three men sat down at the table in front of Conrad and stared at him as if he was an interesting but probably spurious exhibit. Conrad stared back, poker-faced.

"Detective Inspector Davies, CID," said the older policeman. He opened a buff-colored file, glanced at it, then stared at Conrad again. "I'm in charge of this case. I'd like to hear for myself the story you told Sergeant Evans. The constable will take it down, then you can sign a statement.

Of course, you don't have to say or sign anything without consulting a lawyer. That is your right under law."

"Why should I call a lawyer? I want to do everything I can to help." Conrad smiled at the three watchful faces, but nobody smiled back. "One thing, before I start: Is the girl all right?"

"She's ill, Mr. Jessup, very ill. But not dead, if that's what you mean."

"That's exactly what I mean. What else is there to mean?"

Davies sucked his pipe and did not reply.

Conrad changed his tack. "Thank God for that," he said placatingly. "Poor kid."

There was another silence.

"Whenever you're ready," said Davies in a bored voice.

Conrad went through his story again, carefully, pausing between sentences so the young constable could keep up with him.

When he finished there was a pause. The two detectives glanced at each other, then Davies leaned forward. "Are you sure you've told us everything?"

"Everything I can remember."

They glanced at each other again, and again Davies leaned forward. "Am I not right in thinking you visited a dress shop in Knightsbridge the day after the incident? A shop called 'Olivia's'?"

The note of cunning struck Conrad as funny but he did not smile. "That's right. I was looking for a present for my wife."

"Why that particular shop?"

"It's rather famous."

"But rather expensive?"

"A present's a present."

"Any special occasion? Birthday perhaps? Anniversary?"

"Just a present. Something to cheer her up. She's been very down recently."

"I see." Davies paused again. "No other reason?"

75

Conrad shrugged, spread his hands, and smiled, he hoped, disarmingly. "Of course there was. You know it as well as I do. I saw the label on the girl's scarf. I was curious. Scared stiff but curious. I wanted to see where she came from. I wanted to find out who she was." He stopped and smiled again at the unforgiving face opposite him. "I'm sorry. I should have told you straight off. I suppose I've read too many detective stories."

Davies looked at him with distaste. "I think, Mr. Jessup, you haven't read enough."

Conrad started to laugh, then stopped when he saw the others were not joining in. The two detectives were studying the wooden tabletop and seemed embarrassed by his show of mirth. The young constable went on writing furiously.

Davies relit his pipe and rubbed his blue jaw. "I wouldn't want you to lie to me, Mr. Jessup."

Conrad's self-assurance drained abruptly away. "I wouldn't want to either. Please believe me." The base of his spine felt cold. He realized he was no longer altogether in control. "Look, I'm sorry. I apologize. The thing is, I don't know why I went into that shop. Curiosity? Perversity? I mean, why not? The whole thing was so weird. For you it's just routine. But me, I work in an office. In the sales department," he added helpfully.

Davies looked at the file in front of him and said, "So I see."

"What do you mean, 'you see'?"

Davies shrugged contemptuously and began to read: "Conrad Richard Jessup. Born eighth of September 1940. Height 5 ft. 11 in. Weight 180 lbs. Son of William Henry Jessup, grocer, and Mary Gwendolen, *née* Maclagan. Both parents now deceased. Educated Gospel Oak Primary and William Ellis. Six O Levels. A Level in Art, failed in English and History. Granted a place at St. Martin's School of Art

76

but did not take it." He looked at Conrad over the top of the file. "I wonder why?"

"You know it all. You tell me."

"As you wish. Joined World Electric, November 1960. Promoted to assistant sales manager, 1967. No promotion since. Isn't that rather odd?"

Conrad said nothing.

"Do you want me to go on?" When Conrad still did not reply Davies said meditatively, "Assistant sales manager. What else do you do, Mr. Jessup?"

Conrad shivered. "I paint. You know, pictures."

"I know. St. Martin's and all that." He looked again at the file. "These pictures, do you sell them?"

"Not so far."

"I see." Under their bushy brows, Davies' eyes were grayish and hooded. The lines around them were gloomy. He looked like a man who did not approve of pleasure. "Do you have any other source of income?" he asked in a bored voice.

The chill which had begun at the base of Conrad's spine had spread all through his body. He hugged himself and muttered, "Sometimes."

"I don't quite understand, Mr. Jessup."

"I said, sometimes." He put his hands between his knees and rubbed them together vigorously. "I mean, sometimes I gamble. The horses. Cards. I used to do a lot of it but I stopped. It was getting on top of me."

"And now?"

"Now only sometimes, more rarely. Much more rarely. But I don't tell my wife."

"Is that because you're a loser, Mr. Jessup?"

"I used to be, but not anymore. Not since I tailed off. But win or lose, she doesn't like it. Women don't, mostly."

Davies pursed his lips in a schoolmasterly fashion. "Mostly you can hardly blame them." He surveyed the papers in front of him again. Conrad waited, knowing what was coming.

"Am I to understand, then, that you have been winning recently?"

"Two wins, that's all. A few weeks ago I won a lot on a horse. Then I had a good win at poker the other night."

He felt a little warmth beginning to creep back into his hands and feet. "That's right. On the night in question I was playing poker until two-thirty and there are six people who will vouch for me. I can give you their names. With pleasure."

"So you shall, Mr. Jessup." Davies still did not smile. "And how much did you win?"

"Two forty pounds. Cash."

"I see. And where is the money now?"

He knows, thought Conrad. That, too. Aloud he said, "In an envelope at the back of a drawer in my workbench in my studio."

"Just two hundred and forty pounds?"

"Not at all. I told you, I won a lot of money on a horse."

"How much is a lot?"

"Well over nine hundred quid. But I gave some to my wife."

"I thought she didn't know you were gambling again."

"I told her I put half a quid on an outsider and it came up."

"I see. What was the real story?"

"It was an outsider all right. Artist's Moll. Fifty to one at Kempton Park. I put twenty pounds on its nose and it won. A miracle. And that's not a story. I can tell you which bookie it was. They must keep a record."

"That will be very helpful." Davies scribbled a note, then looked at Conrad for a while without speaking. The expression of distaste on his face was intense. Finally he said, "Isn't that an excessively large sum of money to put on a fifty-to-one outsider?"

"That's what gambling's about. Sometimes you get a hunch."

"Just a hunch? No inside information?"

"Just a hunch."

"I see. Do you often get hunches like that?"

"If I did, I wouldn't need to work for a living, would I?"

"And the money. What did you do with the money?"

"I told you, I gave some to my wife. The rest is in the envelope with my poker winnings."

"How much in all?"

"Eleven forty pounds. Nine hundred from the horse, two forty from the poker." Conrad paused, then looked Davies mournfully in the eye. "But you know that already, don't you?"

"Yes, we know that already."

Conrad leaned forward and tried to work up a little indignation. "What right have you to search my house? Where does this bloody dossier come from?"

Davies surveyed him with his cold eyes and did not blink. For the first time, he sounded angry. "Let's not play any more games, Mr. Jessup. I know you thought you were going to enjoy yourself in our little interview, but that's all over now. You're in trouble, Mr. Jessup, bad trouble. A girl has been savagely assaulted and robbed. We have reason to believe she was carrying a substantial sum of money. You were in the vicinity when the assault took place. You have admitted to finding the girl and we have a witness who saw you soon after. You phoned the police but refused to leave your name. The following day you were seen by me and my colleague here"—the young detective grinned smugly—"at a shop with which the girl is associated. Naturally, you are under suspicion. Naturally, we take out a warrant against you. Naturally, we search your house. And there we discover an envelope hidden away in a locked room containing a large sum of money. We are, of course, within our rights. Your lawyer—should you now decide you need a lawyer—will confirm that. But what I will tell you, since you don't seem to understand, is that this isn't a game and neither you nor we are children. The sooner you have that clear in your mind, Mr. Jessup, the easier it will be for all of us."

He leaned back with the air of a man who has done his reluctant duty, and lit his pipe.

Conrad was trembling and when he spoke his voice was thin and unsteady. "But if I'd attacked her, why in God's name would I telephone the police?"

Davies' anger faded. He spoke patiently, as though explaining to a child. "You may have bad habits, Mr. Jessup, distasteful habits, but there's no reason to believe you're a professional criminal. Things can happen in hot blood which you don't mean to happen. You panic, you want to get help. But anonymously. You think, perhaps it'll be all right, she'll live happily ever after, I'll be forgiven. That's not hard to understand. The trouble is, forgiveness doesn't come so easily."

"But you know I didn't do it."

"On the contrary. I know you could easily have done it."

"There are six people who can vouch for me until two-thirty."

"Who can vouch for you at three o'clock? Your dog?"

"The girl. She'll tell you it wasn't me."

"The girl is unconscious. She may not live."

"If you know all that about me, you must know about her. Where she had been, who she was with."

"I am not at liberty to say." Davies pursed his mouth primly. His tweed jacket, his pipe, his air of bullying rectitude were overwhelming. Conrad felt like a schoolboy. Powerless, resentful, longing to be loved.

"Look," he pleaded, "a girl like that doesn't walk across Hampstead Heath on her own at three in the morning for no reason."

"You do, Mr. Jessup."

"I'm not young, I'm not a girl, and I'm not rich, for that matter."

"Indeed." Davies smiled grimly and Evans smirked. "But why precisely were you walking on the Heath at that unlikely hour?"

Conrad shrugged wearily. "The constable here has it down already, but if you want it again, I'll tell you again. I started by walking the dog down the road as I always do. Then I felt kind of sorry for him. He's a working dog, a collie, full of energy. It's like having a dope addict on your hands. He has to have his daily fix on the Heath. Anyway, I didn't feel sleepy. I'd been concentrating, playing cards, I wanted to unwind. I knew that if I went straight to bed I'd just go on playing the hands over in my head. I thought a walk would tire me out, make me sleepy." He shivered. "Never again."

"Why didn't you tell your wife where you'd been? She said you were out with a client."

"Like I said, she thinks I've stopped gambling. She thinks all that is over."

"Why didn't you tell her what happened on the Heath?"

"I tried to but she wouldn't listen. We've been having a bad time together and she was angry when she saw how late it was. I suppose she thought I'd been with another woman. She just didn't want to know."

"I see." Again Davies surveyed him with his cold, bored eyes. "You lie to her, Mr. Jessup. For her own good, you would say. So why shouldn't you lie also to us? For *your* own good."

"It's not the same."

"Isn't it, Mr. Jessup?" Davies pushed back his chair, yawned, stretched, and raised his eyebrows quizzically at the other detective, who shook his head.

"Very well. The constable here will show you your statement. Read it through and make sure it's correct, then sign it. Then perhaps you'll be kind enough to give Detective-

Sergeant Evans the names of the people you were playing cards with. And the name of your bookie." He paused, then added casually, "Oh yes, you can phone your lawyer now, if you want."

Conrad mopped his forehead. A few minutes ago he had been freezing, now he was running with sweat. "I don't have a lawyer. The only time I ever needed one was when we bought our house. I think I used the company solicitor for that." Then he added, as though by way of apology, "I haven't even made my will."

"As you like."

Davies stood up and Conrad stood with him, automatically, just as he would have stood for his headmaster.

"I'll see you later," said Davies and nodded to Evans, who was holding the door open for him.

12

CONRAD SAT ON THE EDGE of the bunk, hands clasped between his knees, and stared at the inscriptions on the cell wall.

"Janey is a good girl."

"Andy Potts of Salford was here. 5 Aug. 1974."

How could one stolid police sergeant have gutted his home like a herring and come up with all the answers?

"Arsenal rules, O.K.?"

Where did the dossier come from?

"I love Liz. Pete Rouse, 17.6.73."

A handful of parking tickets and one visit to the police when the dog went missing in pursuit of a bitch.

"Keep Bradford White. J.S. 2 Jan. 76."

It had finished up in the kennels under the police station, covered in mud, stinking of dog sex and grinning foolishly. Conrad had collected it for the price of a dog license and a small fee. He too had been grinning foolishly.

"Franz Kafka Is Innocent, O.K.? F.R. Dec. 73."

He grinned again now and scratched his neck. It seemed a slender base for a criminal record. So where had the dossier come from?

"Billy," "Jake," "Henry," "John."

They would have questioned Betsy and Horace. But how far would that have got them?

"Pat," "Joe," "Don," "Brian," "Charlie."

Somewhere in some central computer there must be a tape on everyone. The dog-owners and dog-haters, the innocent and guilty, the employed, unemployed and unemployable.

High up on the wall someone had scrawled "REPENT! REPENT!" in large deep letters. Just below it was written neatly, "Courtesy of the Management."

He had never believed in God but the idea of some all-knowing electronic device was not beyond his imagination. It made him feel queasy.

"Liverpool," "Glasgow," "Dublin," "Portsmouth," "Bristol." Names and places and dates. It occurred to him that prison made people homesick and historically minded. It inspired them to make a bid for a place in the scheme of things.

"Jesus Christ was here. 12 March 1971."

"So was Napoleon. 10.5.1812."

They were probably watching him now. The idea of such attention made him feel sleepy. Such devotion. Such concentration. He lay back on the bunk and read, at eye level.

"Tell them they were wrong."

No date, no signature.

For some reason, this reassured him. He lay back on the bunk, closed his eyes, and promptly fell asleep.

The sound of the key turning in the lock woke him. He sat up at once, unwilling to be caught off guard. A stout, gray-haired policeman came in with a tray of food, nodded in a not unfriendly way, but did not speak. There were lumps of gristly meat, tinned peas, and potatoes marbled with frost. The tea tasted metallic and left a furry deposit on the back of his teeth. But he ate everything, wiping the plate around with his slab of bread and margarine, then sat meditatively running the tip of his tongue backwards and forwards along the coating of tannin on his teeth.

Backwards and forwards, backwards and forwards.

From the high barred window a patch of sunlight moved from "Paddy, Belfast, 6 June 1970" to "George Wills, Manchester, 1974." Small sounds filtered down the passage. Footsteps, blurred gruff voices, the distant sound of the telephone. He could feel the barrier of his skin, tight across the bridge of his nose, weary under his eyes, and a vague irritation in his scalp. He wondered whether to scratch immediately or wait until the irritation built up and scratching would give him pleasure. Still wondering, he began to scratch.

He tried to imagine what a prison sentence would be like. Whole years of nothingness. Plus Paddy, George, Joe and Bill. Boredom and fear. Every detail known, every move predicted.

Feet clumped down the passage, a door opened, then clanged shut, a key turned noisily, then the feet marched heavily away. From another cell a reedy voice began to sing:

> *Ay belong ta Glasgee,*
> *Deear auld Glasgee toon ...*

The feet paused at the end of the passage and a voice roared, "Quiet." The singer swore weakly, then subsided.

As the silence returned, Conrad understood that his real disadvantage was innocence. If he had attacked the girl and stolen her money, he would at least know where he was. There would be facts to conceal, a story to spin, a game to play. But to be innocent was to be powerless. Because he knew more or less nothing, they could prove more or less anything. No one would believe him. It made more sense to cosh someone over the head for money than to walk your dog on Hampstead Heath at three in the morning.

The air was cool and smelled of Lysol. Nevertheless, he began to sweat again profusely.

The patch of sunlight shifted around the top of the wall, then disappeared. He inspected the scribbles and signatures again to make sure he had missed nothing. He took out his pen and wrote "Michelangelo loves Leonardo," but did not sign it. He tried to picture the thousands of cells scattered across the country with their millions of names, but all he could come up with was blackness. The way some people live.

He sat down on the bunk again and pulled out his diary. The scribbled notes and appointments seemed to concern someone he had never met, but the section, with diagrams, on mouth-to-mouth resuscitation seemed suddenly full of meaning: "Time is of the essence. The chance of recovery 3 minutes after the victim stopped breathing is 75 percent, after 4 minutes 50 percent."

So he could have helped. Now he knew.

"Place your mouth over the mouth of the victim, closing his nose with your finger or your cheek. . . . Blow into the air passages until you see the chest rise and feel the lungs expand."

He studied the diagrams and thought about the girl. The newspaper had said "assault." So had the police.

"You're not going to believe me, officer, but this started as the kiss of life."

Cells like this were filled with loonies like that. Maybe he was more guilty than he knew. If he worked at it long enough, he would finish up confessing.

The key turned again in the lock and the stout policeman came in. "Follow me, please, sir." His voice was polite and he held the door open respectfully. He led the way down the painted brick corridor, up a stone staircase, and into the main police station with its pale varnished wood and bright paintwork. Conrad was surprised how innocuous it seemed. How sane. How comforting.

Davies' office was full of afternoon sunlight and the pleasant smell of pipe tobacco. Blue bars of smoke drifted in the shafts of light. He waved Conrad to a chair, then sat in silence for a moment, looking at him sternly and with distaste.

Finally, he said, "You have helpful friends, Mr. Jessup. The people you were playing cards with have confirmed your story." He sounded disappointed.

Conrad opened his mouth to speak.

Davies went on: "You'll also be glad to hear that the girl has recovered consciousness and what little she has said leads us to believe it was not you with her when she was attacked."

Again Conrad opened his mouth and again Davies interrupted, "However, nothing is settled yet. We're releasing you, but you must hold yourself available in case we need you again. Which we will. Notify us if you move or have to leave town. Is that understood?"

Conrad shrugged sullenly. "I suppose so." He felt more angry than relieved.

Davies tamped his pipe with his thumb, then began to relight it carefully. He gave this task a great deal of attention, as if to imply that it was more interesting than Conrad. Without looking up, he said, "Do you have any questions?"

Conrad glared at the grizzled hair and narrow forehead bending intently over the pipe. "I'd like the name of the girl and the hospital she's in. I'll send her some flowers. It's the least I can do."

"Is it?" Davies went on puffing and tamping. "Sergeant Evans will deal with that. Anything else?"

Conrad leaned forward. "Why me?" His voice was sharp and accusing. "What's it all about?"

Davies leaned back comfortably in his chair and exhaled a cloud of blue smoke. He watched it rise through the bars of sunlight and spread across the ceiling. Then he surveyed Conrad in a leisurely, contemptuous way, as if the laboratory specimen had suddenly sat up and spoken, thereby revealing that it wasn't, after all, worth studying. "Surely you're not that stupid, Mr. Jessup?" he asked pleasantly. "I can't believe I haven't explained myself already. Who else was there? Think of it that way."

"You've explained yourself all right. What I don't understand is how you know so much."

"Do we?"

"Everything."

Davies grinned. "Maybe there isn't much to know." He leaned back contentedly and puffed his pipe.

Conrad realized that he was outclassed. "Thanks," he said. "Thanks very much."

When he got to the door Davies said, "You've been lucky this time. But remember, we'll need you again. So be available. Don't go away. Don't do anything rash."

"I don't have any choice in the matter, do I?"

Davies smiled happily. "That's right. You don't have any choice." He lit another match and bent again to his pipe.

13

THE YOUNG DETECTIVE drove Conrad home in an unmarked car and did not speak. Like Davies, he seemed disappointed. He grinned maliciously as he left and touched the curls of his forehead in a mock salute.

"We'll be seeing you."

Conrad ignored him.

He wandered into the sitting room, poured himself a drink, then sat scratching the dog's ears and staring at the new painting which still leaned against the fireplace.

Maybe that, too, would be used in evidence against him.

They had given him a packet when he left the police station. He emptied the contents onto the floor. Birth certificate, marriage certificate, medical card, passport, and the manila envelope from his studio. He counted the money and was surprised to find none was missing. He assumed that because it was gambling money—unearned, unofficial, marginal—they would take their discreet cut. Once again, he had underestimated their seriousness.

He climbed up to the attic to put the envelope back in its hiding place. The padlock was in place but the studio was tidier than when he had left it. Otherwise they had left no sign.

Four o'clock.

They had taken eight hours of his life. So far.

Any minute the boys would be home from school. He

wondered where Betsy had got to, remembered the two whiskey glasses, then shrugged.

How could he argue now?

Not that he wanted to argue.

Not that he had ever wanted to argue.

He went back downstairs and clicked his tongue at the dog. It leaped up immediately, quivering with expectation, and ran to the front door. Just as Conrad unhooked its leash from the hall stand, the telephone began to ring.

"Hullo."

Silence.

"Hullo."

Silence again, not even the sound of breathing. Yet he was aware of a vague presence at the other end, of someone waiting, listening, making up his mind. Or hers.

"Hullo," he repeated more loudly.

There was a faint rustling sound, like a distant laugh.

"Fuck off," shouted Conrad.

He was about to slam down the receiver when he remembered something. "Franz Kafka Is Innocent, O.K.?'" He paused a moment to see if they appreciated the joke, but there was still no sound, so he went out, slamming the door behind him. By the time he reached the gate the telephone was ringing again. He walked on.

The Heath was full of mothers pushing prams. Children and dogs ran in the strong sunlight. He walked briskly to the place where he had found the girl. The grass was trampled and the brambles spread out, but otherwise there was no sign of anything unusual.

A heavily built man was sitting on a bench nearby, reading a newspaper. His clothes were dark and his black shoes highly polished, but he wore no tie and sported a Zapata mustache. He glanced briefly at Conrad, then went on with his paper.

Conrad picked up a stick, threw it for the dog, and marched on. When he had gone fifty yards he looked back.

The man was watching him. He had put down his paper and had a bulky notebook on his knee.

Kim bounded ahead, zigzagging along mysterious, pungent tracks, urinating against certain trees and ignoring others, following its own nose and its own rules. It moved in great arcs around the path, circled back, dashed ahead for no discernible reason, then returned panting, feigning obedience, but in reality hoping for Conrad to throw it another stick.

When he reached the long bushy slope which looks across to Ken Wood Conrad stretched himself out in the deep grass, took off his jacket, and folded it neatly for a pillow. It still smelled faintly of the cell, a mixture of urine and disinfectant, the institutional smell of poverty. He unbuttoned his shirt to the pleasant warmth of the sun and lay watching the rooks circle above the wood. Small clouds, like puffs of white smoke, hurried across the sky. The air was bright. A group of children, playing on the opposite side of the little valley, were calling excitedly to each other.

What had the police told Betsy and Horace and what would he tell them?

It occurred to him that he was about to lose both his wife and his job, but somehow the prospect failed to stir him.

He stretched out an arm lazily and rubbed the grass with his palm. It felt silky and cool. Buttercups nodded at him at eye level, swaying faintly on their thin hard stems, the undersides of their petals so bright with yellow light that they seemed wet. He listened to the trees simmering gently behind him. Kim lay at his feet, forepaws crossed, ears pricked, tongue lolling with pleasure.

"Let it all go," Conrad told it.

The dog reached its head forward and licked his hand.

When he got home Betsy was out in the kitchen cooking the children's supper. She gave him her slightly blurred version of a tragic look and said, "For God's sake." Her eyes were puffy with crying.

"Don't *For God's sake.* There's no percentage in it. A mistake was made and now it's been cleared up. *Finita la commedia.*" Then he added irritably, "Anyway, I'm the one in trouble, not you."

"You should have told me."

"You didn't want to know, remember? I could have assassinated the Pope and you still wouldn't have wanted to know. So don't start getting indignant now." Her red-rimmed eyes and victimized air seemed a deliberate provocation. He stuck his fists in his pockets and carefully lowered his voice. "Listen, the girl's all right. She'll identify the man and that'll be that. In fact, she probably has already. That's why they let me go."

Betsy seemed not to have heard him. "You're gambling again. All those lies about a client. It's just like it used to be, except that now I can't take it anymore."

"No, it's not. Those days are dead and gone. I've given up losing."

She swung around on him in fury. "You make me sick. You have one lucky evening and suddenly everything's different. You'll go back next week and they'll skin you alive as they always have."

"You don't understand. It's an attitude of mind. In the long run, losers lose and winners win. That's the beauty of it."

"Now you tell me. Well, I'll tell you something: I'm not staying around for the long run. I'm not going through all that again, so you'd better make up your mind what you want, me or the cards."

He looked at her in amazement and said nothing. Even Betsy, Our Lady of Routine, whose life he thought he knew from morning tea until the three colored dots faded on the television screen, was proving unpredictable. She stood by the stove, legs planted stolidly apart and shoulders squared, in one hand a frying pan full of sausages, in the other a spatula. Her eyes blazed, her curls bristled, the blood glowed in her cheeks. Yet there was no sign of booze. She had strengths he had never dreamed of. He felt left behind.

When he smiled at her and reached out a hand she turned away brusquely and started shoveling food on to the children's plates. She does have a life elsewhere, he decided. A lover. And was again surprised to feel neither angry nor jealous, but relieved.

He went back into the sitting room, took down the muddy painting which hung above the fireplace, and put his new picture in its place. He looked at it critically, nodded, clicked his tongue. After all these years of false starts, there it was. The genuine article, complete in itself, containing all the answers. Just like Betsy. And he realized that, just like Betsy, he didn't give a damn.

"So what?" he muttered. "Big deal."

He carried the old painting up to the attic and dumped it face to the wall with all the others. Folly and conceit. Like the terrorists blowing up restaurants. Like the policemen who knew all the answers. Like the inscriptions on the cell wall. Whistling in the dark.

He took out the manila envelope and counted the money again, dealing out the notes expertly, like cards. That, at least, was a pleasure which did not fail. He was on his way. He began to hum to himself: "They can't take that away from me." But the tune reminded him vaguely of something he no longer wished to remember, so he stopped.

When he went back downstairs the boys were wolfing sausages and baked beans. But they paused when he came into the kitchen and looked at him with interest, almost with respect.

"Tell us what it was like."

"Cosy. Like *Dixon of Dock Green*. You've seen it already."

"Did they beat you up?"

"Did they give you a truth drug?"

"Don't talk with your mouth full," said Betsy.

Conrad said, "The man in charge didn't look like Kojak,

he looked like my headmaster. Which put the fear of God in me more than Kojak would have done."

"But what did they *do*?"

"Nothing. There were no bright lights, no rubber truncheons. They just asked me questions. You know what they say in the papers: 'A man is helping the police with their inquiries.' Well, that was me. I helped them with their inquiries. And when they realized I couldn't help them anymore they let me go."

"Is that all?"

"Don't sound so disappointed."

"At least it was exciting."

"It's an excitement I could have done without. So could your mother."

"Eat your supper before it gets cold," said Betsy.

"Then you can watch the real thing on telly," said Conrad.

His wife was watching him coolly from under her bristling curls and seemed unamused by his attempts to jolly her through the children. "When do you want to eat?" she asked.

"Go ahead without me. I'm going to the hospital to leave some flowers for the girl. I owe her something."

Betsy surveyed her husband bleakly. Her skin seemed grainy with fatigue and depression, as though her pores too had been weeping.

"My, but you do live a full and busy life."

She pushed the words out theatrically, but sarcasm was not one of her things and neither she nor Conrad was impressed.

He shrugged. "Just lucky, I suppose."

He wondered what her boyfriend was like and if she was already quarreling with him. The idea gave him a certain grim pleasure. Let them get on with it.

He paused in the hallway and called, "See you later," in an unnaturally friendly voice, then closed the front door behind him before she had time to reply.

14

THE STEELY-LOOKING WOMAN from the dress shop was sitting by the girl's bed, her hands clasped in her lap, her head bent under its silver casque of hair, as though in contemplation. A thin young man with bushy eyebrows and a prematurely lined face was sitting on the opposite side of the bed, staring at the bandaged girl, who seemed to be sleeping. The two watchers sat so quietly, almost formally, on either side of the bandaged figure, that they might have been posing for a *pietá*. Their faces had the bloodless, slightly waxy look of a Sienese painting. The room smelled of sickness although there were flowers everywhere: on the bedside table and the television set, along the walls and camouflaging the ominous machines with dials and dead gray screens.

Conrad held a bunch of roses in front of him by way of excuse. He closed the door softly and muttered, "Miss Pelham?"

The silver-haired woman put a long finger to her lips and nodded warningly toward the bed. At that moment the girl opened her eyes and looked at him. He remembered the odd way her eyes curved down, then sharply up again at the corners, but their color surprised him: remote greeny-blue, like ice in a crevasse. They were nothing like his painting. Because her hair was hidden under a turban of bandages and her face was almost as pale as the pillows, her eyes seemed unnaturally large and definite.

Conrad hovered at the door.

"Yes?" said the older woman. She had a faintly foreign accent.

"They said I could come up for a moment."

"Yes?" said the woman again.

Conrad took no notice of her. He spoke to the girl: "I'm the chap who found you on the Heath. I've brought you these." He pushed the roses forward hopefully, but nobody moved to take them.

"So you're the fellow." The older woman looked at him critically. "I see." She nodded to herself, as though her worst fears had been confirmed.

The young man uncrossed his legs and smiled bonily. "Did they give you a hard time?"

"Hard enough."

"But all's well that ends well."

"If it ends well."

"Hasn't it?"

"They aren't committing themselves."

"They never do. But you can't blame them, can you?"

"I'm not."

Conrad crossed to where the young man was sitting and put the roses on the girl's bed.

She fingered them idly, as though to test if they were real. "How lovely." When she smiled her rather goatish mouth seemed curiously innocent.

"I'm glad you're all right," said Conrad.

"A miracle," said the older woman.

The girl said, "Thanks to you." Her voice seemed to come from a long way off. She made another effort: "I'm sorry you've had trouble."

"We don't know your name," said the other woman.

"Conrad Jessup."

"Well, Mr. Jessup, we're all very grateful. My name is

Elizabeth Staff and this is Timothy Leyton, Miss Pelham's fiancé." Then she added grimly, "You and Olivia have already met. So to speak."

"Olivia, like the shop?"

Mrs. Staff looked at him sharply and said, "How . . . ?" Then her face froze in a wintry smile. "We have known each other a long time," she said.

There was a pause. Mrs. Staff's wintry smile faded. Timothy drew in a long, whistling breath through his teeth, then exhaled slowly in a sigh. Olivia looked at Conrad quizzically. But when he smiled at her she smiled back.

"Have they caught the man?" asked Conrad.

Another pause. Mrs. Staff and Timothy glanced at each other briefly, then she said, "Not yet. He seems to have disappeared."

"How come?"

Mrs. Staff looked at him with distaste. "Nobody knows him. Olivia met him at a party, but no one seems to have invited him. He must have just wandered in. A gatecrasher." Then she added, as if to forestall argument, "It does happen, you know."

Conrad nodded sympathetically. "They'll get him in time."

"Let's hope," said Timothy.

Mrs. Staff took no notice of them. "Yet he seemed presentable enough," she went on. "Or so Olivia says."

The girl said nothing. She was fingering the roses and seemed not to be listening. Her face was calm and remote.

"Tell me," said Mrs. Staff casually, "how did you happen to be there?"

"I was walking my dog."

The woman stared at him, blank-faced, and said nothing.

"The police have my statement. *They* believe me."

Timothy coughed. "You keep rather odd hours. If you'll forgive my saying."

"Only sometimes. And sometimes I don't sleep. You know how it is."

97

"Not really." Timothy also studied Conrad in silence for a moment. Then he said, "A lucky coincidence."

"Thank the dog," said Conrad brightly. But nobody smiled.

"Ah, yes, the dog." Mrs. Staff nodded, but her face still registered nothing.

Timothy turned to her and said very distinctly, "God alone knows what might have happened without the dog."

The woman nodded back at him. "Correct. Perfectly correct."

There was another silence. Finally, Conrad said, "I'd better go."

"Yes, you'd better," Mrs. Staff answered at once.

"May I come back?"

The older woman opened her mouth to speak, but Olivia said, "Please," so she held her peace.

Timothy opened the door for Conrad. He shook his hand languidly and said in an intimate voice, "We're terribly grateful, you know," then closed the door firmly behind him.

A plainclothes detective was sitting at the end of the corridor, reading a newspaper. Conrad studied him while he waited for the lift, but the man pretended not to notice.

Another detective was on a bench in the entrance hall, opposite the reception desk. Conrad stared at him too. He was amazed how easily he recognized them and wished he felt as confident about the people upstairs.

15

HORACE ALPORT questioned Conrad for a long time in what he imagined was a thoughtful, statesmanlike way. He expressed shock, he expressed concern, but in carefully modulated tones. And when Conrad tried to complain about the police, Horace said, "Well, you can't blame them, can you?" Just as the young man at the hospital had done.

This time Conrad decided to be indignant. "Do you really think I had something to do with it?"

"Don't be ridiculous. But you must admit it was stupid not to leave your name."

"Why? Just to save them a couple of days? They'd have suspected me, whatever. So let the bastards sweat for their living."

"Don't get worked up. Paranoia is bad for the bowels."

"You're out of touch, Horace. These days it's supposed to be the one true wisdom. Anyway, even paranoids have their enemies. Or so they say."

"Of course they do."

"If you can't blame the police, then don't blame me."

"I'm not blaming you. Nobody's blaming you anymore. Not even the police."

"That's right. They're all blaming the man who got away. Very convenient."

"As long as they're not blaming you."

"I think it stinks. Those people at the hospital, they know

more than they're letting on about the fantastic disappearing man."

Horace looked at him gloomily and shook his head. "You're letting me down, sunshine. You know what? You sound disappointed you're no longer the prime suspect." He leaned across the desk, his florid face full of concern. "Are you sorry they let you go?" he asked.

Conrad sat still for a moment to attend to this. Finally he shrugged. "That's a good question. I wish I knew the answer."

Horace leaned back contentedly. "You're a funny little sod, sunshine. You really are."

Conrad tugged an imaginary forelock. "Thank you, Mr. Alport, sir. I aim to amuse."

Horace put his elbows back on the table and resumed his serious expression. "What worries me is not all this nonsense with the police. That's just a ludicrous mistake. It's the gambling that worries me."

Conrad closed his eyes a moment, then said, "Poker's not gambling. It's a game of skill. Ask anyone who plays." He tried not to sound surly.

"You could lose a lot of money and then where'd you be? Back where you were a couple of years ago, that's where."

"It was a social game with friends for small stakes. And as a matter of fact, I won."

"How small is small?"

Conrad looked the older man in the eye and wondered how much the police had told him. Under the earnestness he thought he detected a flicker of genuine curiosity. Time to bluff, he decided, and divided by ten.

"I made twenty-four quid. A nice little going-home present."

Horace seemed satisfied. "No harm in that." Then he added placatingly, "I just don't want to see you getting into that kind of trouble again."

"It's the other kind of trouble that worries me."

"Don't let it. That's all over."

"I don't know what to think."

"Then don't. If you must think, think dirty. That's my motto." As usual, he roared with laughter at his own joke. The examination was over.

Abe called during the afternoon. "I hear you got problems," he said.

"That's one way of putting it."

"Maybe I can help. Want to meet for a drink?"

"I doubt if you can, but a drink would be nice."

"Six o'clock at the Ritz, then. The Winter Garden."

"I'm grateful. Really."

"Don't be. I was going to call you anyway."

As Conrad was putting down the receiver, he had a thought. "Hey," he said, "how did you get my number?"

"Herb, of course."

"Oh, yes, Herb. Of course."

Conrad arrived on time but Abe was already installed at a little gold-legged table, reading the *Financial Times*. His back was toward the reclining bronze nymph who dominated the room.

"See that guy over there?" Abe nodded toward a soberly suited gentleman with white hair and a whiskey complexion who was sitting with a surprisingly young girl. "A year ago he was worth four million. Now he's scraping around trying to hustle up a few gee to put in his back pocket and tide him over the next twelve months."

"What happened?"

"Property. What else? Talk about getting your fingers burned. This was worse than the Great Fire of London."

"Poor bastard."

"Don't lose any sleep. He'll get by. So he's having to sell his second Rolls Royce."

"The girl's young enough to be his daughter."

"Granddaughter." Abe wiped his mouth with a stiff white

handkerchief. "I just hope she likes company. Old Hugh's a great one for party games. I asked him why once and he said, 'The truth is, I feel so lonely when I screw.' It's the only joke I ever heard him make and I still don't know if he was trying to be funny."

"He's not got much to be funny about now."

"I think you can safely say that at the moment he's in a situation where jokes don't apply."

Abe sipped his drink and shifted his large body in the chair. His suit was expensive but irredeemably rumpled, as if no tailor could cope with the shifting bulges, sweat, and uneasiness of his large body. But his hands were small and neat, the hair on them darker than the hair on his head.

"Tell me about it," he said, then sat impassively while Conrad told him, not interrupting, not even nodding. He was so still that Conrad was afraid he had gradually stopped listening and was brooding on something else. This made him anxious. The more he talked, the more he realized how isolated he was, and how bewildered. He needed an ally, a listener, even if the only bond between them was the desire to do each other down over the poker table. At least that meant Abe might take him seriously, and he had a sudden, disproportionate urge to be taken seriously by someone. So he talked on in a low urgent voice while Abe sat perfectly still and watched the ice slowly dissolve in his whiskey glass.

When he finished the fat man took a long, thirsty drink. "It sounds like you're off the hook," he said. "So what bothers you?"

"The girl bothers me. The creeps around her bother me. The police bother me. I mean, how the hell do they know so much about me? And for no reason. A handful of parking tickets and one lost dog. What sort of criminal career is that?"

Abe shrugged. "Maybe they know about everybody. You pay taxes, don't you? That's one computer that has you taped. And I mean taped in every possible sense. Then there's Social Security and National Health and the Passport Office, not to mention the company you work for and the people who insure you and the other people who supply you with credit cards. You're on the books, baby, you're known. We all are, more or less." Little beads of sweat stood out on his upper lip, despite the carefully regulated temperature of the hotel.

"It gives me the willies," said Conrad.

"You better get used to it, friend. That's the world we live in." He took out his handkerchief again and wiped his upper lip. "You got kids?"

Conrad nodded.

"It'll be worse for them. Console yourself with that."

The man with white hair got up, pulled back the little table for the girl, and followed her out. He nodded to Abe as he passed, and smiled grimly.

Abe watched them go. "Sometimes I'm glad I'm not a fly on the wall. That's going to be one heavy interlude I'd prefer not to witness."

Beads of sweat formed again on his upper lip and along his hairline. It occurred to Conrad that his size was disproportionate to his strength and that he probably wouldn't live long. He felt suddenly fond of this overweight stranger, with his sweats and glooms and curious friends in power.

He said again, "It gives me the willies."

"You mean Hugh and his spinner?"

"I mean the police."

Abe signaled to the waiter for more drinks. He glanced quickly at Conrad, then glanced away. "You sure they got nothing on you?"

"You know where I was until two-thirty. You're my alibi, remember?"

"Yeah, I remember. They called me up. It was just like being back in New York, only more polite. It almost made me homesick. Almost."

"Why did you leave?"

"These days I'm no longer sure, but then it made sense. Two wives on my back scrabbling for alimony. And when it wasn't them it was my old ma, God rest her soul, telephoning every morning at nine-o-five, right on the button, like she was computerized. I asked her once, 'Why the o-five, Ma?' and she answered, 'I don't vant I should vake you up.' Get it, Conrad? In her world people only woke up on the hour, just like the news bulletins. Crazy and driving me crazy with her. So I split. My kid sister stayed and now she's in the bin. A nice kosher place on Lon-Gisland, as they say in those parts. The poor bitch is so far gone she doesn't even know the old lady's dead and there's no reason to be gaga anymore."

When the waiter arrived he called Abe "Mr. Gauss" and squirted soda into his whiskey without being asked. Abe said, "Thank you, Arthur," and smiled amiably.

"Do you go back?" asked Conrad.

"Not often. It got kinda complicated. I was involved in this big deal, see, and it was highly profitable. But that has its problems. If you make a killing, you don't necessarily make friends in the process. That was another incentive for coming to England. But the property boom was just starting and before I knew it I was involved again. Same game, different ground rules. I guess I couldn't stop myself. Once a wheeler-dealer, always a wheeler-dealer."

"And now?"

"Now I wheel less but I'm still dealing. I know people, I do favors, I fix things. I work out the percentages. One way or the other, it's all poker." He shifted uneasily on the fragile chair. "The main thing is to keep out of the system, stay between the lines, maintain a low profile. They can still screw you, of course, but not so easily."

"The other night you said we might do business together. What made you say that?"

"You're a player. You know the odds. Or that's my impression."

Two heavily made-up women came up the steps of the Winter Garden, surveyed the room briefly, then settled at the table vacated by the man with white hair. Both had fur coats slung around their shoulders.

"Mink in this weather," said Conrad. "What are they trying to prove?"

"Sable. And that's what they're trying to prove."

"What?"

"That they're beyond mink." Abe kept his eyes on Conrad. "Do you know the odds?"

"Only at the poker table." Conrad watched the women, who seemed to be quarreling. "Elsewhere I don't know a thing anymore. A few days ago I was an aging junior executive who used to gamble and was trying not to. Then a society girl I'd never seen gets knocked over the head and robbed. Lo and behold, the police pull me in and treat me as if I had a record. Now, of course, I do have a record. But all I did was take my bloody dog for a walk at an unlikely hour. What kind of crime is that?"

"Don't take it so hard. There may be nothing to worry about."

"It doesn't feel that way."

Abe studied him attentively but not unkindly. Then his depressed, jowled face relaxed and he smiled like a child. "I know a few people in the police. Maybe I can help."

"How?"

"Ask some unofficial questions, that's all." His face settled back into its habitual gloom. "But don't bank on it. This kind of problem is a bit outside my range. Money, yeah. Money is easy. But you're not supposed to hurt people. Except in the line of duty or business, of course. And that's a job for professionals."

"I didn't hurt anyone. But I've been thinking: maybe the girl was hurt in the line of business."

"How come?"

"The police said she was carrying a lot of money. So

what's an elegant young girl doing with a wad of money on Hampstead Heath at three in the morning? And with a perfect stranger, a chap her friends say she'd just picked up at a party."

Abe smiled again. "You're about to tell me."

"A connection. The guy's her connection. She's going to buy dope. That's why they're all playing it so close."

Abe leaned back in his chair and laughed appreciatively. The tire of fat around his middle wobbled and sweat broke out on his face again. "I'm like you, Conrad, a gambler. Horses I know about. Horse is not my scene."

Conrad also laughed, since it seemed to be expected of him. He swallowed some whiskey and pulled out his hand-kerchief to wipe his foxy mustache. But when he saw how soiled and rumpled his handkerchief was he blushed and stuffed it hastily back into his pocket.

"The other day on the tube I was buttonholed by a mad-man who thought I was part of a plot against him. At the time I felt sorry for him. Now I'm beginning to feel he was right. There are plots everywhere and if you go around thinking the world is as it seems you are at a disadvantage."

Abe nodded like a kindly uncle. "Don't take it to heart, my friend. It's not a question of plots. It's just that people tend not to be more honest than is strictly necessary. There are survivors and there are schmucks. The survivors are the ones who work out the odds in advance and take the proper precautions. Like I said, it's all poker. One way or another."

One of the women was looking at Conrad, but when he caught her eye she pursed her lips irritably and said some-thing to her companion. They both laughed.

"Take my advice," said Abe. "Join the club. It's bigger than you think." He looked at his watch and signaled to the waiter. "I gotta go," he said. He signed the bill without reading it, gave the waiter a pound note, and began to lever himself out of his chair.

Conrad leaned forward. "Listen," he said, "while I was sitting in that cell I had a revelation."

Abe paused halfway up, like a whale about to blow.

"I realized that what was wrong was I hadn't done a thing. If I'd really coshed that girl and nicked her money, I'd have somehow been in a better position. I'd have known what to hide, I'd have known how to defend myself. As it was I didn't know which direction they were coming from."

"So?"

"So I decided it's time I stopped pussyfooting around. If they're going to hang me anyway, it might as well be for a sheep."

Abe laughed. "What are you planning to do, stick up a bank?"

"I haven't made up my mind yet. Got any suggestions?"

Abe remained poised, as if by a miracle, on the edge of his chair. "Maybe." Then he beamed at him affectionately. "Meanwhile, just be careful. Stay cool. So you're beginning to discover that you don't know the difference between shit and shoe polish. A little late in the day, if I may say so. Maybe you also don't know about trouble. Think about that before you do something rash."

Conrad stood up. He felt he had made a fool of himself and blushed again. "It was just an idea. I thought it might appeal to you."

Abe struggled to his feet. Although he was not much taller than Conrad, his great belly and heavy shoulders made him seem enormous. "It does. And I'm full of admiration. I just wouldn't want you to do anything stupid."

"I wasn't planning to."

In the lobby a party of elderly people in evening dress were braying at each other in powerful county accents. Abe eyed them coldly, straightened his tie, but did not do up his collar button. "What you need at this moment, friend, is money. Nothing like it for cheering you up."

"At this moment and at all other moments."

Abe shrugged. "Particularly at this moment, by the look of you."

One of the party-goers gave a brief shout of laughter. Abe rolled his eyes to the distant ceiling. "There's a horse running at Newcastle on Saturday. Summer Lightning. If they start overnight, they still can't beat him. You should get twenty to one."

"Why such good odds, if it can't lose?"

"That's a long story. And I shouldn't be telling you this, anyway. So do me a favor: keep your bets small and spread them around. Go to fifty bookmakers if you want, but bet in tenners or less. Otherwise the odds will shorten and we'll all be screwed. O.K.?"

"O.K."

There was another violent burst of laughter, full of self-congratulation.

"Talk about laws," said Abe. "There should be a law against that."

16

THERE WAS A SMALL eye-level window in the door and he watched the girl through it for a moment before he went in. While he was doing this he was aware that he, in turn, was being watched by the plainclothes detective at the end of the corridor.

She was lying with her eyes closed. The pillows, sheets, and the great burnoose of bandages around her head were staring white and made her face seem old. Even her lips seemed drained of color.

Elizabeth Staff was sitting beside her as before, leaning forward and talking. Her mouth moved with great emphasis and Conrad thought how easy it would be to lip-read someone with a death's-head face. She was holding the girl's hand in both of her own, clasping it with her left, stroking it slowly from wrist to fingertips with her right. The heavy rings glittered on her moving fingers. The two women seemed more intimate than mother and daughter.

Conrad turned and nodded to the detective, who took no notice. Then he knocked loudly on the door, paused and went in. Mrs. Staff lifted her taut wintry face to him and did not react. He was astonished that anyone could be so in control as to register nothing at all. Maybe that was how she saw the world: as nothing, but with distaste.

The girl, however, opened her eyes and smiled at him.

Despite her bandages and her pallor, she seemed somehow more solid, as if she had gained weight during the last few days. The room was still full of flowers but the ominous medical machines had been cleared away.

"I came to see how you're getting on."

"Did you?" said Mrs. Staff.

"Better," said the girl. "It aches a bit, that's all."

"Thank God," said Conrad emphatically, though he was not sure if he meant it for her sake or his.

Mrs. Staff folded her hands in her lap and said nothing.

"But I'm still tired," said Olivia. "You don't know how tired."

"I can guess."

Mrs. Staff got up abruptly. "I must make a telephone call. You talk to Olivia. Amuse her." She went out, still without smiling.

"How does she keep it up?" Conrad asked.

The girl laughed in a ghostly way: a quick puff of breath and a small noise at the back of her throat. "That's just her manner. She's very kind really. At least to me."

"I've played poker against people like that. And usually lost."

Olivia looked at him amused, her eyes clear and dispassionate. "Is that your thing?"

Conrad squirmed on his chair. She too had his number. "Just from time to time," he mumbled. "It breaks the monotony."

She nodded sympathetically. "Anything to break the monotony. But anything."

There was an awkward pause. A door opened in the passage outside and a voice, over the voices of the television, said brightly, "Bye, darling. Bye till tomorrow." Determinedly cheerful, trying to mask the relief.

"Have they found the man yet?"

"Not that I know."

"How could he just disappear? It doesn't make sense."

110

"Nothing makes sense about that night. I suppose I'm to blame."

"You still can't remember anything about him?"

"If I could, they'd probably find him."

"I suppose."

He studied the delicate lines of her face carefully, trying to order them in his mind for future reference, future paintings. The slanting, ice-blue eyes were too remote for someone so young.

"You're very philosophical about it," he said.

"What else is there to be? I've learned my lesson."

"It might have been your last."

"But it wasn't. So . . ."

Her voice trailed away and there was another pause. There seemed nothing left to say. Maybe, he thought, she really does know nothing.

"Is there anything you want?" he said at last. "Anything I can get you?"

She shook her head, then smiled at him ironically. "What about you? What is it you want?"

"I'd like to paint you."

Her eyes widened mockingly and she raised her eyebrows. "You paint too, as well as gamble?"

He smiled back at her. "I'm a man of parts." Some kind of barrier between them had fallen.

"Well," she said thoughtfully, "I don't see why not. Once I'm out of here and this bloody turban's gone and my hair's grown back a bit. I don't see why not."

"That's something to look forward to. How long do you think they'll keep you?"

"They're not saying. They never do."

Mrs. Staff came back into the room and Conrad got up immediately. He turned at the door and said, "I'll see you."

"Please," Olivia replied, and smiled again.

Mrs. Staff looked at her quickly, then at him, but said nothing.

17

AFTER THE HOSPITAL there seemed no point in going home. So he went to a private club above a dairy in North Kensington where four gloomy Greeks and two West Indians were playing five-card stud. He left after midnight, having lost twenty pounds slowly, and was jigging his way through the side streets between Ladbroke Grove and the Harrow Road when he first noticed that the car was following him. It was a silver Cortina, with two large men in the front seat. He went on carefully, keeping meticulously to the speed limit, even down the long empty stretches. He assumed they were waiting for him to make a mistake, then on would go their peaked caps and out would come the breathalyzer.

They were still behind him at the Harrow Road traffic lights. When he moved off sedately he thought they would leave him, knowing he had recognized them and was being a good boy. But at the next lights they were still there, right on his tail, not bothering to pretend. He turned left down the dingy avenue, right and left through the dogleg at its end, staying under thirty. The Cortina remained a steady twenty yards behind, as though guided by remote control.

On the long straight up to the roundabout behind Maida Vale a Jaguar swished past them at speed, roared into the roundabout with a brief, bright flash of brake lights, then disappeared. The Cortina stayed where it was. Conrad began to sweat. If it was the police, it wasn't an ordinary patrol car. He could not think who else it might be.

He also could not think what business it was of the police or anybody else what he was doing at twelve-thirty-four in the morning.

"Shit," he muttered and put his foot down on the accelerator. As he came up to the roundabout, he went through the gears instead of braking and swung left as the traffic light beyond began to change. The Cortina came after him, ignoring the red.

He went across Maida Vale into the dim side roads behind the council flats, over the railway bridge where someone had painted "PSYCHIATRY KILLS" in large ragged letters, through more side streets into West End Lane. He went up and down through the gearbox so that his brake lights would not warn them when he was about to turn. He touched sixty through the curves of West End Lane, tires protesting loudly, and the other car was no longer in sight when he passed West Hampstead station.

The lights were with him all the way. By the time he swung off up Lyndhurst Road, he thought he had lost them. But at Finchley Road the lights were red, the traffic heavy. He kept the car in gear and flipped the engine impatiently, watching his rear mirror and hoping they had missed the turning.

Just as the lights began to change he saw headlights sweep around the curve at the bottom of the hill, closing on him fast. He swore and let in the clutch with a bang. The rear of the car shimmied from side to side as the tires tried to grip, then he was off uphill again into the shortcuts he had known for years. He left smoke on the air and the smell of burning rubber.

He switched off the car lights as he turned into his own street. The pub traffic was gone. Nothing moved except the trees against the lamps. He parked a few yards from his house and sat listening to the engine creaking as it cooled. The car was full of the smell of hot oil.

He waited a moment, listening, and watched the tangled shadows of the trees move across the front of his house. Only the bedroom lights were on. The whole street slept.

Let them sort that one out, he thought, and opened the car door just as the Cortina came around the corner, its tires screaming. He sat there, half in half out of the car, lit by the courtesy light as though for inspection.

The other car roared past, then braked heavily fifty yards up the road. A man came out at a run, but Conrad was already out of the car and up the steps of his house. He thanked God for the teenager who had shot out the street-lamp and thanked Him again that Betsy had left the hall in darkness. As a sign of disapproval. But bless her, all the same.

He ran up the stairs two at a time and into the bedroom. She lay as usual propped against the pillows, reading a magazine. She looked at him resentfully and opened her mouth to speak.

"Switch off the light," he ordered.

Her eyes widened, her mouth closed. She did as she was told.

He went to the window and inched the curtain aside. A large man was walking along the other side of the street, studying each house in turn. Even under the dull lights his curly hair glowed bright ginger.

"What's happening now?" Betsy whispered plaintively.

Conrad whispered back, "I wish I knew."

She came and stood beside him and peered out of the slit between the curtain and the wall. At that moment the man with ginger hair seemed to look directly at them. But he moved on without pausing. They watched him pad up the street, examining house after house.

"He's not the police," said Conrad, "or he'd know my address."

The Cortina came slowly back down the road, its headlights full on. It paused at Conrad's car and the driver leaned out to test the lock. His face was pale and fat. His bald head, with its tonsure of dark hair, gleamed. Then he drove on to where the other man was waiting. They conferred briefly, then the car drove away. The man with ginger hair strolled on down the road.

Betsy sniffed loudly and went back to bed. "Now what are you doing?" When Conrad did not reply her voice rose accusingly. "What are you mixed up in?"

"I wish I knew," he repeated. In the dim light that filtered through the curtains he could see her face, round-eyed and uncertain. "I'm not doing this to get you. In fact, I'm not doing anything."

She sniffed again. "Yes, you are. You're mucking up my life. My life and the boys'."

"For God's sake, don't cry. Not again."

But it was too late. He left her snuffling and fumbling for Kleenex and marched downstairs. He switched on the hall light, called the dog, and walked angrily off down the street. He could see the man with ginger hair outlined against the shop lights at the end of the road.

Damn them, he thought, why should they make me hide? Anyway, they don't know who I am. I could be anyone, just a fellow taking his dog for a late-night pee. Then he remembered what had happened last time he had done that and began to walk more slowly.

When he got to the main road the man had disappeared. Conrad turned with relief and began to walk home. He had only gone a few yards when someone stepped out of an alley between two shops. It was the man with ginger hair.

He stood with his legs straddled, his arms hanging loosely. "Aaah," he said. He was grinning.

Conrad said nothing. He made a move as if to walk on, but the man lifted an admonishing, carroty finger: "A word with you, friend."

"What the devil do you want?" Conrad tried to sound managerial.

The man smiled at him almost fondly. "I've got a message," he said. "Stop meddlin'. You're gettin' into things that ain't none of your business. Get in too far and you'll get 'urt."

"A message? What the hell are you talking about?"

"You know, friend. Don't pretend you don't."

"I'll report this to Davies."

"Who the fuck's 'e when 'e's at 'ome?"

Conrad studied the grinning face in front of him. It was as freckled as a child's, but the lips were thick and one front tooth was broken. "You don't know Inspector Davies?"

"Never 'eard of 'im. But I'll tell you one thing, friend: the blue beetles can't 'elp you. And if they could, they won't."

The wind gusted down the road, bringing a spatter of warm rain. The dog stood attentively at Conrad's side, its head cocked. He wondered how it would react if the man moved suddenly. Probably bark and lick him, thinking it was a game. And this, like the grinning face in front of him, made him angry again. "I don't have to eat this shit," he said, and made a move to pass.

"You don't 'ave no choice," the man answered. But he stepped back and did not try to stop him.

As Conrad walked off down the road he could feel the man watching him. So he went slowly, determined not to be stampeded. The dog trotted sedately beside him.

When he reached the pub the man called after him, "Eh, mate."

Conrad paused but did not turn.

"I like yer style," said the man with ginger hair.

Conrad sauntered on, even more slowly. He felt curiously elated. He could handle it. He was used to this sort of thing.

A year before, he had got himself into the bookies for over a thousand. They asked nicely, then less nicely, and finally they made threats. So he wrote them a check and put what cash he had left on a horse that could not lose. It did and the check bounced. The next day two burly men came to the door at breakfast time, pushed Betsy aside, and went around the house inspecting things. One of them had an eagle tattooed on the back of his right hand. They took his hi-fi, his camera, his television set, and Betsy's old Morris. When he complained that all that added up to more than he owed, the man with the eagle said, "You forgot the interest."

It was the loss of the television set that finished Betsy. She left immediately with the children and went to her parents' home, where there were no interruptions to her viewing. He had to grovel to Horace Alport and rent a new set before he collected her. He also made her a promise not to gamble again.

He walked slowly past his house, wondering how he could get in without being seen. But before he was halfway to the far corner a car turned into the road, stopped, and drove past him. It was the Cortina. Both men were in it and they were laughing together. He waited until the car was out of sight, then doubled back indoors.

The voice on the telephone was as bored as ever: "Hampstead police."

"Is Inspector Davies there?"

"I'm afraid not, sir."

"What about Sergeant Evans?"

"Both off, sir. Shall I put you through to the duty sergeant?"

"It doesn't matter."

He went upstairs. The bedroom was in darkness but when he switched on his reading light Betsy was staring at him sullenly.

"Well?" she said.

"Well nothing."

"I can't take any more."

"So be it. But *you* asked."

He got into his pajamas and went into the bathroom. When he returned Betsy was still staring stolidly in front of her. He climbed into bed, suddenly flattened with fatigue, and took her hand.

"Look," he said, "I'm in some kind of trouble."

"What kind?" She lay quite passively and her voice was uninterested.

"I wish I knew."

He squeezed her hand but she took it away abruptly.

"I've come to a conclusion about all this."

"Which is . . . ?"

"It's not my business. You've chosen to leave me out, so let's keep it that way." She turned away from him.

He lay staring at the shadowy ceiling. He was so tired that his body seemed to be dissolving into the bed, as though his frame were sinking down through his flesh. In the morning, he thought, all that will be left will be white bones on the white sheet and a little dry powder where there had once been all this busyness.

Nothingness.

Blackout.

Total eclipse.

It was a sweet thought.

He made a great effort and said slowly, "All we ever get now is a few moments on the way to sleep. I wish I understood how it happened." His voice felt heavy in his mouth. He did not know why he was bothering.

Betsy said briskly, "It's a bit late to think of that," and pulled the blanket around herself in an ostentatiously irritated way.

He made one last effort, as though lifting a great weight.

"Fuck it," he said, and fell asleep.

18 THE FOLLOWING MORNING the Cortina had gone. In its place was a blue Hillman which tagged along behind Conrad without any pretense at disguise. The driver was the man with ginger hair. He was alone but the car had a radio transmitter aerial and Conrad, watching in the rearview mirror, saw him talking into a microphone.

He drove straight to the police station and parked outside. When the man with ginger hair scowled at him as he went past, Conrad raised two derisive fingers.

The open window in Davies' office looked out onto the gardens of the expensive houses between the police station and the Heath. The sunlight streamed peacefully in.

"I have a complaint," Conrad began.

Davies' mouth twitched slightly. Amusement? Conrad wondered. Pleasure? But he said nothing.

"I was followed last night, all the way from Kensington to home. A silver Cortina with two men in it. One fat and pale and mostly bald, the other a big freckled bastard with ginger hair. Ginger was still there this morning, but in a blue Hillman Avenger. He's on his own this time and probably parked down the road."

Davies watched him impassively. He was wearing a light-weight suit, a knit tie, and a pale striped shirt. The elegance of his clothes seemed out of place on his somber frame, like the hint of good humor.

"How do you know they were following you?"

"I asked. I came to the conclusion they were trying to intimidate me and that made me angry. So I took the dog for a stroll and confronted them. Or, rather, one of them: ginger and freckles."

Davies clucked his tongue disapprovingly. "Rash," he said. Then he added, "That dog of yours is a permanent source of worry to me, Mr. Jessup." He was having difficulty in concealing his amusement.

"Are they your men?" Conrad made an effort to sustain his indignation, but the policeman's levity undermined it. He began to feel foolish.

"Perish the thought."

"Then whose are they?"

"I'm not at liberty to say."

"But you know?"

"I have an idea, though I could be wrong."

"Then they're official? They're not gangsters?"

"I'm not at liberty to say."

"I'll get a lawyer on to you. There must be a law against intimidation and harassment."

Davies' silent mirth increased. "I warned you at the start you'd probably need a lawyer, but you wouldn't listen."

Conrad leaned forward and raised his voice. "You mean you're going to do nothing about it? They threatened me and you're going to do nothing? I'm a respectable citizen. I pay taxes. I vote. I have my rights under law."

Davies' face became solemn again. He looked at Conrad with new interest. "They threatened you?"

"They told me that if I didn't stop meddling I'd get hurt."

"Did they, now?" Davies became thoughtful. "That was rather unwise."

"Thanks," said Conrad. "That's one way of putting it."

"Most unwise. And not lawful, of course, not lawful at all."

"So what are you going to do about it?"

Davies sighed. "Nothing. There's nothing I can do. It's not under my control."

Conrad leaned back in his chair and exhaled wearily. "I give up," he said. "It's all beyond me." He stared out of the window at the peaceful gardens and the jumbled backs of the houses. The sky was pale blue, like a thrush's egg, and slightly hazy. "What should I do?" he asked finally.

"If I were you, I'd do what they say: stop meddling." Davies' voice was remote but kindly. He sounded almost sorry.

"I didn't know I was meddling."

"That just goes to show, doesn't it? Keep to your own turf, Mr. Jessup. It doesn't pay to get involved in things you don't understand."

He opened the door for Conrad and shook his hand in an avuncular way. "Don't hesitate to get in touch with me again if you need me. I'm nearly always here." The ghost of a smile was back on his face again.

Conrad paused in the corridor outside the closed door. He thought he heard a snort of laughter.

The blue Hillman slotted into the traffic behind him and followed him to the office. He made no effort to shake it off, but as he drove into the company parking lot he realized he was trapped. There was nowhere he could go and nothing he could do without their knowing about it. It irritated him not to know who "they" were. Or what "they" wanted of him. Or why "they" should wish to trap him. He wondered how he would be able to place all those bets. He brooded on this problem and tried to encourage his anger in order not to think about the alternatives to anger.

Margy bustled in with a cup of coffee almost before he

had sat down, murmuring, "How about a nice chocolate biscuit?"

Duval arrived next, solicitous but more wolfish than ever and gleaming with triumph.

Horace waved cheerily as he passed and boomed, "Fighting fit, eh?"

Others smiled at him more or less nervously over the glass partitions. A few merely stared.

He understood that he had become interesting. After all those years as a piece of office furniture, he had at last acquired interest. It was not a quality to be desired.

At the usual Friday sales conference he sat at the back of the room and had nothing to say. But the others kept asking him his opinion, and when he reluctantly gave it, they deferred to him as if he alone had attained that special wisdom which comes through grief and age. Even Horace, who usually drove through the meeting like a stagecoach, listened patiently, nodded, and said, "Well, yes. You're the man with experience in this." "Experience." The word came up again and again. It made Conrad certain that his days in the office were numbered.

After the meeting the whole sales staff went over to the pub, a tight knot of men moving in convoy, Conrad safely in the middle with Horace, who bombarded him with dirty stories as if everything was perfectly normal. There was no sign of the man with ginger hair.

Conrad ate a sandwich and drank his beer quickly, then elbowed his way out to the Gents'. Nobody followed him and when he had finished the short passage to the bar was empty. He paused, expecting some sober-suited, threatening presence to materialize, then slipped out of the side entrance and hurried down the alley, trying not to run. He looked back when he reached the corner. Nobody.

In the next half-hour he crisscrossed from street to street and found ten bookmakers' shops. At each he put ten pounds to win on Summer Lightning in the 2:30 at Newcastle the next day.

"Where did you get to?" asked Horace when he got back to the pub.

Duval snickered and said, "Been walking your dog again?"

"A touch of the green-apple quickstep," he announced loudly. "After which I needed some air."

"Say no more." Horace held up his large hairy hand. "Spare us, please, the details."

"The green-apple quickstep, Duval old pal. No more, no less."

"It's the exciting life you lead," said Duval. "It can't be good for the digestion."

"More likely the exciting curry I ate last night," Conrad replied. And nothing more was said.

On the way home from the office he stopped at seven more betting shops to place his ten-pound bet. He assumed he was still being followed, but no longer bothered to look. He drove slowly and loitered at each stop to examine the day's results and chat with the punters.

If they wanted to follow him, let them sweat for it. He hoped they were being decently paid for their trouble and wondered if they too were on to Summer Lightning. That depended on who was employing them, which was not an idea he was willing to consider in any detail.

That evening Betsy did not speak to him and he could smell the whiskey on her breath. The face she turned to him was closed and set, but when she settled in front of the television her expression softened and became dreamy, as though she were somewhere altogether different. He was certain she had a lover and was again surprised to feel only relief.

He ate his dinner in the kitchen on his own and thought about going back to the hospital. The girl seemed to be lodged in his fantasies like a shard of glass, catching the light and sending it flickering back into odd corners of his mind.

Anything to break the monotony, she had said. He remembered the way her lips moved and the cold color of her eyes.

But anything. Including the man with ginger hair?

He went into the sitting room and sat for a while, staring at the new painting, wondering how he had managed to do it. The face on the canvas blurred together with the face of the girl in the hospital bed, confusing him. They seemed to contain everything he himself lacked: life, richness, possibility. Also menace. Yet it was he who had painted the picture. It was all beyond him.

Finally, he went up to the studio and put a fresh canvas on the easel. Immediately, his mind went blank. The surface was primed and ready. But the idea of starting all over again made him faintly ill. He pottered about for an hour, cleaning brushes, peering at his sketchbooks, counting his money again, then went back downstairs.

Betsy was already in bed with the light out, lying with her back turned belligerently toward him. He climbed in beside her and picked up a book. After a while she rolled over and said in a flat voice, "Maybe you'd better go."

He put down his book and stared at her with interest. "What do you mean, go?"

"What do you think I mean?"

"Just like that?"

"Don't be naïve. It's been falling apart for years."

He did his American-Jewish accent. "So now you tell me."

"It's too late for funny voices, too late for anything. Why don't you just go? Clear out, beat it, scram, vamoose. Take your pick, but get out."

"Don't cry." He did not touch her. "Why now? Just because I'm in a bit of trouble?"

"Damn you." She cried louder. "Go away. Let me be."

"Just like that," he repeated, and picked up his book

again. He could see no reason to argue. The boys, now he came to think of it, would probably be glad to see the back of him. He brooded on this a moment, then said, "I'll take the dog."

"Fuck the dog," said Betsy, and went on crying.

Conrad read himself to sleep.

He dreamed he was out in the country under a bright, peaceful sky scattered with fluffy clouds. He was walking with Kim along the edge of a field toward a long low building. As he came near, he saw it was not a barn, as he had expected, but a brick tunnel with a curved roof, quite low. When he stood in the entrance his head almost touched the bricks at the top of the curve. The sunlight flooded in. The end of the tunnel was lost in darkness but ten yards away, in the dusty light, the roof was thick with cobwebs and a colony of spiders was moving about busily. They were black and big as his fist, but too far away to bother him. The sun was warm on his back, the dog panted contentedly beside him. When all is said and done, he thought, what harm can they do me? Behind him the green corn moved in the breeze and the larks dipped up and down, singing their hearts out. He told himself there was nothing to be afraid of.

Suddenly, one of the spiders scuttered along the roof straight toward him, making for the light at tremendous speed. He ducked his head into his shoulders, but it was too late. The thing caught in his hair and dropped between his open collar and his throat. When he clapped both hands to his chest in horror he could feel it squirming against his heart, sinewy, determinedly alive. He knew that nothing worse could ever happen to him and started to shout, "I'm going to die. I'm going to die." He was still shouting and struggling when he woke, but Betsy did not stir.

He lay on his side staring at the early sunlight which seeped across the floor. His hands remained clasped to his chest, his knees were drawn up, he was trembling. After a few minutes he rolled onto his back and searched the ceiling. There were no spiders. Even so, the terror did not subside.

He got up, dressed quickly, and walked with Kim through the empty streets, across the Heath to the pond. No one seemed to be following him and the pond was empty, apart from the keeper reading his newspaper in his hut. He swam out to the raft, the dog paddling beside him, making sharp excited noises. Then he rolled onto his back and surveyed the willows bending to the water and the birds coming and going. The dog circled him, bright-eyed, still making hysterical, whimpering sounds. He lay for a while perfectly still, stretched out on the water, then swam slowly back to the landing stage. As he toweled himself down, he realized that the chill muddy water had washed away his fear.

He whistled all the way home and cooked himself a large breakfast while the others slept on. Three more bets to place, then he must set about finding himself a room. He was on his way at last and didn't much care where to.

19

SUMMER LIGHTNING CAME in at twenty to one, two clear lengths ahead of the even-money favorite, Bodega. It was an early race and Conrad spent the rest of the afternoon touring the betting shops to collect his money. When he arrived home he went straight up to the studio, took out the manila envelope, and counted the notes neatly into piles of one hundred pounds. What had begun a couple of months before a twenty-pound gesture of despair was now 4,743 pounds. He wished he had not spoiled his run by losing twenty to the Greeks.

He put the forty-three pounds in his wallet and counted the rest again to make sure it was real. His hands were unsteady and he kept pausing to smooth his mustache. Finally, he stacked the notes together, secured them with a rubber band, and wrapped them in a piece of gray plastic. Since his luck was running, he wondered if he should go down to one of the clubs to play a little poker or see what happened at the roulette table. Then he remembered that luck had nothing to do with his latest win. He was on to something as unpredictable but far more complicated. Again he felt apprehensive, as in his dream, and looked quickly around the room. But there were no cobwebs, no spiders.

When he went into the sitting room Betsy looked up from the television with a face like rock. "Well?"

"Well what?"

"I thought you were going."

"You really mean it?"

"I've been, remember? Now it's your turn."

"Keep it up," said Conrad. "You're doing fine."

She seemed not to have heard. "You're into something nasty. I don't know what it is, because you haven't told me. Because I don't want to know. All I know is, I don't want any part of it. Not for myself, nor for the kids."

"So sweep me under the mat." He looked at her with distaste and patted the wad of money in his pocket for luck. "Is that what your boyfriend wants?"

She blushed fiercely, started to get up, then sank back into the armchair and turned her face to the television set, which emitted a roar of laughter.

"That's none of your damn business," she said.

"Hasn't he done well?" said the television set, then applauded loudly.

Conrad went upstairs and packed a suitcase. When he came back down Betsy was sitting as he had left her, except that now she was nursing a glass of whiskey.

"Where are the boys?" he asked.

"At the Robinsons'."

"What will you tell them?"

"The truth: that we're going to live apart for a bit."

"That'll be jolly."

"How much do they see of you, anyway?"

Conrad dumped his suitcase in the back of the car, then, followed by the dog, he went to the phone booth down the road and called Abe.

"Wife trouble?" said Abe. "Tell me something new."

They arranged to meet at a pub in Soho. Conrad was relieved not to have to face the opulence and decorum of the Ritz knowing there was a dog waiting mournfully in the passenger seat of his car.

He arrived early, bought himself a beer, and settled into a corner. The place was almost empty and the calm late-afternoon light flooded through the open doors. He watched the customers drift in, men on their own and couples full of talk, and wondered which of them was following him. The idea seemed to him so pointless, so disproportionate to the triviality of his life, that he was unable to grasp it properly. Yet they had seemed to know what they were after. He envied them their conviction, their sense of purpose; he felt he should be flattered that they had chosen him.

Maybe the madman on the tube hadn't been so mad, after all. Maybe he had even known a thing or two.

He got up and went to the Gents'. When he had finished he examined his face in the cloudy mirror: thick, surly mouth under the drooping mustache, foxy coloring, faint touches of gray. Portrait of the Artist as a Middle-aged Gambler. He touched the packet of money in his pocket superstitiously, thinking: The one true end. As long as I have that they can't really get to me.

"Why do I bother to paint?" he asked the face in the mirror, and felt a sudden surge of relief, just as he had when he realized Betsy had a lover.

When he came out Abe was standing at the bar. His cream shirt was silk, his tie discreetly patterned, his dark suit faintly lustrous.

"Just like the movies." Conrad was genuinely admiring. "'Stick with me, babe, and you'll dress in silk.'"

"My working clothes. I'm playing at the club and a guy's gotta keep up appearances."

They took their glasses to the corner table. The bar was filling up, but there were no faces Conrad recognized and no one seemed interested in him.

"Still contemplating a life of crime?" asked Abe.

"Not at the moment, thanks to you and Summer Lightning."

The fat man smiled benignly. "I told you she was a good little horse. How much did you get on her?"

"Two hundred. In tens."

"That should tide you over."

"Is she running again?"

"Save your money. Next time you won't get better than two to one. Today was special."

"Apparently. And I'm very grateful."

"Think nothing of it. Just a favor to a friend. Now tell me your next problem."

"You seem to be running a one-man citizens' advice bureau."

Abe shrugged. "I help you, you help me. I'm not in the philanthropy business."

"So far it's been pretty one-sided."

"Who knows what the future holds?"

"Fun and games, naturally. 'Nods, and becks and wreathèd smiles.' "

"You mean from the little woman?"

"Forget the little woman. That's all just a happy accident. An inevitable happy accident, if you see what I mean."

"Then what's the problem?"

"It comes in two sizes: one squat and bald, the other big and ginger."

He told him as quickly as he could, and without fuss, while Abe sat with his unwieldy bulk poised forward and his head cocked, like an alert hippo.

When Conrad finished Abe held his glass up to the light and studied the movement of the bubbles. He shook it a little but the result seemed to fill him with melancholy. "Beats me why they're following you." He set the glass back down on the table carefully. "The police don't need it. Anyway, that's not their style."

"I believe Davies—though don't ask me why. On the other hand, he knew about it."

"That could mean a private agency. They're supposed to inform the local fuzz when they stake out an address. That way they stay kosher if there are complaints." He mopped his

face with a handkerchief, then added casually, "Of course, it could be MI5 or something like that."

Conrad stared at him. "MI5? What's that supposed to mean? The drug squad I could understand."

"Maybe the drug squad, then," said Abe placatingly. "Not that they're all sweetness and light."

"But why MI5? Why should they get into the act?" His voice rose. A young couple standing at the bar turned and looked at him with surprised faces. Then the boy winked at the girl and the girl giggled. Conrad ignored them. "How come everyone knows about this except me? Yet I'm the one in the middle who's getting all the shit."

"Take it easy," said Abe. "I don't know a thing. Just guessing."

"Funny sort of guess."

"I told you I had a pal in the police. So I called him and asked him to check it out for me. But when he got back to me he was kinda evasive. You know how I mean: he wouldn't say yes and he wouldn't say no. But I got the impression there's something fishy about that girl and her buddies, and he was trying to warn me off. Mind you, that could have meant drugs. Those characters are not what you'd call the League of Distressed Gentlefolk."

"That's all very well." Conrad's head was beginning to ache and he felt obscurely insulted by Abe's kindly, concerned manner. "What's all this crap got to do with me? First it was the police, now it's MI5 and the drug squad. Next, I suppose, it'll be the CIA and the KGB. What kind of outrageous bloody game is this? I'm not James Bond, I'm Conrad Jessup, Assistant Sales Manager, father of two and, since this afternoon, of no fixed address."

He glanced at the young couple at the bar. Though their heads were averted they were still watching delightedly and the girl was still giggling. His anger drained abruptly away. "All I want to do is get on with my lousy little life."

Abe said quietly, "Then why go on seeing that girl?"

Conrad spread his hands. "I like her. She intrigues me. She is also very attractive. It makes a change, for Christ's sake, after twelve years with a woman who is married to a television set."

"London, my friend, is stuffed with pretty girls. Indeed, the beaches of the world are strewn with delectable pebbles. Each more unspeakable than the last. Believe me."

"Oh, I believe you. Nevertheless . . ." He got up. "How about another drink?"

"Perrier," said Abe, and when Conrad raised his eyebrows disbelievingly, he added, "Like I said, I'm going to the club. I never drink when I'm working."

When Conrad came back with the glasses Abe said, "Got anywhere to stay?"

Conrad shook his head.

"I got a place you can use. Just around the corner. It's in a new block, mostly offices, and the landlord's a pal of mine. He lets me rent it cheap because he doesn't want some unknown quantity moving in and then installing a whore. Which would screw up the value of the property, right?"

"Are you sure?"

"Quite sure. It's mostly empty, but for ten quid a week how could I refuse? So I keep it for visiting clients or an afternoon snooze. Sometimes an afternoon lay. Things like that, strictly tax deductible."

"I'll pay, of course."

"Whatever makes you feel good. Just use it till something better turns up."

"What about the dog?"

"What dog?"

"Mine. He's in the car."

"You left your wife and kids, but you brought your fucking dog along?" Abe looked at him fondly. "You know something, Conrad? You're the last of the big sentimentalists. How, in Christ's name, do you manage to win at poker? Tell me that."

"Just lucky, I suppose."

"That, my friend, is not what the game's about."

"So they keep telling me."

Conrad left the pub first and walked straight to Soho Square, where his car was parked. He glanced back once but there seemed to be no one following him except Abe, dawdling watchfully along fifty yards behind.

Kim came bouncing out of the car as if released from a life sentence, urinated on the nearest lamppost, then on the railings, then began to bark excitedly.

"Knock it off," growled Conrad, and glanced apprehensively around. But no one seemed to be interested.

When he reached the building in Dean Street the glass door to the entrance hall was locked, but Abe, lurking inside just out of sight, opened it immediately. They watched the street while they waited for the lift, but nobody passed.

The flat was a single room with neat anonymous furniture, like a motel. There was a little kitchen opening directly off it and a bathroom across the tiny hall. The windows along one wall looked onto a courtyard and a jumble of roofs, behind which reared the blank slab of Centre Point.

"A small place but your own. For the time being."

"I'm grateful."

"Forget it."

Abe settled himself in the one armchair while Conrad unpacked. The drawers were all empty, but there were towels in the bathroom and sheets in the cupboard in the hall. Nothing seemed to have been used. It was as though the place had been furnished and equipped specially for him, like some marvelous, unexpected present.

"I'm really grateful," he repeated.

"Stop saying that."

Conrad went into the kitchen and opened a tin of dog

food he had brought from home. While he was out of Abe's sight, he slipped the bulky packet of money in the vegetable crisper in the fridge.

As he did so, Abe called, "Why not put on a suit and come down to the club with me?"

"That game's too high for me."

"Not anymore it isn't. But you don't have to play. Come and watch. We could eat there first."

Kim gazed at Conrad with emotional eyes.

"Why not?" he said.

At the door he patted the dog's head tenderly. "Poor bastard," he said. "It's going to miss the Heath."

"What about you?" asked Abe.

"Me too. But less, definitely less."

20

AT KNIGHTS' CLUB the curtains were closed against the gathering dark and the staff were all smiles.

"Good evening, Mr. Gauss."

"Perrier as usual, Mr. Gauss?"

While they were in the bar a sleek dark man came up to them and inclined his head in a courtly manner. "Playing tonight, Mr. Gauss?" When Abe nodded the man said, "I'll reserve your usual seat, sir."

They ate in a somber room with a high, paneled ceiling and when the bill came it was stamped "Complimentary." Abe left a large tip.

After dinner they wandered through the gambling rooms where the deep carpets and velvet curtains blotted up the sounds: the click of chips and rattle of the roulette balls, the faint swish of cards from the shoe, the croupiers quietly intoning their litany.

Conrad's fingers began to itch and his pulse quickened, although the decorum and churchly hush unnerved him. He was not used to such civility. In the old days he had frequented the big flashy casinos where there were crowds and noise and gamblers flown in from New York on special junkets and a small army of solid, apparently unemployed men in dark suits and white shirts who stood around and watched the customers. That was how he had imagined

Vegas: wide open, fast-moving, and mostly Jewish, but with shady, Mafia overtones. The stir and excitement partly reconciled him to his dreary life in the suburbs. He used to play poker in the vast card room upstairs with dubious businessmen and housewives from St. John's Wood who called him "darling." He had done rather well.

But this was another world: hush and discretion and obsequiousness, high Regency rooms, the chandeliers glimmering, the servants uniformed, and pervading everything, like incense, a sense of ritual, almost of sanctity. When the conversation rose for an instant above a summery insect drone an imposing silver-haired presence in a brown tuxedo commanded "Shushshshsh . . ." and spread his hands soothingly, as though in benediction.

"The Pope?" whispered Conrad.

"The head barman," Abe replied.

The man had the stout, authoritative air of an elderly family servant. Waiters scattered at his nod, nervously and self-effacingly, like so many discreetly intimidated children.

"Wow," said Conrad.

They went up another flight of the curving staircase to a room where there was more roulette and rows of tables set out for backgammon. People were beginning to drift in in twos and threes. The summery hum intensified but remained subdued.

Abe slumped down at one of the backgammon tables, picked up the dice, and began to throw them again and again, as if he were looking for something. Finally, he yawned, stretched, and said, "Time to work." They crossed the landing and paused outside a closed door. "I'll introduce you so you can get back in later," he said. "But give me time to play myself in."

The room was smaller than the others, high and narrow, and contained a single felt-covered table, like an elongated kidney. A Chinese dealer sat at the dip in the kidney's center, his back to the curtained windows, eight seats curving around him. Six were already occupied by middle-aged men with pudgy gray faces, who greeted Abe like old friends.

He turned to a man in a brown dinner jacket who stood by the door. "This is my friend Mr. Jessup. He's not playing tonight, but he'll be back in later to watch."

The man inclined his head to indicate deference. "Delighted, Mr. Jessup."

Abe took his seat at one end of the table, loosened his tie, and counted the large oblong chips the man at the door handed him. As he left, Conrad saw him surreptitiously easing his shoes from his feet.

He wandered back across the landing. The backgammon tables were beginning to fill up, but only a handful of people were playing roulette. He watched them for a while, then went downstairs.

The main room was more crowded now, although the atmosphere remained churchly. Conrad moved among the roulette and blackjack tables inspecting the polite, bored faces. At least half the men were squat and bald, like the driver of the Cortina. For a painter, he thought, I have a lousy memory for faces. The man with ginger hair was easy. He even had a broken front tooth to make it easier. But there were no ginger-haired players at Knights'. Naturally.

He settled finally at a table where the players seemed least geriatric and stood for a while, trying to see if there was any pattern in the way the numbers came up. He bought twenty pounds' worth of chips and piddled away ten pounds in as many minutes on random numbers and combinations. There seemed to be no rhythm at all to the run of the ball.

There never is, he told himself, and wondered vaguely how much he had paid to learn that simple truth. A mug's game. He had read the books and studied the systems: Martingale, D'Alembert, Cancellation. None of them worked. There were runs, of course, but the house percentage always beat you in the end. So in the old days he had only played roulette seriously when he was running out of control, not caring whether he won or lost, just wanting to have done with everything once and for all. A mug's game for a mug's ambition. Why, then, this uneasy sense of arousal? Why did his fingers itch?

He picked up his remaining chips briskly, straightened his back, shook his head, and was unable to leave.

"Seventeen, black," said the croupier.

The languid figures around the table stirred and seemed to waver. The croupier pushed the neatly piled stacks toward the winners, the players dipped and leaned, reaching this way and that to place their bets, then they settled again nonchalantly, pretending not to watch the ball. Yet the tension vibrating through them was almost audible. His dog would have heard it and begun to fret.

The wheel turned smoothly, the ball buzzed in its groove, and Conrad examined the heavily made-up face of a woman on the other side of the table. Her mouth was twitching nervously but her eyes were blank as mica.

"Twenty-four, black," said the croupier.

It occurred to Conrad that the last four numbers had all been black, so he pushed his remaining tenner onto the red and it came up. That put him back where he had started.

While he waited for the croupier to pay him, he watched the woman opposite. She was looking down, counting her remaining chips and biting her underlip. She seemed on the edge of tears. But when she glanced up and saw him watching her, her eyes were murderous.

Time to go.

He cashed in his chips and was halfway up the stairs when he heard his name being called.

"Mr. Jessup. Mr. Conrad Jessup wanted on the telephone."

He stopped and waited, feeling suddenly cold.

"Telephone call for Mr. Conrad Jessup," the well-bred voice repeated.

Down in the lobby the staff were all smiles as usual. Conrad closed the door of the telephone box and leaned his back against it.

"One moment," said the operator. "I'll put you through."

Then a man's voice he did not recognize said, "Conrad Jessup?"

Conrad said nothing.

"Are you there, Mr. Jessup?"

Conrad shivered, but his hands were sweating.

"Yes," he said.

"Just checking," said the voice, then laughed pleasantly and rang off.

"I hope you're enjoying your evening, sir," said the uniformed gentleman behind the reception desk.

Conrad stared at him blankly, then hurried up to the poker room and perched himself on a chair against the curtains behind the dealer. He was still shivering. Abe looked up and winked at him. The pile of chips in front of him had grown considerably and he seemed pleased with himself. But when he saw Conrad's ashen, unsteady face he raised his eyebrows questioningly, then frowned. Conrad shrugged at him. There was nothing to be done.

Which seemed logical, since he had done nothing, anyway.

The last place at the table had been taken by a young man with a pitted face and a mop of black hair. His jacket was over the back of the chair, his shirt collar open, and the knot of his tie was pulled down to the middle of his chest. He shifted around continually in his seat and seemed obscurely angry.

Conrad watched the dealer flip out the cards in a smooth arc, announcing each in turn. He tried to think about the voice on the telephone, but it reminded him of no one he knew. There was something odd about the vowels, something that had once perhaps been a foreign accent. But he wasn't sure. It seemed safer to concentrate on the game.

A gray-haired man with a long, witty face bet the mandatory five pounds on his ace. Two other players saw him and the young man raised twenty pounds on a queen. Only the gray-haired man saw the bet, but when the next card was dealt he checked immediately.

"Sixty pounds." The young man threw his chips into the middle as though he were throwing down a gauntlet. He was showing a queen and a four to the other man's ace and six.

"Your sixty," the gray-haired man's voice was gentle, almost soothing, "and raise the pot."

"A hundred and eighty," intoned the dealer immediately.

Conrad's head began to clear. The menacing voices faded.

The young man pushed his chair back from the table and glared angrily at the other man's cards. Then he leaned forward and counted his remaining chips. Finally, he pushed in the bet, leaving himself four five-pound chips.

The Chinese dealt again, an eight and a three.

"Twenty pounds?" said the older man in the same gentle, faintly enticing voice.

The young man glowered at him, then pushed in his last chips. "Go on," he said to the dealer, "hit me."

Abe winked again at Conrad, who raised his eyes to the ceiling. His confusion had faded with the voices. He felt unexpectedly lucid. He watched the gray-haired man admiringly, grateful to know that not everything was out of control. Despite the evidence of his own messy life.

The dealer flipped out the last cards, a ten and a jack. Immediately, the older man turned over his ace in the hole.

"Hard luck," he murmured.

The young man flushed vividly. "Another five hundred," he called to the smooth gentleman at the door. Then he turned to the gray-haired man: "Hang about, Lou. One of these days I'll take you." His voice was harsh and unsteady.

The other man smiled at him. "I'm sure you will, Dave."

His smile was open and bright, like that of someone years younger.

The curtains were drawn, the door was closed, the room was silent. Only the dealer spoke, announcing the cards as they were dealt and folded, and the size of the bet. Between hands the players murmured together occasionally, but in hushed voices, like worshipers in church. They seemed transformed by the silence and concentration and sums of money involved. After a while Conrad was no longer aware of how coarse the faces were, with their heavy features and pallid complexions, nor of the slumped, unhealthy bodies. They gradually assumed a kind of dignity which went with the strictness of the game. It was a classical occasion, almost beautiful.

He realized that this was what he had always been waiting for. Like falling in love. He felt he had come home at last.

Only the young man with bushy hair seemed out of key with the decorum and formality. He chased cards, bet like there was no tomorrow, and continued to lose. The others watched him patiently, murmured sympathetically when he complained of his luck, and waited their turn to take him.

By one o'clock he was down two thousand and had had enough. The other players wished him well and told him that, sometimes, these things happen. That's how it is. Whenever you get good cards someone has better. Sometimes. It happens. There was no hint of irony in their condolences and he left looking pleased with himself and saying he would be back. Which was the point of the exercise.

"Only the tigers left," said Abe, and nodded at Conrad. "Want to play a hand or two?"

Conrad shook his head. He felt stiff and old and sleepy. The seat made his bottom ache. Even so, he preferred not to go back to Dean Street just yet. On his own. So he shifted uncomfortably on his chair and watched the cards fall.

But the game had gone quiet, and when he caught Abe's

eye half an hour later, the fat man glanced at his watch and nodded.

The dealer sent the cards around again, one down, one up.

On the second up card Abe was showing two eights. He bet fifty pounds, about half the pot. Three eights, thought Conrad; he's trying to suck them in. Abe fixed his melancholy gaze on a point halfway between the pile of chips in the middle and the dealer's right hand.

The other players, however, were not tempted. Each of them folded, more or less reluctantly: ten, king, jack. Only Lou, showing a nine and ten of hearts, saw the bet.

The dealer sent around the cards again: to Abe the ace of spades, to Lou the six of hearts.

Without hesitating, Abe bet a hundred pounds, again about half the pot. Lou stared thoughtfully at the money in the center, then saw the bet.

Abe's melancholy expression did not change, but he made a faint, irritated movement with his head and the quality of his stillness altered, as though his whole body were tense. He hasn't got his three eights, Conrad thought. It's a double bluff: betting less than the pot not to suck Lou in against a cinch hand but in order to seem as if that was what he was trying to do. But how does Lou know?

The dealer dealt for the last time: to Abe the jack of diamonds, to Lou the deuce of hearts.

"Possible flush," said the dealer. "Two eights to bet."

There was a long silence while Abe studied the four hearts facing him. Finally, he said, "Check." The tension had gone from his big soft body and his face seemed suddenly haggard.

"Bet the pot," said Lou at once, in his gentle voice.

"Possible flush bets four hundred and ten pounds," the dealer announced.

Lou counted out the chips and pushed them into the center. He sat indolently in his chair, one hand resting on the table. His fingers were square and carefully manicured.

He waited, his eyes demurely down, his face expressionless.

Abe shifted his weight uneasily from ham to ham and continued to study the cards. He was sweating heavily. Finally, he leaned back and grinned. "Son of a bitch," he said. "You've got the eight of hearts in the hole. It stands to reason." He flipped over his down card to show a second ace. "Aces-up," he said. "But I can't call you." His voice was admiring, almost affectionate.

"Very wise." Lou was also smiling. "But tough too."

"Tough, my ass. I made it too cheap. I tried to box clever and all I did was offer you odds." Abe mopped his streaming face with a handkerchief. "That's how it is," he said. "Sometimes you get the elevator, sometimes you get the shaft."

He pushed back his chair and got up. "Gentlemen, I'm going to quit while I'm still ahead, like my momma told me."

Lou said, "Who would have thought you had a momma?"

"Sure I did. But she also quit while she was ahead. God rest her soul.

"What happened?" he asked, as they crossed the landing to the cashier's desk.

What had happened to Conrad three hours before no longer seemed particularly interesting. Besides, he felt sleepy. "That Lou," he said, "he's really good."

"The best. But you haven't answered my question."

"How do you beat him?"

"You don't. Not in the normal course of events."

At that moment, the well-bred voice on the intercom said, "Mr. Jessup. Telephone call for Mr. Conrad Jessup."

"What the hell?" said Abe. When he saw Conrad start down the stairs toward the lobby he gestured to the main gambling room.

"On the right," he said. "In the passage."

The voice Conrad did not recognize was as pleasant as ever. "Glad I caught you, Mr. Jessup. There's something I thought you'd like to know."

At the end of the passage was a room containing a large

baccarat table. The figures slumped languidly around it seemed even more bored than those playing roulette. But the chips they were playing with were bulky oblong objects in bright colors which Conrad recognized from the poker game as multiples of a hundred pounds.

The voice said, "The name of your wife's lover is Ryan Belling."

Conrad watched the croupier shifting the cards and chips deftly about the table. He wielded his palette like a pizza cook. Conrad yawned.

"What does he do, this Ryan?"

"Use your brains, Mr. Jessup." The man at the other end laughed amiably. "He works for television. Independent Television. What else would he do?"

Timothy Leyton was sitting between two white-haired women, a cold bony presence, one arm hanging loosely over the arm of his chair. He seemed disproportionately young and appeared to be losing. His mouth was tense and his metallic eyes, under their bushy brows, were vaguely bewildered.

"Why are you telling me this?" asked Conrad.

"We want you to have all the facts."

Timothy Leyton pushed back his chair and stood up. He nodded to the other players and murmured something Conrad could not hear.

An elderly lady, wearing a diamond necklace, rose with him. "Past my bedtime." Her voice was unnaturally sharp and penetrating. She smiled nervously around the table. There were no chips left in front of her and Conrad wondered how many thousands she was down. He turned away as Timothy stretched and straightened his tie, and saw Abe standing at the end of the passage, looking at him quizzically.

He cupped his hand around the mouthpiece and said, "How did you know where to find me?"

The man laughed again. "Easy. Just another fact."

144

"One more fact, then. Who the fuck are you?"

"What sort of a question is that?" The man coughed—a small, deprecating noise. "I'm not a fact, Mr. Jessup. I'm a hypothesis." He rang off.

Conrad put down the receiver slowly and turned to where Abe had been standing. But Abe had gone.

Timothy Leyton tapped him on the shoulder. "What a nice surprise." He held out a languid hand. "I didn't know you were a member."

"Just visiting. It's a bit out of my range."

"Oh, the money goes around, you know."

"So they say. Did you go your way tonight?"

Timothy shrugged. "This hasn't been one of my evenings. But you can't win all the time, can you?"

"Apparently not."

"A coffee?" Timothy took him by the elbow. "It's too late for a drink, alas."

"Thanks, but I've got to be going."

Timothy's mouth stretched in a spectral smile. "A pity." He let go of Conrad. "Be a good chap." His voice was suddenly intimate. "Go and see Olivia. She asks after you."

"How is she?"

"Every day a little bit better."

"I'm so glad." He was also glad that Abe was nowhere to be seen.

"Then go and see her. *Please.* The poor thing gets so bored."

"Of course."

He moved away but Timothy walked with him down the noble, curving staircase. When they reached the lobby there was still no sign of Abe.

"Are you alone?" asked Timothy.

"A friend brought me, but he's left."

"Ah, well. No one I know, I suppose?" When Conrad did not reply Timothy turned toward the dining room. "Soon, I hope," he said.

"Of course."

Abe was waiting in the shadows beyond the car park. "You catch on quick," said Conrad.

"Being dumb isn't how I make my living."

While Abe unlocked his car Conrad watched the door of the club. It had been raining earlier and the streets glistened under the lamps. The leaves of the plane trees muttered together conspiratorially.

"For a guy who's never visited the joint before," said Abe, "you seem exceedingly popular."

Conrad got into the car. "Drive first, talk later. And jig around a bit to make it hard for them."

He sat sideways, watching out of the rear window, while he told Abe what had happened. Abe nodded and said nothing. He took side turning after side turning, stopped suddenly, reversed down a one-way street, doubled back the way they had come. But there was no sign of a car following them.

"It's a put-on," Abe said at last. "The guy's a joker."

"I wish I could believe you. A month or two ago I was pining for action. I might even have appreciated the joke. Now I almost envy Mr. Ryan Belling."

"Like the proverb says: Be careful what you want; you may get it."

He drove twice around Trafalgar Square, once very slowly, once very fast, then shot off up Charing Cross Road. He seemed to know what he was doing and to enjoy doing it.

"Cops and robbers," he said. "It makes me feel young."

"So long as you're having fun."

When they reached Foyle's Abe swung suddenly left down a side street and under an arch. As he slowed momentarily to turn left into Greek Street, he said, "Go." Conrad slipped out of the car and flattened himself against the mock-Tudor doors of a pub. He waited a couple of minutes, but no one passed.

When he reached the house in Dean Street he paused at the outer door and surveyed the street, then he went upstairs, collected the dog, and walked slowly around the block. There were lights on in an upstairs club, and the sound of loud music. He passed two bleary couples, hand in hand, and an elderly whore who smiled at him. A car went by quickly. But when he returned to the flat the street was still empty.

He let himself in with relief, suddenly overwhelmed by fatigue. But he slept badly in the strange bed and must have talked in his sleep because at one point he woke to find Kim licking his hand and gazing at him anxiously. The sky behind Centre Point was already gray. He fell asleep again fondling the dog's head.

21

THERE WAS STILL NO ONE around when he came down the following morning, though the streets were full of litter, some of it in black plastic bags, some not. The sky was pale and clear, the air was warm. Sunday morning.

In Soho Square a tramp was stretched out on one of the benches, sunning himself peacefully. His bundle was under his head and all his various upper layers of clothing were unbuttoned: a filthy raincoat which had once been brown, a polished blue suit jacket, four dingy cardigans, and a collarless shirt. But underneath it all his woolen vest was immaculately clean and the flesh between its top and his curling white beard was fresh and pink.

While the dog busied himself in the shrubbery Conrad fished a fifty-pence piece from his pocket and offered it to the old man.

He sat up immediately and shook his head. "No, thank you, sir. I don't think so. But kind of you all the same." He had a gentle, educated voice and smiled sweetly, despite his ruined teeth. His eyes were as blue and innocent as nursery china.

Conrad blushed furiously.

"Father Christmas is alive and well and living in Soho," he told the dog as he bundled it into the back of the car.

But secretly he was envious. If you don't accept handouts,

maybe you don't get onto the computers. Social Security, National Health, Old Age Pensions. Just like Abe had said. No handouts, no computers. So that's how it's done, he thought. A pity I don't have the temperament.

As he drove away, he glanced into the driving mirror. The tramp was leaning forward and staring after the car in a way that made Conrad uneasy. He seemed to be muttering to himself.

Primrose Hill was full of noisy children and yawning, irritable parents. Conrad parked near the Zoo and walked lazily past the playground. The swings and slides were doing brisk business—to and fro, up and down, round and round—and in the adults' enclosure a solitary man, no younger than Conrad, was performing on the high bar. With great solemnity, he pulled himself up until the bar was at his waist, paused, body taut as a propeller blade, then gyrated slowly until he was hanging again from the bar, legs at right angles to his torso, toes pointed. He stayed like that for maybe half a minute, then suddenly flicked his legs through his arms, somersaulted, and dropped lightly to the ground. Conrad watched from a distance, smiling vaguely and wondering how it would be to have a body like a precision instrument. Would it be a protection against whoever it was who was after him and whatever it was they were trying to do to him? He labored on up the hill, the dog running around him in ecstatic circles. There seemed no reason to believe that physical strength would make the slightest difference to the situation he was in, and the other strengths had always been beyond him.

"There are survivors and there are schmucks," Abe had said. Conrad was unsure which category he qualified for, but he was certain his present troubles contained subtleties which were as lost on him as they would have been on the middle-aged gymnast performing so beautifully on the high bar.

Abe had also said, "It's all poker. One way or another." But that was no longer a consolation.

When he got to the top of the hill he stopped and looked back over London, blue and hazy in the morning sun. A group of German tourists were arguing loudly about the landmarks, but when one of them turned to Conrad and asked him he could not answer properly.

"The Post Office Tower." He pointed and the German nodded.

"The Castrol Building."

"*Ja.*"

"Over there's the Hilton, I think."

The German nodded again and gestured eastwards toward the City.

Conrad shrugged. "Sorry," he mumbled.

When he had come here as a child there had been only St. Paul's raising its gold cross above the swarming, indeterminate sea of roofs. Now he could scarcely pick out its dome among the clutter of slabby glass buildings, halfheartedly pretending to be skyscrapers. In what seemed no time at all the London he had known had become as remote and irrecoverable as Ur of the Chaldees. He was puzzled that it should have happened so swiftly, without his noticing. He felt he should have been told.

A puppy came bouncing up to Kim and tried to provoke it into a game. The sheepdog piddled belligerently against a bench and growled.

"Kim," called Conrad. "Behave yourself."

The excited voices of the children in the playground rose in the still, warm air and something stirred vaguely at the back of his mind.

Trees, he thought.

Something to do with being a child on Primrose Hill.

He walked slowly down the other side of the hill.

Suddenly, the image assembled itself complete: a great white mass of blossom, like a snowdrift. It had seemed enormous, but of course he had been very small. "Smell that," said his mother. He remembered her neat soft mouth and well-shaped arms and the piercing, heady scent of the blossom. "That's mayflower, dear. Sometimes they call it hawthorn. Isn't it beautiful?" He inhaled, then inhaled again, thinking, Aren't you beautiful, too? The smell stayed with them all the way to the top of the hill, then enveloped them again as they made their way home to tea.

Irrecoverable. Dead and gone, like Ur of the Chaldees.

It was the third tree from the bottom, there was no mistake about that, although it seemed now curiously small and stunted, and it was far too late in the year for blossom. He studied it, thinking: It contains my past. My childhood is stuck to its spikes like gossamer. My past. His father had died of a coronary occlusion, his mother had died of cancer of the liver, and he had chosen not to go to art school. It was better to play out the hand he had been dealt.

He turned and walked back on the grass around the edge of the park. At the gate to Regent's Park Road he glanced up the hill. The German tourists had gone. A solitary tall man was standing in their place, gazing down toward him. In the bright sunlight his ginger hair seemed almost on fire.

22

THAT AFTERNOON he went back to the hospital. Since he knew he would return in the end, there seemed no point in putting it off. He drove with all the windows open to the pleasant summer air. On the radio a clear pure treble voice was weaving an intricate pattern, on and on, as though heaven really existed and there was no end to it. Then a helicopter clattered overhead, flying low and drowning out the music. He wondered what they were after on an empty London Sunday afternoon.

The chopper disappeared toward the river, but a few minutes later it passed over again, the red light in its belly winking steadily.

Most of the flowers were gone from Olivia's room and her head was no longer bandaged. She had brushed her hair forward so that it lay thinly over the place where the wound had been, giving her a lopsided look. He could smell her perfume in the hot room, light and sweet, mingling with the hospital antiseptics. She did not seem surprised to see him.

"They let me go tomorrow. I feel like the end of term." She gave him her slightly goatish smile.

He smiled back. "Amazing what a couple of days will do."

"I must have looked awful."

"Not awful; just wan."

"What's the difference?"

The smoke from their cigarettes rose through the sunlight and hung in fragile planes under the ceiling.

"Will you be leaving London?"

"I don't think so. What's the use?"

"Good," said Conrad. "Then I can paint you."

"Oh, yes," she said coolly, "there's that, isn't there?"

"Having second thoughts?"

"Why should I? I've never been painted before. It'll be an experience."

"Not necessarily for you. But for me, yes."

"Then who am I to deny you it?"

"I don't know," he said, "I really don't know who you are. I haven't a clue."

"Let's leave it that way, then. Finding out is always a disappointment."

"That depends."

He half rose from his chair, leaned forward, and kissed her on the mouth. Her tongue fluttered under his, then she began to nibble gently at his underlip. For such a slim girl her breasts were unexpectedly full.

They stayed like that for what seemed a long time. When Conrad finally opened his eyes he found she was still watching him with amusement. The curious upward curve of her eyes gave her a sly look.

She said, "Do you think you'll get much painting done?"

He sat back in his chair: "We'll have to see, won't we?"

"Yes," she answered, "we'll have to see."

They sat for a moment, eyeing each other. Finally Conrad said, "I saw your fiancé last night, old Timothy."

"I know. He told me. Dear old Timothy."

"He plays in a very heavy game."

"And you? What kind of game do you play?"

"Strictly small-time." He grinned at her. "But I have hopes."

"Oh, yes," she answered coldly, "I'm sure you do. All sorts of hopes. Everybody does."

"What else is there to keep you going?"

"That depends on whether you win or lose."

"These days I just play poker. On the average, I seem to win."

"What about away from the table?"

"Less good. Since that night I found you on the Heath, I've been on a losing streak."

"I hate to think I'm a jinx."

"Don't fret. The gambling's been going well."

She shrugged. "You can't have everything."

"So they say. But it seems a shame."

Her mood changed abruptly. She looked at him seriously and the mocking note disappeared from her voice. "What's been going wrong?"

"All sorts of things. For starters, I've left my wife."

"That's pretty dramatic." But she seemed pleased, as though he was in some way flattering her.

"It's been coming a long time."

"Well, then . . ." She started to smile, then changed her mind. "What else is wrong?"

"There's been someone following me."

He watched her closely, but she looked him in the eye and said, "How absurd. Are you sure?"

"Quite sure."

"It must be the police. Maybe they don't believe you."

"Maybe. Do you?"

"Naturally."

"Then tell them," he said.

"Of course I will, if they ask me."

"Do they ask you?"

"I haven't seen them for a couple of days. But they're bound to." She paused, then the sly look came back into her eyes. "It couldn't be anyone but the police, could it?"

He widened his eyes in an innocent expression he had practiced at the poker table. "Who else is there?"

She shrugged and looked away. "No one at all. That was a silly question."

Conrad leaned back in his chair and lit another cigarette. "Any news of the guy you were with?"

She shook her head. "Not a sign. He seems to have vanished into thin air."

"Maybe that's why they're still after me."

She smiled at him with relief. "That must be it." She raised her face toward him and said, "Kiss me before the others come back."

Her mouth seemed even softer than before and she moved her breasts against his shirt front. After a little while, he slid his hand down the bed, pulled up her nightdress, and caressed her belly, then her thighs. They parted immediately for him.

"Like silk," he whispered in her ear.

She went on rubbing herself against him, moving her head to and fro on the pillow.

"Tell them to lay off me," he whispered, and she managed to answer, "Whatever you say, sir."

Suddenly her body hardened and began to arch up and down, and her mouth widened over his.

She lay back against the pillows, her face flushed and smooth. "Jesus," she murmured. Then she started to giggle. "I didn't know I had such a short fuse. It must be all this lying around in bed." She stroked the back of his neck and looked at him with large eyes. "You don't mind, do you?"

"Mind?" he answered. "I'm flattered."

As he bent to kiss her again, there was a knock at the door. Conrad sat back quickly and Elizabeth Staff came in.

She surveyed them icily. "Sorry I interrupted."

Conrad glowered at her and did not speak, but Olivia said, "Oh, hello," and gave her a vague, affectionate smile.

She took a bottle of cologne from the bedside table and dabbed her cheeks and neck. The sharp clear scent rose in the heat.

Conrad rubbed his mustache and suddenly under his nose he had the secret smell of Olivia herself. His groin ached and he shifted uneasily in his chair.

Mrs. Staff studied their flushed faces, then said to Conrad, "We weren't expecting you." Her dress was green and she wore a large emerald on her finger. When she brushed an invisible spot from the side of her taut face her complexion seemed to pick up the greenish coloring, like a mask etched in acid. "I didn't think you'd be back," she said.

"Olivia asked me," he replied. "I'm sure you remember."

"Oh, yes, you were going to paint her, or something improbable." She made a faint dismissive movement with her hand and turned her cold face away.

Her anger was disproportionate and made Conrad uneasy. He was certain the two women were lovers.

Not to mention old Timothy.

What sort of vipers' nest had he fallen into? He looked at the pale girl in the hospital bed, with her lopsided hair and fragile convalescent air, and wondered what she was after. She was beyond him, like a creature from another planet inhabiting a dimension he had never guessed at. The swelling in his groin slowly subsided.

He knew it was time to go, but resented giving in without a struggle, knowing that Mrs. Staff would assassinate him directly he was out of the room. He rubbed his mustache again and inhaled Olivia's mushroomy smell. He was ahead for once, so he might as well enjoy it while he could. He smiled at the older woman and asked in a jovial voice, "How are the inquiries going?"

She gave him her wintry look. "You'd better ask the police. They aren't telling me."

"I'd have thought they'd keep you informed. That's not very nice of them."

"The police aren't in the niceness business. They never are, not even in London." She sounded like a woman who had had experience in these matters, though that might just have been the effect of her foreign accent and the weary lines around her cold, slightly hooded eyes.

"But your own inquiries?"

"I'm a fashion designer; I don't make inquiries. All I could do is ask the people at the party, and they told me precisely what they told the police: nothing."

"It seems unbelievable."

"Really?" She looked at him with venom, although her voice was cool and restrained. "All sorts of people gatecrash. Perfect strangers butt in where they're not wanted. It happens all the time. Surely you know that."

Despite himself, Conrad blushed. "They have to be asked. They have to be encouraged."

"Apparently not."

Conrad decided not to provoke her further. "Well, I'm sorry. But it's a pity that this swine should get away with it."

She shrugged contemptuously. "What do you know about swine and *schweinerei*, Mr. Jessup?"

"Probably not enough," said Conrad sadly. "Are you an expert?"

"I have had what is called a European education, God help me."

For the first time, it occurred to Conrad that she might be an interesting woman. "I don't envy you that," he answered.

"It has its advantages," she said, "in the long run. The problem is to live long enough for the long run to count."

"You seem to have managed that."

"Oh, yes." Her anger had gone and she seemed genuinely amused. "I suppose I have. But you see, I contrived to get out before it all started up again."

"Out of where? Germany?"

"Poland," she said. "I left just after the war, while everything was still confused. Luckily for me."

"Why tell me?" he asked.

"Because," Mrs. Staff said patiently, "you don't seem to understand. You think this is some kind of game we are playing and nobody but you cares about the brute who attacked Olivia. Well, you're mistaken. Olivia is very dear to me, like my daughter, and I care more than you could possibly imagine. But we have got nowhere. The man has simply disappeared." Her cold eyes had widened and she spoke slowly, seriously, emphasizing the words. Her accent was stronger than before.

"I'm sorry," said Conrad. "But I'm not meddling for the sake of it. I'm the one in the middle. I won't be clear until this man is found."

"Of course." Mrs. Staff's face reassumed its chilly disdain. "You have your own problems. But Olivia can't help you with them."

"I know." Conrad looked over at the girl who was lying back on the pillows, her face pale and smooth again, the sexual flush gone. "That's not what I was asking her." In repose, her face was soft, almost translucent. For a moment, he saw her as, somewhere, she really was—too young, too vulnerable—and his heart went out to her. Then he remembered that she had brought him only trouble.

He got up, took her hand and squeezed it. "See you soon."

"Please." She smiled back at him, a smile without afterthought. It was as if sex had restored her innocence.

Mrs. Staff watched them, stony-faced.

Conrad went back to the little flat and spent the evening thinking about Olivia and the clear look on her face. He made sketch after sketch, but the look eluded him. Finally, he went to bed without washing his hands in the hope that some faint scent of her would linger on to keep him company through the night. But he slept without dreaming and woke feeling cheerful.

The next evening, however, when he came out of the office late, having stayed on to finish a sales report, the man with ginger hair was waiting in the car park. He seemed angry. He clenched his teeth, as if he were having difficulty in keeping his voice under control, and said, "'Ow many times d'yer 'ave to be told?"

Conrad ignored him and began unlocking his car. But the man took him by the shoulder and swung him around, saying, "Keep outta it, d'yer 'ear?" Then he thumped Conrad with great accuracy in the solar plexus.

Conrad doubled over, emptied of all breath and unable to breathe. He sank to his knees, retching with the effort to fill his lungs. The asphalt plane of the car park tilted and turned.

By the time he got to his feet again, the man had gone.

23 INSPECTOR DAVIES leaned back complacently. "You can't say you haven't been warned."

Conrad's anger evaporated under the policeman's level, unsympathetic gaze. He felt terribly depressed. It was never going to stop. He studied Davies' face for a point of weakness and found none. There would be no forgiveness. He shivered, despite the heat, and realized that he had had this insight months ago, even before his troubles started. He remembered sitting in the kitchen at home on a soft May evening, the door open to the garden with its thin grass and struggling flowers, the television banging away in the next room. Betsy and the two strangers who were his sons already mesmerized in front of it. And he had thought: It will be like this forever. In summer the door is open and the light comes in. In winter it is dark outside and the kitchen is thick with the smell of frying. Those are the only differences: the degrees of light and the amount of fresh air. Evening after evening I will go upstairs to a blank canvas and further proof of my inadequacy. Or maybe I will play cards. Eventually, I will die, but the seasons will go on, the evenings will lengthen and shorten, the television will continue to blare.

It had not worked out like that, yet the sense of being locked into a system he could not control remained unchanged.

"In ordinary circumstances," Davies continued, "I would advise you to go away until things calm down. But under the terms of your release I can't."

"Thanks."

Davies went on as if he had not heard, "So I can only suggest you maintain a low profile. Keep to yourself, live quietly. Avoid those people."

"Which people?"

"Come now, Mr. Jessup. You know as well as I."

"It's not the girl's fault."

Davies smiled condescendingly. "What makes you so sure?"

"Everything."

Davies lit his pipe and went on smiling. "You're a romantic, Mr. Jessup. Not that that has anything to do with the situation you're in, but it may just stop you getting out of it again."

"That's none of your business."

"Don't excite yourself, Mr. Jessup. Naturally, your temperament is not my affair, but the trouble it has got you into is." He paused to tamp his pipe, then lit it again. In one of the gardens beyond his open window a blackbird was singing passionately. "If you will forgive my asking, what does your wife say?"

"She doesn't. I've moved out." Conrad glared truculently at Davies and saw that he was having difficulty in suppressing his amusement. "But you know that already, don't you?"

"Naturally." The policeman's merriment and condescension seemed to increase every moment. "I was waiting for you to tell me your new address. We have to know, remember?"

Conrad studied the complicated club symbol on Davies' tie. There really was no way out.

After he had written down the address Conrad gave him, Davies seemed to relent a little. "It's for your own good." He sounded almost apologetic.

161

"You cannot imagine," Conrad replied, "how much you remind me of my headmaster."

Davies decided not to be offended. "Do I take that as a compliment?" he asked in a jovial voice.

"Take it how you like, since it obviously gives you pleasure."

"It's a hard life, Mr. Jessup, and a hard job. We must take our little pleasures where we can find them."

He held open his office door for Conrad and shook his hand warmly, as though they were good friends.

Abe was waiting at the flat when Conrad got home that evening. The dog had its head on his knees and was gazing up at him operatically while Abe scratched its ears.

"I reckoned you'd have to be back soon, because of the pooch, so I let myself in."

"Make yourself at home. After all, it is your home, not mine."

"Don't think like that. It puts you at a disadvantage."

Conrad started to laugh, but it made his solar plexus ache. "That's all I seem to be at these days." He told Abe what had happened in the car park.

Abe listened attentively, his great bulk sprawled in the armchair, his hand beating time to some private rhythm in his head. Kim came and settled himself guiltily at Conrad's feet. He scratched its white throat with one hand and stroked its black head with the other. After a little while, the creature rolled over onto its back and offered its belly to be scratched. When he obliged it stretched its long jaws in a foolish grin.

After Conrad had finished his story, Abe sat staring thoughtfully at the floor without speaking. Finally he said, "If it's drugs, you got off easy. Those boys are more likely to fuck you over with a razor than a fist."

"But why me?" asked Conrad plaintively. "It's not my scene. I'm like you, I belong to the whiskey generation."

"Don't take it so hard."

"That's what everyone keeps telling me."

Abe sucked his cigar with fat, strong lips. "Maybe it's not dope, maybe there's something else going on." He exhaled noisily and studied Conrad as though his face might contain some clue to the mystery.

"Jealousy," said Conrad. "I think that Staff woman is a dike, and she and Olivia sleep together. Or have done."

"What about the fiancé?"

"Old Timothy? He's no competition. He's one of those languid, upper-class gits who looks as if he goes in all directions at once. He probably joins in."

"That doesn't leave your girlfriend Olivia anywhere very agreeable."

Conrad blushed. "She's young. Maybe she just got caught up in it."

"So now you're cantering up on your white charger to rescue her? My, my." Abe inhaled luxuriously and stretched. "Just make sure, my friend, that she wants to be rescued."

"I make no claims." Conrad poked at the dog's stomach with his toe. Kim flapped his forelegs up and down twice and grinned harder. "I fancy her and I think she fancies me. In her peculiar, sideways manner."

"Just don't put too much money on it," said Abe. But when he saw Conrad's surly, offended expression, he wagged his hand placatingly and added, "I mean, think about it. How come they're going to hire a guy to beat up on you just because they're jealous? Nobody does that, especially in the classy world you say they inhabit. Like where in Knightsbridge do you hire a muscle man? Harrods? Universal Aunts?

"Look," Abe went on, "if this Mrs. Staff and Timothy Leyton had felt so strongly about you and their little girl, they'd have confronted you. Like challenged you to a duel or something; choose your own backgammon board."

"So what's your theory?"

"None at the moment. But I've heard something that

might interest you. What do you think the fiancé does for a living? Your buck will get you ten if you guess right."

"If he actually works, I'd say a City bank. But he looks to me like a gentleman of leisure, a remittance man."

"Nope. He's the next best thing: a civil servant. He's a private personal assistant to an under-secretary to an under-secretary at the Ministry of Defence."

Conrad whistled. "You've got to be joking."

"I kid you not, my friend. He's a kosher civil servant. Took the exams after Oxford and passed. So he's not as dumb as he looks. Think about that."

Conrad went into the kitchen, took ice from the fridge, and poured two whiskeys. Behind Centre Point the dull sodium glow showed heavy clouds. A little rain spattered against the window. He handed Abe a glass, then sat down again on the edge of the bed. The whiskey tasted fresh and cold. "But civil servants don't gamble," he said.

"Right," Abe answered. "Think about that too."

They sat for a while in silence, listening to the rain pattering against the window. Finally Abe finished his drink and heaved himself up from the deep chair. "There's a game at Herb's tonight. You wanna play?"

"Not tonight. I'm too tired and too down. I'd lose."

Abe shrugged. "Have it your own way." He paused at the front door and said, "Stay loose. I'll call you tomorrow." Then he was gone.

Conrad sat on for a while, scratching the dog's ears and brooding. After about an hour, he got up reluctantly and walked in the rain from Soho to Regent's Park. He stood at the edge of the dark empty spaces while Kim busied himself with the fresh scents released by the rain and the trees moved heavily in the wind. He peered anxiously about, but no one seemed to be following him.

By the time he reached home again it was dark. While he was waiting for the lift, he thought he saw a cigarette glowing in a doorway on the opposite side of the street. He was debating whether or not to go over and investigate when the lift arrived. He shrugged and muttered, "Why bother?"

But when he closed the door of the flat behind him he was panting fiercely, like a man who had been running a long race. He leaned against the door, listening to the breath rasping in his chest, and realized that once again he was afraid.

Maybe it's the police, he told himself. Maybe they're trying to protect me at last. But he wasn't convinced and during the night he kept waking from unsavory dreams, thinking he heard noises in the corridor outside. However, the dog never stirred and that comforted him sufficiently to sleep again.

24 THE CERTAINTY that he was being followed began slowly to unnerve him. He saw figures lurking watchfully in doorways or loitering down the street after him. Even at night when there was no one about he could feel them watching him. He would swing around suddenly and stare up at the windows of houses he had just passed. Invariably, it seemed to him that a curtain had just slid back into place. He thought he could hear the rustle of the settling cotton and feel against his neck its faint vibration on the air.

He became obsessed with signs and omens. This shirt was lucky, that one wasn't. Never wear a blue tie on Wednesday or a red one on Friday. He watched which lampposts the dog peed against, trying to see if there was a recurrent pattern which affected the events of the day. One morning he was woken by a pigeon strutting and rolling its *r*'s on the window ledge. It filled him with terror. He was still trembling when he reached the office an hour later. The whole world became a cipher it was imperative for him to interpret. It was like the worst days of his gambling fever, except that now he was too unnerved even to gamble. He scrutinized the daily lists of runners, looking for magical names and messages, found none and placed no bets.

Once he telephoned home, hoping for comfort. Betsy was out and he spoke to the boys, who were polite but unenthusiastic. He could hear the television booming remorselessly away in the background.

The police left him alone and Abe, when he called, seemed to have lost interest. This made Conrad more anxious than ever. He felt abandoned.

At lunchtime he avoided his office colleagues, walking long distances to pubs where he could be sure of meeting no one he knew, although he was convinced he was putting himself at risk by doing so. The back of his neck bristled all the way and he glared at innocent people who happened to be behind him in the street. Once he tried to pick a fight with a tall young man in jeans who was dawdling along in his wake. When the young man shouted in alarm to a policeman on point duty Conrad ducked into Marks & Spencer and left by a side door beyond a counter piled with cold meats and pies in neat packages.

At the office Duval could scarcely contain his triumph. He seemed swollen with glee, taller, fatter, sleeker. Every time he saw Conrad he lit up like a fairground with hilarity and self-satisfaction. Horace, however, became increasingly somber. It worried him that a member of his team should be opting out of the ritual cheerfulness; it reflected on his own efficiency as a manager and his private conviction that he could control everyone and everything he came in contact with. His conversations with Conrad were full of long pauses, heavy with sympathy, which Conrad understood to be invitations to confide. He ignored them. At first Horace made a show of disappointment, then he grew daily more impatient. Conrad knew it was only a matter of time before he was fired; all that was lacking was an excuse.

Yet he continued to work well, attending to the details of sales and delivery and spares and maintenance with the same absorption as he attended nightly to the furnace glow behind Centre Point—as if each might yield some clue which would solve his ridiculous dilemma.

So every day and for the greater part of each night he

gave himself up to a terrible concentration on detail. Secretly, he knew that there were no clues to be found and that the situation was beyond him. But at least the concentration kept him sane and he was grateful for that.

It seemed as if the summer would never end. The showery spell had passed and the long days stretched out cloudless and hot, the swifts and swallows wheeling high up in the milky blue sky, the parks full each lunchtime with picnicking office workers exposing their lobster flesh to the healing sun. The men on building sites were shirtless, the girls in the streets paraded lovely backs and shoulders and arms.

Duval surveyed the typing pool like a sultan, rubbed his hands, and asked, "When did you last see so much meat on the hoof?"

"We're becoming a banana republic," Horace boomed back. "We have the weather, the inflation, the unemployment, and the corruption. All we lack is the bloody bananas. If we had them, United Fruit would take us over and our economic problems would be solved."

In the whole office only Margy stayed loyal to Conrad, and patient, although the heat made her suffer. By nine-thirty in the morning the armpits of her dress were already dark, her large soft shoulders glistened and little rivulets of sweat ran from her hair into her neck. When the chocolate bars melted on her desk she switched to boiled sweets. Finally, when the heat did not relent, she turned to soft drinks—Coke, Pepsi, Tizer, Cream Soda, and fizzy orangeade —which she offered to Conrad tentatively, as if they were Valentines. His gloom upset her, but she asked no questions, for which he was duly grateful. He thought of confiding in her but decided against it, not because he did not trust her but in case she let something slip. What and to whom he did not know, but he began to feel they could all be in it —Alport, Duval, and the others, their tittering secretaries, even the maintenance engineers and the doorman who had failed to notice the ginger-haired man lurking in the car park. It was best to keep to himself.

Early each morning he drove to Hampstead Heath with the dog and swam in the chill wooded pond. The amber water restored him to himself and blotted out the offensive dreams which visited him nightly. The dog paddled behind him out to the raft and back, snorting and making sharp, nervous sounds. Although it swam well, the sight of Conrad in this strange element drove it slightly crazy. Once, as Conrad drifted peacefully on his back toward the landing stage, Kim turned and tried to climb onto his shoulders, forcing him under. He spluttered to the surface and punched the dog hard on the side of its head. It swam away whimpering, but when he got out it was waiting as if nothing had happened, crouching with shining eyes, excited and pleased with itself. When Conrad swore at it, it wagged its tail encouragingly. Its horny nails had drawn a double welt, like a love mark, from his shoulders to his left nipple.

On his way back into town he sometimes drove past his old home. He stared up at the bedroom curtains still drawn against the morning sun and tried to decide which was the boyfriend's car. Ryan Belling. Not, he realized with surprise, that he gave a damn. He was relieved that Betsy and the boys were being taken care of: one responsibility less. Even so, he was puzzled not to feel jealous.

Kim, sitting beside him in the passenger seat, its head out of the window, whined briefly and wagged its tail at the familiar street. "Not this time," said Conrad, and patted its head. At least he still had the dog, and more gambling money than he had ever dreamed of.

Nevertheless, the evenings gave him trouble. He walked in Regent's Park, where the flowers wilted and the grass was yellow-brown, then ate cheap and read the evening paper, while Kim panted beneath the table like an old steam engine. But when he settled himself for his nightly vigil at

the window of the tiny flat, the city seemed curiously unquiet. He thought he could hear dull thuds in the distance
and faint shouting. The air was full of dust and seemed
to vibrate. Each morning he searched the papers for reports
of the night's outrages, but found nothing. He told himself
the terrorists were gone and that the noises he heard came
from television sets elsewhere in the building. He tried to
convince himself that this was the trouble with television:
it made it impossible to distinguish between real horrors
really happening and the fantasies dreamed up in the back
lots at Burbank to entertain him in the prime viewing hours.
But he did not believe it. Something was up, something was
wrong.

Finally, the strain of waiting and listening night after
night was too much for him, so he went back to the poker
table. At least it passed the time and took his mind off his
troubles. Although he lost in moderation, he was glad of
the company.

Abe was at Herb's game, playing with authority and winning. He greeted Conrad cheerfully, as if nothing had happened, and looked faintly surprised when Conrad took him
aside after the game and asked, "Why the sudden silence?"

"No news is good news."

"I feel like I've got the plague."

Abe's expression became sorrowful. "Don't let it get to
you, old friend."

"You try it."

"I empathize, Conrad, believe me. And I'm working on it."

"That's all very well."

"I know, I know. But nobody's bugging you, right?"

"Right."

"And you're not seeing the girl?"

"Right."

Abe looked relieved. "Well, then, what's there to worry
about?"

Conrad shrugged. "It's not that easy."

"You don't have to tell me. But as of this moment they're leaving you alone, right? So maybe it was all a mistake. Whoever made it found out and now it's all over."

"I'd like to believe you."

"So believe me. What can you lose?"

"More than I thought."

"Don't take it so hard," said Abe serenely. "Remember the old adage: ' "Cheer up," they said, "things could be worse." So I did and they were.' " Then he peered at Conrad's somber face and added, "Just a joke, pal. No hard feelings."

But when Conrad phoned Abe's office a few days later he was told that Mr. Gauss had had to go abroad unexpectedly and they were not certain when he would return.

He spent a long evening brooding on this and his other misfortunes, and the next morning looked up Olivia in the telephone book. He was surprised to find she was listed and even more surprised when she answered the telephone herself and seemed pleased to hear him.

"It's been weeks. I should be insulted." Her voice sounded young and fresh, a world apart from his own shabby troubles. It seemed to him incomprehensible that he should have hesitated so long.

"I wanted to call, but I thought there might be objections."

"Who's to object?"

Conrad left that one alone. "How are you, anyway?" he asked.

"A changed woman. My hair's growing back again. You don't know how much better that makes me feel."

"I'd love to see you."

"You shall. Just say when."

"How about tomorrow?"

"Tomorrow is fine."

When he put down the receiver he felt cheerful for the first time in weeks. That evening, after he had walked the dog, he changed his shirt, took a hundred pounds from the packet in the fridge, and strolled to one of the big, gaudy clubs where he knew there would be action. He went straight upstairs to the card room and sat down at the ten-pound game with the usual Greek professionals and car dealers from South London. It was like old times. The game was tight and silent, and nobody seemed to be enjoying it. After an hour, he had lost thirty pounds. He got up, went to the lavatory, washed his face and hands and wrists in cold water, and thought about Olivia's clear voice on the telephone welcoming him. Then he returned to the table, refreshed and sure of himself. By midnight he was sixty-five pounds ahead. He cashed in his chips, went home, and slept deeply for the first time in weeks.

25 OLIVIA OPENED THE DOOR to him. The lines had gone from her face and her bare arms were faintly tanned. She kissed him lightly on the mouth, then turned away immediately, leaving a faint smell of shampoo on the air. He took this as a good sign and was filled with unreasonable hilarity.

The windows of the upstairs drawing room reached from the floor almost to the ceiling. There were window boxes outside which made them seem as if they opened onto a garden instead of a dusty Knightsbridge side street. But the geraniums in the boxes were ragged and the windows needed cleaning. The room, too, was luxurious but run-down. Outsize cushions and filled ashtrays were scattered between the chairs and sofas. A joss stick burned among the invitation cards on the marble mantelpiece, which was supported by two lugubrious caryatids. There were mirrors on all the walls and photographs of Olivia wearing exotic clothes, so that everywhere she turned she was reminded of herself.

"I didn't know you were a model," said Conrad.

"I'm not. I used to do it for Elizabeth occasionally. She paid me in dresses."

"Why not professionally?"

"It didn't work out." She shook her head irritably. "Also I couldn't stand the people. Too many poofs and the talk was all the same. You'd think they were Rembrandt, the way they carried on."

"It seems a pity."

She shrugged. "If you make it, the money's sensational, but you pay in other ways." She patted the thin hair on the side of her head. "Anyway, that avenue, as they say, is now closed to me."

She poured drinks and settled herself on one of the cushions in front of the empty fireplace. Conrad sat down by her. The mournful caryatids stared down their noses at them disdainfully. Olivia picked up an old cigarette tin lying by the fender and began to roll a joint.

"Where's Tim?" asked Conrad.

"Oh, he'll turn up. He always does."

She closed her eyes as she inhaled and kept them closed while she held the smoke in. Conrad studied her face, trying to analyze how the strange curve of her eyes blended with the line of her jaw and the way her hair fell. She looked like a sensual saint. He wondered what small movements of pleasure were going on in her head.

She opened her eyes suddenly and exhaled. She seemed to find his rapt expression amusing. "My," she said, and handed him the joint.

He was careful to keep his eyes open while he smoked.

"Does Elizabeth live here?"

"On and off."

"Is this off or on?"

"Off. She's away for a couple of days."

"That's nice," he said.

Olivia took no notice. "You didn't bring your paints and stuff," she said.

"I didn't know they were invited. I didn't bring my dog either."

"Oh, you have a dog. What else do you have?"

"Two sons. But they stayed with my wife when I left."

For some reason, this seemed to interest her. "Were you married long?"

"Long enough."

"Is that why you left?"

"That's one way of putting it."

"How does it feel?" She studied his face carefully, as though looking for signs.

"Why should you want to know? You're not the marrying kind, are you?"

She shook her head. "Breaks, departures, divorces—all the little deaths fascinate me."

"After what you've just been through, I'd have thought the big one would fascinate you more."

She shrugged. "Go on, tell me. How does it feel?"

He inhaled the joint again and sat in silence to attend to this question. He could feel a vague stirring of laughter, far off, somewhere at the back of his skull, like a voice from the past. It reminded him of something. He closed his eyes briefly and once again he saw the great snowy mass of hawthorn and felt his head sway with the scent. Was it his mother laughing?

He smiled at the girl without reservation. "Nothing," he said. "I don't feel a thing."

"Lucky you," said Olivia.

"At the moment, however, I feel nice." He gave her his beatific smile again. "At one with the world, and all that."

"You should do," she replied. "That stuff comes from Ecuador. Very high class, very expensive."

Conrad went on smiling. "I thought it was you," he said. He eased toward her on the cushion and kissed her neck. She sat perfectly still, inspecting the joint, then took another toke and closed her eyes as before. His mouth moved slowly along the line of her jaw to her ear. When she did not respond or open her eyes he slid his hand up under her striped T-shirt and began to caress her breasts.

She exhaled reluctantly, opened her eyes, and moved his hand away. She looked at him wearily and said, "Later."

Conrad rolled back to where he had been sprawling. "Later there'll be Tim."

"One pleasure at a time."

She passed him the joint, got up lazily, and switched on the television. A large woman in a hunting tunic was urging a large horse over a five-barred gate.

"Must we?" asked Conrad.

The horse cleared the gate and gathered itself for a water jump. It cleared that too, apparently without effort. The audience applauded.

"It's even funnier when you're stoned," said Olivia.

The horse rose to a simulated brick wall. It seemed to clear it, but at the last moment dropped a back foot and knocked off the top layer of bricks. The audience exhaled a noisy sigh of sympathy and the commentator began whispering solemnly into the microphone, as if describing some royal occasion in Westminster Abbey.

"I used to know people like that," said Olivia, as the horsewoman, looking angry, cantered through the exit from the arena.

"I bet you did. They must be even more boring than the modeling lot."

"Boring enough," Olivia replied. But she seemed annoyed that he had mentioned it.

He sat up on the cushion and wondered why he was there. He studied her fine, somehow expensive limbs in their deliberately shabby jeans and T-shirt, her pouting mouth and hair hanging forward, the know-all expression in her eyes, and thought: Rich and spoiled and vain, just like all the unattainable girls in the magazines. That's why I want her, he decided. It's a form of social climbing. Through her I will measure the distance I have moved from my dreary domesticated life.

Yet the idea depressed him. He had been hoping for something more.

He smiled at her nervously and said, "Don't get cross."

She got up again, collected the vodka bottle from the bookcase, set it between them on the floor, and rearranged herself on the cushions. "Save your aggressions," she said, "I've been got at enough. The police seem to think it was my fault I was nearly killed. And then Elizabeth . . ."

Instead of finishing, she took another drag from the joint.

"She hates my guts," Conrad put in.

Olivia shrugged. "The Poles are complicated people."

"And possessive with it."

"She doesn't have any family."

"Do you?"

"Yes and no. They're separated. Daddy's in America now and Mummy's down in the country with her boyfriend. Which means I get the house to myself and that's nice."

"Why does Mrs. Staff resent me so much? I can't do any harm."

"I suppose she thinks you're after something."

"I am: you."

He grinned at her, but she was smiling vaguely at the television where a burly man with a heavy jaw was making it all look easy. He wore a scarlet jacket and his black horse shone like his riding boots. The crowd was in ecstasies.

Conrad put his hand over Olivia's in the hope of regaining her attention. She shook her head impatiently. "No, not me. Something else."

"What else is there?"

She glanced at him briefly, then turned to the screen again. "You'd have to ask Elizabeth."

"What's your opinion?"

She studied him quizzically for a moment, her head on one side. Then she stubbed out what was left of the joint and smiled. "Oh, I believe you. I think it's me you're after."

She leaned over and kissed him on the mouth. While she bent over him, he pulled her T-shirt over her head and began to stroke her elegant breasts, murmuring something unintelligible even to himself, a noise at the back of his throat expressing satisfaction. He buried his head in her shoulder and inhaled gratefully the delicate, rousing scent of her skin. It was as if her whole body were faintly permeated by her secret juices.

"Jesus," he managed.

She undid his shirt and eased it off him, then bent to attend to his belt. When she had undressed him she stood up to take off her jeans. She hesitated a moment, one hand in her hair, looking down at him. The last of the sunset through the high windows created coppery shadows around her belly, breasts, and ribcage.

Conrad gazed up at her with wide eyes and slack mouth. Beautiful, he thought. But at the same time she made him vaguely uneasy. The taut line of her body hinted at violence somewhere far back, something malicious and faintly sinister, like a girl with a snake. She reminded him of a painting he had once seen. Signorelli? he wondered, but could not remember.

Out loud he said, "Just as well I didn't bring my paints. I'd never have done you justice. In this light you look like an Old Master."

"Old Master, my eye," she answered. "More like young mistress."

She lowered herself onto him and began to rock to and fro, from side to side, moving to some private music in her head.

He reached up to her breasts and said, "I could really fall for you."

She went on rocking quietly to the unheard, complicated melody. "That would be a stupid thing to do," she said.

"Why so sure?"

"I know me. It's not my style."

When he started to say something she put her fingers in his mouth and moved them over his tongue. The sly, ironic expression was on her face again. "Don't spoil it," she said. "I thought we were going to be such friends."

Then the expression faded and she began to work away, her thighs opening and closing on his chest like wings. He came abruptly and without warning but she took no notice, laboring on and on until she had brought herself to a climax. Her eyes were wide open, fierce and without depth. He watched them, sane and emptied out before her, and realized what their odd shape reminded him of: she had the eyes of a wild cat. It also occurred to him that she had no idea he existed.

She rolled off him and they lay side by side in their sweat, fingers entwined, while the last of the afterglow vanished from the sky. The room was lit by the flickering light from the television, where a woman was reading the news. This struck Conrad as funny. He nodded toward the screen and said, "It's like making love in front of an older sister."

Olivia raised herself on one elbow and peered at the television. "She has hot eyes, but I bet she'd pretend not to notice."

The lady newscaster was registering ladylike interest in the latest forecast of doom from the Chancellor of the Exchequer. His jowled face replaced hers briefly. Then she went on to report a nonevent from the Common Market. The terrorists, apparently, were taking the day off. Conrad felt obscurely relieved by this. He sat up and poured vodka into both their glasses.

"What about Tim?" he asked.

"Oh, Tim." Olivia did not sound interested. "We understand each other."

"That's nice."

"Nice enough," she answered irritably. "Better than the body-and-soul bit."

"Is that what you get from Mrs. Staff?"

Olivia's irritation increased. "You ask too many questions. And furthermore, don't get indignant on my behalf, thank you. My problems are my own."

"After what we have just expressed to one another, can't I be curious?"

"What we have just expressed to one another gives you no rights at all."

Conrad shrugged. "As long as I know."

He got up and began to pull on his clothes. Looking down on her slim, shadowy body on the cushions, he wondered how many times she had had sex in this room, and with how many different people. How many men? How many women?

His vanity was wounded and the place demoralized him: the Queen Anne windows and marble fireplace, the decorous street outside. And under these symbols of the high life, the faint suggestions of seediness and corruption: the dust and disorder of the room, and the girl lying there oblivious, her elegant body still slippery with sweat. He sighed. All my life, he thought, I've been watching people like this from a distance and wondering what they were like. Now I know. When all is said and done, they're not much to write home about. He sighed again, wondering why, in fact, he had ever left home.

He emptied his glass and refilled it. "Ever since I found you on the Heath," he said accusingly, "nothing's gone right."

Olivia pulled on her jeans without getting up, arching her back and wriggling them over her hips. "You've told me that before. Do you think it's my fault?"

"I've been followed," Conrad went on, "I've been threatened, I've even been beaten up in a mild way."

"And you think I'm to blame?" She buckled her belt and sat up. He watched regretfully as she pulled her T-shirt down over her breasts. Good-bye to all that. She caught his yearning look and said sourly, "Spare me your paranoia."

"Take it easy. I just wish I knew what's happening. Why should I blame you?"

"Why, indeed? Blame yourself or tell the police."

"I've done both those things."

"Then leave me out of it." She stood up and ran her hands down her sides as though she were smoothing a dress.

"Hey," he said. "Remember me? I'm the guy who just made love to you."

"Then don't start being a bore because we've finished."

"Not another word. Let's go somewhere and have dinner."

The idea seemed to cheer her up. "Grouse," she announced. "Grouse are in. Take me to Boulestin and buy me a grouse."

He bowed deferentially. "Whatever you say, your Highness."

But when they got back to the house after dinner, lights were on in the upstairs drawing room and the tall windows were open. When Conrad switched off the car's engine they could hear the sound of a woman singing.

"Tim's back," said Olivia.

Conrad listened: a come-on voice, but very musical.

Call me at the station,
The lines are open.

"Joni Mitchell," he said. "For a civil servant, Tim's a real swinger."

Olivia looked at him sharply. "How do you know he's a civil servant?"

Conrad blushed. "Someone told me. I thought it was you, but maybe it was him. I don't remember."

She opened the car door. "Do you want to come in?"

"There's no point." He leaned over to kiss her, but she was already out of the car. She waved briefly.

As he drove away he thought: Now she's going to go upstairs and have sex with him. Instinctively, he thought of it as having sex, not making love. Nevertheless, the idea depressed him.

181

26 HE KNEW THERE WAS SOMETHING WRONG when he opened the flat door and the dog was not there to greet him.

"Kim," he called, "Kim," and whistled softly.

To his left he heard the sound of halfhearted scratching, then a muffled whine. When he opened the bathroom door the dog stared up at him dejectedly. It seemed groggy and rather embarrassed, as if it knew it had been made a fool of. It came forward unsteadily, wagging its tail, and put its head sorrowfully on Conrad's lap. He scratched its ears and murmured consolation, "Did someone slip you a Mickey, then, you poor old fool?" The dog groaned softly in accompaniment.

The medicine cabinet was open and the top was off the lavatory cistern. The handbasin was full of toothpaste and the filleted tube had been squashed down onto a bar of soap.

Conrad crossed to the living room and switched on the lights. "Boy," he said.

All the drawers had been pulled out and their contents emptied on the floor. Trousers, jackets, blankets, and sheets were jumbled together in front of the cupboard. The divan bed lay on its side, the sacking ripped from its bottom to show its springs. Piles of stiff white flock hung from a gash in the side of the mattress.

In the kitchen, too, all the drawers had been emptied,

and the doors of the oven and icebox were open. He blessed whatever sad flicker of vanity or caution had impelled him to take his gambling money with him. He poured himself a drink and went back into the living room, where the windows were wide open to the night.

When he set the divan back on its feet he saw that someone had drawn on the wall a frontal study of a massively erect penis rising from two hairy testicles. The drawing had been done with a felt-tipped pen and contained a good deal of loving detail. Whoever had done it was not without talent. Underneath was written in large neat capitals:

BLESSED ARE THE MEEK,
FOR THEY SHALL INHERIT THE EARTH.

Conrad stared at the wall, thinking: They knew what they were about. The name of the game is rape—a sudden, violent eruption into one's privacy. He shuddered and looked quickly around the room to make sure they weren't still hiding somewhere. Nasty, brutish, and short, he thought.

Then he dialed Abe's number. The telephone rang for a long time and when Abe finally answered his voice was bleary with sleep.

"Oh, it's you." He brightened slightly. "I just got back tonight. What's up?" He was silent for a moment after Conrad told him, then said briskly, "Hang in there. I'll be right over," and rang off.

By the time Abe arrived Conrad had got most of the spillage back into the drawers and cupboard, and had remade the bed. But there were still handfuls of ticking on the floor and he had not yet replaced the back of the television set.

Abe looked around the room admiringly. "Well," he said, "they really fucked you over."

"Not me, just the flat, thank God. But I think they slipped the poor dog something."

Abe looked at the old sheepdog, which lay gloomily on its side by the bed. "He's lucky. They'd have killed him if they hadn't been worried about the noise." He pushed the dog with his foot in a friendly way. Automatically, Kim rolled over onto its back and groaned mournfully. Abe balanced above it on one leg, rubbing its stomach gently with his toe. The dog's hind leg began to scratch in time to the movement of Abe's foot. He stared at the dog meditatively for a moment, then began to prowl around the flat.

When he had finished he nodded and said, "Thorough," in an admiring voice. Then he studied the drawing on the wall and added, "Witty, too."

"God knows what they were after." Conrad sat dejectedly on the bed. He felt faintly offended by the other man's levity. The drink, the grass, the girl, then the heavy alcoholic meal, and now this. Once upon a time, in another life, he had been a married man with earnest painterly ambitions. Now his only ambition was to sleep. If he slept deeply enough, maybe he would wake up in the shabby terraced house in Hampstead with his wife beside him.

Abe went into the kitchen, poured himself some whiskey, then settled into the armchair. His mere size was somehow comforting.

"They were paying you a compliment," he said. "They really think you're after something." He paused and when Conrad did not reply he added encouragingly, "Put it this way: at least they're taking you seriously."

Conrad weighed the compliment carefully and decided he was not flattered. "All I was after was the girl. As I told her this evening." He closed his eyes and concentrated, trying to take the measure of the weariness in his body. It seemed to penetrate right into the marrow of his bones. When he opened his eyes again he found Abe watching him appraisingly. "What am I supposed to be after?" he asked.

Abe shrugged. "Information, I guess. I think these people

are very hot for information—the kind they call classified."

Conrad began to giggle. "You mean they're spies? Olivia and her upper-class twit of a fiancé and that Charles Addams dress designer? You've got to be joking."

Abe was not amused. He looked at him somberly and with disapproval until the spasm had passed. "That's how it is these days. Not telescopic sights and electronic toys and all that stuff. Just someone who knows where interesting things are and when they're being moved from one place to another. Then all you need is a tourist with a camera. You'd be surprised how much a professional can learn from a simple snapshot. What the hell; these days most intelligence work is done by aerial survey, anyway."

"I don't get you."

"Come on, pal, don't play simple with your uncle Abe. That upper-class twit has access to information. He works for the MOD, remember?"

"Why should he bother?"

"Because he's like everyone else, he needs the cash. He gambles, right? But not poker, like us sensible guys. He plays games of chance, chemmy, roulette, things you can't control. That kind of activity can get you into deep trouble. Need I tell you? Moreover, his friend and yours, little Miss Olivia, is an expensive number to maintain."

Conrad studied the large melancholic presence dumped in the chair in front of him, looking for signs of humor. "You're dreaming," he said.

Abe shook his head. He seemed as weary as Conrad. "Why should I *schlep* over at two A.M. and start telling fairy stories?"

"How do you know all this?"

"I have my sources, like I told you before. I do odd jobs for odd people. All sorts of odd jobs for all sorts of odd people."

"You mean the CIA?" The corners of Conrad's mouth

turned down and he rolled his eyes to heaven, appealing for patience. "Come on, Abe, don't disappoint me. I always thought your pals were in the Mob."

Abe grinned at him and turned his palms upwards. "A guy's gotta live. I have all sorts of friends. I do them favors and they do me favors. I guess you could call me one of God's middlemen. You've seen too many movies, pal. You think the CIA is one thing and the Mafia is another. Equal but separate, as they used to say down South, and each with its own code of honor. Don't kid yourself, baby. It's a crumbling world we live in."

Conrad heaved himself reluctantly from the bed and fetched the whiskey bottle from the kitchen. He refilled their glasses and they drank in silence. Finally he said, "You've got to be wrong about Timothy. I bet he's an Hon., if we did but know it. Eton, Christ Church, and the rest of that scene. Those people are the last of the patriots."

"Not necessarily when it comes to money, pal. That's why the Swiss banks do so well, despite the lousy three percent they pay. Eton, Christ Church, and a numbered account is the rule of the day now."

"Nevertheless . . ."

"Nevertheless, nobody cares anymore. Rich or poor, they're all on the lookout for Número Uno. Like you are, like I am. So don't get sentimental; it ruins the judgment. Moreover, the guy probably thinks: What kind of secrets has jolly old England got these days that are worth keeping? If some schmuck is willing to pay good money to be told when a missile is being sent under drapes from Scotland to Oxfordshire, he thinks: Why not? What's the harm? Remember, he's a gambler. He's got the bug. You've been there, pal; you know which comes first. In such cases patriotism, like the lady said, is not enough."

Conrad bent to the dog again and scratched its ears tenderly. Kim wagged its tail and gave him its Charles

Boyer look. The drug seemed to be wearing off. "You're the expert on middlemen, Abe. Who's Timothy's?"

"Who do you think? One guess and no prizes."

"Elizabeth Staff?"

"Too true. Your fancy Mrs. Staff, she of the spun steel face and silk dresses, is not as kosher as she looks. Of course, she's very big in *émigré* circles. They all love her because she's famous and successful, a smart figure on campus, whereas they live very marginal lives. Talk about patriots. You ever see the old guys in the coffee houses around South Ken.? Silver-haired ex-cavalry officers with ramrod backs and bear wax on their mustaches. Not the swingers who came over to fly Spitfires and screw all the English girls, but the original maniacs who got on their horses in September thirty-nine, lowered their lances, and charged the fucking panzer divisions. Beautiful men, the last of the dodos. And they're still around, living on hopes and dreaming about the mushrooms on their estates in eastern Poland. They can't believe there aren't any more estates and eastern Poland is now part of the Soviet Union. I tell you, kid, somewhere off Queen's Gate the Polish government-in-exile still sits in perpetual session. And they need all the friends they can get, believe me. That's why they love the famous Mrs. Staff. I guess she loves them too, in her funny way. After all, she's been through the same mill. The Nazis shipped her from Auschwitz-Birkenau to Dachau early in forty-five, then we released her and shoved her in a DP camp. A lovely life. Eventually, she wangled her way to Vienna, then to Paris, where she got into fashion. Now it's London and the big time."

"Now I know what she meant by a European education. It's not something to hanker after."

"Or to forgive."

"Meaning?"

"Meaning maybe she hates the Germans more than she

hates the Reds, though I doubt it at this late stage. *Basta ya*, which, in case you don't know, is Spanish for enough already."

"Thanks." Conrad studied the other man's face suspiciously. He realized that Abe was enjoying himself and this puzzled him. "Why should she do whatever it is you think she does?"

"Search me. Maybe her heart's still in the old country. Or maybe she just wants to keep in good in case one day she needs to go back on her own terms. Or maybe she just wants to be loved by the old folks back home. It's an exile's disease. Or could be she just needs the cash. Your guess is as good as mine."

"No, it isn't. It sounds to me like you've got it all worked out."

"So write me a better scenario." Abe settled back in his chair, took a large swallow of whiskey, and mopped his face. As usual, he was sweating heavily, but his sharp dark eyes were cool and steady. He seemed pleased by Conrad's dismay.

Neither of them spoke for a while. Finally Conrad tapped his breast pocket and said, "At least they didn't get my money."

Abe grinned at him fondly. "Don't tell me. You wanted to flash your wad at the girl."

Conrad's gloom increased. "My wad and other things."

"I hope," said Abe in a fatherly voice, "she was suitably impressed by them all."

"She wasn't saying. She's not the type that does. But I suspect she doesn't impress easily."

"I believe you. A very cool young lady, if that's what you like. Me, I prefer them cosier than that, more *heimische*."

"Oh, I like, all right." Conrad brooded a moment, then asked, "But if she's so bloody cool, how did she get herself coshed?"

Abe shrugged. "Beats me. Maybe they had an argument

about money. Or maybe the wrong agency was waiting. Or maybe she was with someone who decided he might as well do the collecting for her. *Quién sabe?* I don't even know why she was there in the first place."

"Or maybe it was dope after all, and maybe you've worked it out all wrong."

Abe raised his right hand and made the sign of the cross. "With faith all things are possible, my son. I'm not the Pope. I never claimed to be infallible."

Conrad emptied his glass. He closed his eyes and felt the fatigue roll over him like a boulder. When he heard Abe get up quietly and cross the room he forced his eyes open again. "What should I do?" he asked.

Abe was standing at the door. "Sleep," he said. "And keep away from that chick. She'll burn you, she or her friends."

Conrad watched him from the bed. His face was slack, his hands too heavy to move. Abe opened the front door, then turned and looked at him sorrowfully.

"And if you can't keep away, try to persuade her she's got it all wrong. Tell her it was a mistake. Maybe she'll believe you. Maybe she'll even get Mrs. Staff to believe you."

He went out into the passage, then turned, shaking his head.

"But I wouldn't give you odds," he said.

27

"YOU LOOK AWFUL," Horace Alport announced, "all trembling and green about the gills, like a frog with shell shock." He loomed energetically in the doorway of Conrad's office. The gray paint and gray steel furniture made his face seem unnaturally florid and his beer belly intolerably powerful.

"I don't feel too bright, if the truth were known."

Horace shook his head. "The truth is there for all to see. What exactly have you been doing to yourself?"

"Blame it on my age." Conrad smiled placatingly. "I've reached the point where each time I blink I'm ten years older."

"Then stop blinking," said Horace. "It's beginning to show." He paused for laughter, but when none was forthcoming he went on more sympathetically, "Don't think I don't know, old boy. Alport's First Law states that as you get older the days get longer and the years get shorter. At nine in the morning it seems impossible that you'll ever make it through to midnight. But by the time you have it's already next month."

This time Conrad managed a thin laugh, though only to show that he appreciated the effort Horace was making.

The big man seemed encouraged by this. He stepped into the room and closed the door behind him. "I was out with that Unirealm fellow last night and he came up with some asshole problem which only you could answer, so I tried to phone you. All I got was Betsy."

Conrad stared at the papers on his desk and waited. The columns of figures were as indecipherable as the Rosetta Stone.

"Why didn't you tell me?" Horace asked.

Conrad shrugged. "Why should I bore you with it? I'm working O.K. and that's all that matters."

Horace sat down heavily, leaned forward on the desk, and thrust his large cheerful face at Conrad. He smelled of bacon and cigarettes. "Conrad, old son"—his voice was thick with sympathy—"you've worked for me longer than you've been married, and that's a long time. Ten years, is it?"

"Twelve." Conrad lit a cigarette in self-defense.

"A long time," repeated Horace. "I'm an old friend, sunshine. I've trodden on your fingers all the way up the company ladder. Christ"—he slapped the desk theatrically— "I went to your fucking wedding."

"Weddings are one thing, separations something else." Horace's imitation of concern irritated Conrad unreasonably. He averted his eyes and muttered, "Anyway, why should I make a pig's breakfast out of it? Maybe it'll all work out."

"She seemed such an easygoing girl."

"These things happen, sport. I had that trouble with the police and Betsy couldn't take it. Couldn't or wouldn't. And there were other things. It just seemed better to clear out for a bit. But I'll probably go back."

"Yet she stuck with you while you were having your troubles with the horses."

"Gambling's private. All the world can see the police at the door."

"Knowing Betsy, I wouldn't have thought she'd care."

"Knowing Betsy," Conrad echoed, "I'm her husband and I don't have a clue. Maybe hidden away somewhere in the ITA is a program planner who has her measure, but you and I, old buddy, we don't stand a chance. For her, everything is part of a serial. Each time we fucked I worried that she'd dissolve us into the next scene before we'd finished. It's unnerving, Horace. It's like having your mother-in-law living with you—an all-seeing eye. I think things would even have been easier if I'd thought she'd had a lover—someone human and boring, with a job and bad breath, like all the rest of us. Then at least I'd have known where I stood. But television: it never fails and it's always there. Who could possibly compete?"

"And who could possibly argue?" Horace spread his hands palms down over the desk, as though soothing the troubled waters. "In other words, you're saying that if you look lousy it has nothing to do with your domestic problems?"

"Right." Conrad leaned back in his chair. He considered his fatigue and what lay beneath it, then he considered Horace whose sympathetic manner seemed oddly out of key with his tempestuous complexion. "I think I'm going to die," he announced. It was the first time he had mentioned the possibility, even to himself.

"Oh, *that*." Horace beamed at him as though it was a secret he had known all along. "What do you know about death, sunshine?"

"Ten years less than you know."

"Don't kid yourself. Death is my specialty. I think about it every day without fail."

"Don't tell me: 'It's being so cheerful that keeps you going.'"

"You think I'm having you on?" Horace leaned suddenly forward and thrust his face even closer to Conrad's. "I tell you true. Every single day. You know why? Because every day I go to the loo; every day without fail I deliver to the cooling waters the muck I carry inside me. You'd imagine it'd be one of the things you'd get used to, wouldn't you? But somehow I never have. I sit there and inhale the stench of my own innards and I think: That's what I'll be like when I'm dead. And sometimes I think: Damn it, I'd rather be dead already; it's not to be tolerated." He leaned back and lit another cigarette, suddenly peaceful again. "That's why I've put a codicil in my will asking to be cremated. No smell then, no corruption. Just a little ash sifting over London."

Conrad looked at him with respect. "So now I know."

"That's right, sunshine. Now you know."

Outside, Margy was pounding her typewriter as though she were trying to test it to destruction. Conrad listened for a while, admiring the energy she put into such boring, senseless work. He wished he was back there in the simple world, doing his job, eating her Polos and thumbing through her magazines. Once upon a time he had even painted one good picture. Another life. Not so bad, either, now he came to think about it.

He smiled at Horace. "People are full of surprises these days. Everywhere I turn someone comes up with something extraordinary."

"It's your sympathetic face, sunshine. It inspires confidence."

"I'm not ready for the responsibility."

"You'll get used to it. It's one of the things that happen with age. All it takes is wrinkles and a few gray hairs, and everybody thinks you know the answers."

"If I wasn't feeling so lousy, I'd be offended."

"Don't waste your energy." Horace glanced at his watch and got up. "Look," he said, "if you're having a hard time, why don't you take a couple of weeks off? It's due to you anyway. Then you can see the missus, talk it over with her at your leisure while the kids aren't around, maybe go off together for a few days." He paused, took a drag of his cigarette, and exhaled with a sigh. "You shouldn't let it all fall apart in your hands without making an effort. It's gone on too long for that."

Conrad smiled at him gratefully. "I never thought of you as a marriage counselor. That's another surprise."

"Oh, I'm full of surprises," Horace answered. "You should know that by now. Two in one morning is a mere nothing."

"Three," said Conrad. "The other is, I thought you were going to give me the bullet."

Horace stared at him. "Just like that? After all these years?" He sounded genuinely hurt. "How could I do something like that?"

"Stranger things have happened." Conrad picked up the sheet of figures on his desk. "What do I do about this?"

Horace grinned maliciously. "Give it to Duval. He's so bloody ambitious, let him do something to prove it." He opened the door, then turned. "You started to tell me, but I got carried away. Why this sudden concern with death?"

"Let it pass," Conrad replied. "It's probably just my age."

Horace marched off energetically through the hammering typists. Halfway to his office he turned and waved. "That's my boy," he bellowed. "I'll see you in a fortnight, bright-eyed and ready to go. Meanwhile, have some fun."

Conrad waved back. "Right," he called. "Right you are."

He collected his things from the office and patted Margy tenderly on the back as he left. Her spine was already damp with exertion. She smiled at him, looking puzzled, but he offered no explanation.

"Holiday time," he said. "End of term."

He was surprised not to find the ginger-haired man waiting for him in the car park.

28 "ALL RIGHT," said Betsy on the telephone. "Come if you want but it won't do any good."

When he answered, "It can't do any harm," she rang off without further comment.

He had the impression that both Betsy and the house were slightly shabbier and sloppier than before. The summer dress she was wearing was rumpled and not quite clean, her hair needed washing. But she was freshly made-up and that seemed to give her confidence.

In the living room all the ashtrays were overflowing and the television was on as usual, although the sound was switched off. Sunlight streamed through the closed windows and the air smelled of old tobacco exhaled through old lungs. When Betsy went out to the kitchen to put on the kettle Conrad examined the stubs: unfiltered Gauloises and Embassies in about equal proportions. His and hers. He wondered briefly what the lucky man was like, then turned his attention to the television, where nervous, long-legged horses were being led around a paddock. The list of runners appeared on the screen and he studied it carefully, but none of the names spoke to him.

The Face still hung over the fireplace. He looked at it critically, admiring the brushwork and wondering how he had managed to do it. It seemed full of light and depth and feeling. It also seemed to have nothing at all to do with him. A gift from God, he told himself, a one-off fluke. Now do what your friend says: Quit while you are still ahead.

He could hear Betsy clattering the cups on the tea tray. "I'm just going up to my studio," he called, and clumped upstairs before she could object.

On the landing the bedroom door was ostentatiously closed. Very quietly, he tried the handle, but the door was locked. He shrugged and pulled down the aluminum ladder.

Immediately he put his head inside the attic the old smell enveloped him and the old nostalgia. What had he been doing all this time? Why had he been wasting himself? He had a sudden childish yearning to start all over again with easel, canvas, and paints, somewhere where the light was clear and there was no Betsy or children or Horace or Abe or Olivia or Mrs. Staff or Inspector Davies or men with ginger hair. To start from scratch with just the dog, which didn't answer back.

The air in the attic was hot and full of dust. The blank canvas still waited on the easel. He looked at it tenderly and ran the palm of his hand gently over its dusty surface. Such disproportionate, unfettered ambition! Then it occurred to him that he still had his four and a half thousand pounds of gambling money and could light out for the sunlit territory whenever he wished.

He found a plastic bag under the workbench and swept into it brushes and palette, carbon sticks and tubes of paint. Carrying it under his arm, he climbed back down the ladder and padlocked the trapdoor behind him.

Betsy was waiting in the living room, sipping tea and staring at the silent television. Two horses had broken from the pack and were fighting it out down the homestretch. Conrad considered turning up the volume, then changed his mind.

She nodded at the tea tray on the floor beside her. "I've

poured yours already. I didn't think you'd be so long. It's probably cold."

Conrad picked up the cup, peered at the filmed surface of the liquid, and put it down again. "Fine," he said.

There was a long pause while they both watched the winner being unsaddled and rubbed down. The camera zoomed in on the lady owner. She was stroking its head lovingly and seemed to be smiling and talking and crying at the same time. Conrad was about to comment on this when the name of the horse was flashed on the screen: Ambo's Girl, 30–1. With odds like that he too would be weeping. The name rang no bells for him, but he wondered if Abe had been on to it.

Betsy got up abruptly and turned off the set. "I've been to see a lawyer," she said.

"Isn't that a bit sudden?"

"Sudden? I've had twelve years to think about it."

He looked at her in amazement and she glared back at him briefly, then bent to pour more tea.

"A bit dramatic, then," he said.

She sat up so suddenly that the tea sloshed into the saucer. He was surprised how angry she was.

"You don't understand a bloody thing, do you? You thought you could just go on and on and I'd sit here and take it. On and on with your horses and your cards and your girls at the office, just as though I didn't exist."

"There weren't any girls at the office."

Betsy took no notice. "You made me feel like a kind of ghost, as if I didn't have any"—she fumbled a moment— "any substance." She looked at him accusingly. "As far as you were concerned, I might have been dead already."

Conrad glanced from her angry, tearful face to the painting over the fireplace, which stared impartially down on them both. Which was the more real for him? Maybe she was right.

197

"I'm sorry," he said.

For some reason that seemed to mollify her. "So am I," she said. "But you see, I don't want to give up yet. There's more due to me before I'm done for."

"Who's talking about giving up?"

"Come on, Conrad," she said sarcastically, "don't play me for a fool. Not at this late stage. You'd given up on me and the kids years ago. I'm not saying that you yourself had given up. You had your painting. I suppose even your bloody gambling was a sign of something or other. But it didn't include me."

Conrad found it hard to argue about this, so he answered, "You had the television. You never seemed to want anything else."

Betsy addressed an invisible listener above the gray-faced screen. "You see what I mean?" She rolled her eyes despairingly to the ceiling. "You're not a serious man, Conrad. I used to think you were serious about your painting, but now I doubt that too. Maybe it was just a way of getting away from me and the kids. At heart, you're frivolous. There's no talking to you."

He roused himself briefly from his lethargy. "What do you know about seriousness, glued to the television all day like a chip to the inside of the freezer? Is your boyfriend so serious, then?"

"At least he takes *me* seriously. I'm beginning to learn."

Now it was out.

"I hope you're happy, then," said Conrad angrily.

"Happier."

They were both silent a moment. Then Betsy got up and poured whiskeys from an almost empty bottle. But when she opened the cupboard Conrad noticed another full bottle on the shelf.

"It was the police, wasn't it?"

Betsy considered this for a while. "That's what woke me up. Yes."

"But Ryan was around before that, wasn't he?"

"How . . ." she began, then shrugged. "Not really."

"You mean, not seriously."

"That's right. You got it. Not seriously."

"Well," said Conrad, "I'm glad you've become so serious about seriousness."

"Better than frivolity."

" ' 'Tis sweating labour to bear such idleness,' as the Bard says."

"The Bard?" Betsy echoed. "Bachelorhood has made you very high-toned."

Conrad grinned at her affectionately. "Maybe I should pretend it's that new seriousness got me, but you'd never believe me. You know what it is, Betsy dear? Softening of the brain. All sorts of old rubbish I haven't thought of for years keeps popping up to the surface, just like I was drowning."

Her anger suddenly vanished and she looked at him with concern. "Is it hard on you?" she asked. "Are you taking care of yourself?" She seemed to be examining him for signs of neglect.

"At the moment," he said, "it's all a bit complicated."

Balancing on the edge of his chair, he leaned across the tea tray and kissed her on the mouth. He had forgotten how nice she tasted, how familiar she felt.

Out of habit she started to kiss him back, then pulled away quickly. "Don't start all that up again."

"For God's sake." He was genuinely indignant. "We're still married."

"Don't get technical, Conrad. I was feeling sorry for you, that's all. Feeling sorry doesn't make a marriage."

"It's part of it.'"

"Not anymore. Not for me."

"You've got very tough."

"Tell me an alternative." She sounded puzzled, as if she really wanted to know.

He shrugged. "I'm not complaining, just commenting."

"That's all right, then."

He changed tack. "What about you, are you O.K.?"

"I'm fine. You don't have to worry about me."

"And the boys?"

"They're fine too." She flared up suddenly. "What do you expect? Even when you were supposed to be at home they never saw you."

"Where are they now? Will I see them?"

"They've gone camping for a week with the school."

"How convenient."

Betsy put on an accent: "A gal's gotta do what a gal's gotta do."

He got up wearily. "O.K., Betsy, you win. Leave it to your lawyer. I won't contest it."

She followed him to the front door. "How do I . . ." she began, then corrected herself. "How does the lawyer get hold of you?"

"Through the office," he answered sweetly. "Ciao." And he went quickly down the grimy steps. She lingered at the door, watching him, but he didn't look back. Through the rearview mirror he saw her wave vaguely at the disappearing car.

It was only when he reached Camden Town that he realized that he had forgotten the picture and his bag of paints and brushes.

"Screw it," he muttered. "I've still got the dog."

29 CONRAD PACED the broad spaces of Regent's Park, head down, like a monk in his cloister. The grass was unnaturally withered by the heat and half of London seemed to be stretched out indolently, not even talking, staring at the sky through dark glasses. Even the children wilted. In the distance, the lake with its oarsmen was like brass.

While he was still living at home he had pictured himself as a kind of suburban Prometheus, chained by a family he scarcely spoke to, a job that bored him, by routines and responsibilities and lack of money. Now suddenly the chains were removed and he was at a loss. I can go away, he thought. For two weeks my time is my own.

He wondered if he should grow a beard, develop a painter's face. He also wondered if he should phone Olivia and ask her to go away with him. Maybe if he could really get through to her his troubles would be over. But he doubted his chances. She was too far off and too taken up with whatever it was which seemed set on doing him down.

Why me? he wondered, but was unable to come up with an answer. It was a random happening, as if certain odd destructive forces had been whirling haphazardly around, without center or direction, and he had merely wandered by. So they had battened on him because he was there. Like a conscript shipped to the front line. For no reason at all people he did not know wanted him dead. If it had been someone else, he would have found it funny.

He picked up a stick for the dog, whirled around and threw it in the direction from which he had come. In the distance he thought he saw a heavy figure with ginger hair sauntering after him. He screwed up his eyes against the glare. There were two of them, the other shorter, fatter, and dark. But they were too far off for him to be sure. His heart began to bump heavily in his chest.

"Kim," he shouted. "Here, boy, here."

The dog bounced up cheerfully, offering Conrad the stick.

"Heel," he said curtly, and began to hurry toward the Outer Circle. There would be policemen outside the American ambassador's home, he thought. Just in case.

When he reached the road he paused and looked back down the long graveled walk. There was no sign of the men. He shook his head and told himself it was all nerves. But he was not convinced.

By the time he got back to Dean Street the idea of going away no longer seemed appealing. Wherever he went they would find him. He sat down on the bed and leaned forward until his face was close to the dog's. "Anyway," he told it, "I couldn't go abroad and leave you behind, could I, old chap?"

The dog licked his nose tenderly.

I can go later when the time comes, he thought. I'm a free man.

He sat staring at the copper and purple sunset, stroking the dog's head and thinking: Sufficient unto the day. Then he phoned Herb and invited himself to the game.

He was about to ring off when he saw Kim watching him reproachfully. "Mind if I bring my dog?" he added.

"You can bring your bloody grandmother," said Herb, "provided she keeps quiet."

Beyond Centre Point the coppery light was slowly turning red. It would be hot again tomorrow. He listened to the traffic droning home and was glad not to be part of it. It puzzled him that he should have slipped back into bachelorhood as casually as he had once slipped into marriage. He wondered if the boys missed him or bore him a grudge, or if Betsy was right and they hardly noticed he had gone. Not that he would ever know. By the time they got around to telling him, if they ever did, it would be too late.

He opened a tin of food for the dog and put a pot of coffee on the stove. Kim wolfed down his heavy-smelling mess in less than a minute, then watched mournfully while Conrad cut bread and fried himself an egg. While he ate he listened to the evening concert on the radio and to the faint, admonishing voices in his head—Betsy's, Horace's— telling him about his past and his mistakes. He knew he should be worried—he appreciated their concern—but somehow the effort was too much for him. He was overcome by pleasant, vague inertia. He seemed to feel his life receding, little by little, drifting away from the shore where other human beings were so inexplicably busy.

Finally, he got to his feet and stretched. "Let's play cards," he said to the dog, and went out, double-locking the door behind him.

The same old faces were around the table, saying the same old things. Yet no sooner had Conrad settled in his seat than the soothing rhythm of the game took him and he began to feel at peace. Slowly his head cleared of everything except the green baize in front of him, the silky, whispering cards, and the bright chips that clicked so delicately and restrainedly when they were counted.

"Happiness," he announced, "is a clear head and a full house."

The others looked at him quizzically.

"You should be so lucky," said Herb. "For that, I'll raise you."

For the first hour the dog sat alertly beside Conrad's chair, waiting for something to happen. It wagged its tail whenever he glanced down and leaped to its feet when he got up to fetch himself a coffee. But as the night wore on it became increasingly morose, despite the titbits Conrad sneaked for it from the kitchen. Finally, it stretched itself out on the carpet and fell asleep, stiff-legged and resigned.

When Conrad next looked around it was hunting rabbits in its dreams. Its feet made tiny, frantic movements, its eyes rolled up in its head, and it whimpered in its attempts to bark without waking. The other players found this peculiarly amusing. Conrad, of course, laughed along with them, although secretly he was offended for the animal's dignity. He was relieved when it sank deeper into sleep, its broad shaggy flank rising and falling evenly, its paws primly crossed.

He won modestly that night, then again the following evening at a game organized by the Irishman, and again at the house of Paul the journalist. London poker, he discovered, was like one of those conjurer's handkerchiefs: pull one out and an endless string followed. Whenever the private games failed he went to the Victoria and played at the ten-pound table, where he also won.

He preferred, however, to play in private houses because he could take the dog with him. He was convinced it brought him luck, although in one corner of his mind he knew he no longer needed to be superstitious. He was playing better because he had no cause to be optimistic. Bad times had made him patient and mistrustful. He concentrated on the cards because the alternatives were too disagreeable. Kim was merely his excuse.

"Brought my mascot along," he would announce when he arrived and, to his surprise, the other players welcomed the idea. They made fun of him, as they made fun of the dog, and this affected their estimate of how he was playing. They seemed offended, as well as puzzled, by the fact that he was winning regularly and were glad when he made a point of telling them how stunningly the cards were falling for him.

"Maybe we should ban that hound of yours from the game," said the Irishman. "He's disturbing the natural order of things. Come without him and we'll see how you do."

Conrad understood that his reputation from the bad old days was at last standing him in good stead.

"Every dog must have his day," he answered, and glanced across the table at Abe, who narrowed one eye in the ghost of a wink.

"Are we here to play cards," Abe asked wearily, "or to discuss lucky dogs and black cats?"

"We were discussing," answered the journalist in a prim Oxford voice, "the miraculous transformation of Conrad Jessup."

Abe shrugged. "Excuses, excuses. Consider the possibility that he may have learned how to play the game after all this time."

"What a wee-ard conception."

"Life, friends, is a weird conception," Abe replied, "as my old mom used to say every time she looked at me."

The fat man and Conrad ate together each evening before the games, drinking Perrier and coffee, talking about cards. They analyzed hands and discussed the temperaments of the other players. Neither of them mentioned Conrad's recent troubles.

Once he asked, "Any news?" He tried to sound casual.

Abe looked him sympathetically in the eye and shook his head. "The line's gone dead."

"I don't know whether to laugh or cry."

"Neither. Just forget it. Maybe you were right after all. Somebody got his signals crossed and now it's been sorted out."

"Maybe."

After that they avoided the subject.

Conrad went on winning. Finally he asked Abe about the big game at Knights'.

"Like the ad says: Try it. You'll like it."

"How would I get on?"

"O.K." Abe nodded judiciously. "I think you'd do O.K. if you play like you're playing now. Also," he added, "you've got enough money behind you not to be frightened."

"How much is enough?"

"You can't sit down with less than two hundred in front of you. Club rules. But you need at least a thousand to be comfortable."

Conrad drew in his breath between closed teeth. "I thought we were having an economic crisis."

"Sure we are, but this is another world, baby. Those guys aren't fools even if—when you're lucky—some of them play that way. If they choose to drop a grand or two, that's their pleasure. So they'll get up from the table hating themselves. But they can make it up again on the telephone the next morning." When he looked at Conrad his sharp dark eyes became almost kindly. "In your book, how rich is rich?" he asked in a patient voice. "Twenty-five thousand a year? Thirty?" He shook his head. "No way. That's just comfortable these days, the kinda bread that gives you tax problems. The really rich don't think like that, not in income per annum. Serious money is like a cancer, it breeds itself. These guys just take what they need, or what their accountants say they should take. There's no time span, no per annum, no real limits. There's just capital in one form or another. And believe me, it has an infinity of forms. It's a numinous presence, like the godhead, and they're its priests: they serve it and it serves them."

"How can you beat them?"

"With skill."

"They say frightened money never wins."

Abe made a small dismissive gesture with his hairy hand. "You're four or five gee ahead, am I right? Gambling money pure and simple. So it won't wipe you out even if you drop a thousand. Which you won't on your present form."

Conrad sipped his coffee and stared at the paper tablecloth. When he looked up again Abe was leaning back in his chair, watching him critically. Conrad had seen that expression over the poker table. In the shabby little Indian restaurant it made him feel uneasy. He understood that something was expected of him.

"How do I get to play?" he asked.

Abe sighed noisily and wiped his sweating neck. "Nothing easier. We'll stop by the club on the way to the game tonight."

"I thought these things took time."

"Not with me, they don't. I'm one of their oldest members. They'll take my word for you."

"Thanks," said Conrad, wondering: What's in it for him?

Abe raised his hand in benediction. "All part of the Abe Gauss service."

He finished his coffee, then peered intently into the cup, as though waiting for some truth to be revealed. But all he said was, "Instant. I dunno how they have the nerve to call the muck coffee."

"Because it contains caffeine."

Abe grimaced. "That must be it."

They called in at Knights' Club and Conrad became a member on the spot. He surprised the club secretary by paying his subscription in cash.

When they were back in the car he turned to Abe: "Twenty-six twenty-five, what kind of sum is that?"

"Guineas," said Abe. "Twenty-five guineas to you, buster. That's the kinda place it is: traditional."

"I'm flattered they deigned to take my money."

"They'd take your gold fillings if they had to."

"Then they'd better join the queue," said Conrad. "There are others in front of them."

The dog, stretched out on the back seat like a traveling rug, groaned mournfully. Conrad reached back and scratched its belly. The dog groaned again. Out of the corner of his eye he watched the streetlights make shadows on Abe's heavy face. Finally he said, "Ever heard of a horse called Artist's Moll?"

Abe grinned and ran his tongue over his lips, as though remembering a particularly good meal. "Uh-uh. Came in at fifty to one, God bless its sweet soul." His tongue moved again over his lips. He seemed to be tasting the money. "How come you got on to it?"

"I liked the name."

Abe took this as a joke and laughed appreciatively. "Sometimes it pays to be a romantic," he said.

Conrad blushed. "Nearly a thousand is what it paid. I put twenty quid on its nose and it changed my life." He paused, and as the truth of what he had said sank in, a wave of depression rolled over him. He shivered. "You don't know how much it changed it."

"Let me guess," said Abe soothingly. He drove in silence for a while through the gathering dark, then said, "Come on, pal, tell me true. Who put you on to that nag?"

"Boredom and despair," Conrad answered. "The old firm. I take it you had a more reliable source of information."

"I guess you could say that. Not that it wasn't obvious to those who knew how to read the entrails." He looked at Conrad quizzically and shook his head. "You mean, you really didn't know?"

Conrad's indignation flared again. "For Christ's sake, what was there to know?"

Abe went on shaking his head. "I thought you were a student of these intricate matters." He sighed. "The favorite was a horse called Silver Arrow, which was running at Newmarket two weeks later. A very good little pony, very short odds. Artist's Moll was this nag's stablemate, just put in to make the pace in the early stages."

"So?" Conrad's depression increased. There was no such thing as luck and he had never been blessed.

"So don't be naïve. Silver Arrow is seven to eight on and Artist's Moll is an outsider nobody's heard of. But she's done some good times in training back in Ireland, which they've managed to keep quiet about. So big deal. They let her go and hold back the favorite. She comes in at fifty to one and the odds on Silver Arrow change for the better in the big race."

"Which it wins?"

"Too true. And everyone lives happily ever after."

"I'm not sure I do anymore."

"You take these things too seriously. It's your bourgeois morality."

"Morality my arse. I thought that win was a sign. I thought the gods were smiling on me at least."

"Maybe they were. You got your money on it, didn't you, without anyone's help? I'd call that a *mitzphah*."

"You're missing the point," said Conrad.

But when he won again that night he was no longer tempted to blame it on the dog.

30

HE PREFERRED TO PLAY until it was light, uncertain of what he would find when he returned to the flat. One morning the telephone was ringing as he unlocked the door, but directly he picked it up a man's voice said, "Sorry, wrong number," and rang off before Conrad could say a word. Twice he thought he saw the man with ginger hair behind him in the street, but when he turned back to confront him there was no one there. Then for a few days nobody came, nobody phoned, and he began to wonder if they had forgotten him.

Maybe I have been forgiven, he thought. But he wished he knew what he was supposed to have done.

He spent a whole morning scrubbing at the drawing of the phallus above his bed but succeeded only in blurring its outline. So he bought a pot of paint and a roller and repainted the wall. Although the new white did not quite blend with the old, the untouched cleanliness of it, like a canvas primed and ready, brightened the flat and at first made him cheerful. But the smell lingered on in the heat, and when he woke to it morning after morning, it reminded him of his troubles.

Each day he slept until noon, then spent the afternoon on the Heath or in one of the parks, wandering aimlessly, swimming, sprawling on the grass with a newspaper, throwing sticks for the dog, which was ecstatic with so much fresh air and attention. Conrad woke each morning to find it staring at him slavishly, and whenever he talked to it, it rolled passionately onto its back and offered its belly to be tickled.

Gradually it occurred to him that he was missing something. While he played poker all night and slept away the best of the daylight, his holiday was seeping away. He felt a dull ache, a sense of loss. Not for Betsy and the children. If he went back now, all he could expect was a lifetime of resentment and recrimination. She would never let him off the hook again. Nevertheless, something was missing. He thought of Olivia's soft mouth and the fall of her tawny-blond hair. All they had brought him was fear and trouble. They were not worth the cost.

Kim put his forelegs on the bed and began to lick Conrad's hand. He turned over irritably and contemplated the freshly painted wall. It offended him that there was still so much untidiness in his life, such unfinished business. If Betsy had decided to shut up shop after all these years, at least she should have got hold of a lawyer by now.

"Once a slut always a slut," he muttered self-righteously.

Then he remembered that she did not know his address. There might be a letter waiting for him at the office. He climbed out of bed, set the coffee percolator going, then sat down by the telephone. The dog followed him around expectantly.

"Only the usual rubbish from the usual firms," said Margy. "I've taken care of most of them. The rest I've passed on to Mr. Duval."

"Nothing else?"

"Just one. Handwritten and marked 'Personal'. I was going to send it on, then I thought you might be away, so I telephoned your home."

She paused and he heard her swallow.

"So now you know," he said encouragingly. "Don't take it to heart."

"I'm sorry."

"It's not your fault."

"I was afraid you'd think I was prying."

"Don't be daft, love."

"I haven't breathed a word to a soul."

The dog had sidled up while he was talking and laid its head on Conrad's thigh. He shoved it away roughly.

"You're a good girl and I'm grateful to you."

"I really didn't want to pry," Margy repeated.

"Of course you didn't. Tell you what: I'll buy you lunch at the Greek's. Bring the envelope."

"You don't have to."

"That's no way to say thanks."

He heard her swallow again. "Thanks, then."

"That's better. See you at one and don't forget the letter."

Margy worked her way through olives, peppers, radishes and spring onions, hummus, taramasalata, three pitas, the special mixed grill with rice, and two chunks of pastry oozing honey. Conrad watched her with awe. Between mouthfuls she expressed her continuing loyalty by complaining about Duval. Conrad felt sad not to be able to work up the appropriate indignation. He nibbled his food and fingered the envelope. He did not recognize the handwriting, which was large and spiky.

When she had finished eating Margy said, "Did you know Mr. Alport's been taken ill?"

"What's up?"

"Nobody's saying but Enid seems awfully upset."

"Poor old Enid. Poor old Horace, for that matter."

"They've brought in Mr. Stockton from Accounts."

"Meaning Horace'll be away some time?"

"They say he's in hospital. But that's not official."

"What's a nice guy like him doing in a joint like that?"

"Maybe they'd tell you if you asked."

"Right at this moment I don't think I want to know. I'm not strong enough."

"That isn't very nice, dear."

Conrad looked at her bleakly. "Don't give me trouble, Margy. I've got enough already."

"Of course you have," she said consolingly. "That's not what I meant."

"Find out where he is and I'll send the old sod one perfect rose and a dozen tit magazines."

Margy flushed and said accusingly, "I thought he was your friend. He's always looked after you."

"It's too late for friends, Margy. I seem to be leaving them all behind."

"Some of us still love you." She made a move to pat his cheek, then thought better of it and got up. "Must run," she said.

She steered herself carefully between the tables and out of the door, as though she were some great ocean liner. Through the window of the restaurant, Conrad saw her pause and stare resentfully up at the hot cloudless sky. Then she moved majestically off down the street, breasts and buttocks swaying.

He sat on over his coffee and opened the envelope. All the letter said was "Dear Conrad, Why haven't you telephoned? I think about you often. Love, Olivia."

He turned the letter over, sniffed the thick yellow paper, then held it at arm's length to study the general effect of the handwriting. It looked like a hedge of thorns. He tried unsuccessfully to connect it with the slim, casual girl and her delicate profile. He wondered if they had made her write, though who "they" were he still did not know. Then he remembered that "they" had already taken his room apart and knew that, like his life, it contained nothing of interest. So why should they bother? It must be her own idea.

For a moment he forgot the anxieties and fears "they"

213

provoked in him and felt unreasonably optimistic. "You're a feckless fellow," he muttered into his coffee. Nevertheless, he remained obscurely elated.

He hurried back through the baking streets, collected the dog, and drove to the Heath for a swim. But the pond was full of schoolchildren who splashed each other and screamed and churned the water into thin mud. He swam out to the packed raft, hung there a minute or two, staring balefully at the scrawny young bodies, listening to their idiot chatter. Then he swam back, dried himself quickly, and walked across to Ken Wood.

He saw them immediately he came through the trees which border the lawns sloping down from the house. Dicky was standing in front of a folded jacket, swinging a cricket bat. Jim and Betsy were watching him expectantly, one on either side and at a discreet distance, while Betsy's lover bowled from another folded jacket. He was older than Conrad expected and considerably plumper. His hair was long and streaked with gray, his florid face bright as a stop light with exertion. When he ran up to bowl the tire of fat above his belt wobbled hysterically. He bowled without moving his left arm, which made him seem curiously lop-sided. But when Dicky drove the ball at him hard and high, the man leaped like a teenager and caught it at full stretch. "Howzat?" he roared, and the others shouted, "Out!" Dicky threw down the bat, his Afro haircut bristling with anger, while his mother and brother applauded the catch.

Scenes from a Family Life. Conrad stepped back into the trees and clicked his tongue at the dog, which had started to trot forward when he heard the familiar voices. He felt indignant. Whenever he had suggested a walk on the Heath they had made excuses: something urgent on television, something they couldn't possibly miss. Or, on the few occasions when they came with him, Betsy would mislay her coat belt when Conrad was already out of the front gate, then one of the boys would be sent back to change his shoes, and they would finish up strung out irritably down the road, moving at different speeds, nobody talking to anyone else. So he had given up asking. He preferred to go on his own peacefully, followed by the dog, and the others never went out at all, so far as he knew, except to school or the shops. Now they were playing cricket together. He felt betrayed.

Jim hit the ball and the plump red-faced man lumbered after it, stopped it with his foot, and threw it to Betsy. She flapped her hands at it vaguely and missed. Ryan roared with laughter and the others laughed with him, Betsy included. So that's what has been missing from their lives all these years, thought Conrad. They are having fun together. Who would have thought it possible? This man has preempted my bed and my sons not with love or tenderness but with jollity. The surge of rage he felt was not of the genitals but of the heart. With his clenched fists hanging inertly at his sides like lead weights, he watched them clowning together on the barbered grass and understood that the real betrayal was not that Betsy should have found herself a lover but that, having found him, joy should have entered all their lives. It seemed to Conrad unforgivable that they should be so blatantly happier without him.

Then the wind shifted in his head, his hands unclenched, and he was filled with sorrow. See what you've missed, he admonished himself. It was worth having after all.

Dicky bowled, pitching the ball wide and short. Jim stepped across and hit it hard, with the sweet of the bat, directly toward the trees. As the lover began to pound after it, Conrad turned and blundered away through the bushes. Their excited voices came after him.

It is as if I had never been, he thought.

At South End Green he parked the car and called Olivia from a public box.

"Come on over," she said.

"When?"

"Why not now?"

"I've got the dog."

"I've been waiting to be introduced."

He lit a cigarette before he left the kiosk and was surprised to find his hands were still shaking. He inhaled and watched the match burn unsteadily down while the blackened end curled trembling upwards. He waited until the flame touched his finger before dropping it.

I hurt, therefore I am.

Now there was only Olivia left.

31

"WHY DON'T WE GO AWAY together for a couple of days?" he said.

Olivia lay back on the cushions and studied him, as though from a great distance. The idea seemed to amuse her. "Isn't this a bit sudden?"

"I said a couple of days, not a lifetime."

"Sometimes a couple of days can seem like a lifetime."

"Bless you too, Miss Pelham."

Olivia shrugged. "I like you, Conrad, you know that, I mean, I wrote to you, didn't I?"

"But?"

"But today you've got a kind of look in your eye." She sat up and clicked her fingers at the dog. "Here," she said.

It went to her immediately, laid its head in her lap, and gazed up at her lovingly. Conrad wondered whether he was offended by the creature's promiscuity or simply jealous.

"Don't worry about that," he said. "I have no moral designs on you."

"A girl can't be too careful these days."

"Maybe I should be flattered after all." He leaned toward her and said, "Don't let's spar around. I'm too weary." He touched the delicate skin in the crook of her arm, then ran his fingers gently down until they meshed with hers. "There aren't many options open to me anymore."

"And I'm one that is?" She smiled good-humoredly. "I've never thought of myself like that before."

"Get used to it. Everyone I talk to these days looks at me as if I was someone I'd never heard of. It happens. You are who you know."

"So you think we should pool our resources?"

"We might do worse."

She shook her head dubiously. "It wouldn't work out. I too have become a liability."

He lifted her hand to his mouth and kissed her fingertips. Her cat's eyes were full of greenish light.

"Maybe I always was," she said.

He answered, "It's a risk I'm willing to take."

"That's nice, but also unwise. I'm in a real mess."

"What sort of mess?"

"All sorts of mess." She took her hand away from his and ran her fingers through the still thin hair on the side of her head. "I have been kind of indiscreet, if you know what I mean."

"I can guess." He reached for her hand but she moved away and looked at him bleakly. For a moment she seemed older than he was and even more depressed. "Is that why they tried to kill you?" he asked.

She looked away and began to fondle Kim's muzzle. "That's not a matter I care to discuss," she said primly.

"Take it easy. I'm on your side."

"That's not the point." She ran her fingers along the side of the dog's mouth, ruffling the soft white fur, then smoothing it down again. After a while she said, "Do you believe in God?"

Conrad made an embarrassed noise in his throat which was supposed to be laughter. "What a weird question."

"Go on," she insisted, "tell me."

"Well, I'm a gambler and gamblers are superstitious. So I used to believe in luck. But now I have reason to believe that not even luck is simple. It can be arranged."

"What's left, then?"

"Sometimes the cards run for you, sometimes against. It's

a question of mathematics." Through the open window he heard a taxi draw up outside. He listened to its engine churning in the quiet street. It occurred to him that in some way he was letting her down. "Why do you ask?"

"I was brought up in a convent. My parents are Catholics. That's why they're not divorced."

"That's a hard one to get over."

"Not with those nuns it wasn't. They turned me off once and for all. Even so . . ." Her voice trailed away. She, too, seemed to be listening to the taxi.

"Well?"

"Well, maybe I didn't get over it." She leaned forward, holding the dog's passive head in both hands. "You see, I went on thinking I had a charmed life. That was stupid of me, wasn't it?"

"Maybe you did, up to a point."

Olivia sighed. "That point has come and gone."

They heard the front door open and close, then the sound of footsteps going toward the back of the house.

"Sometimes, when my luck was really out," said Conrad, "I used to think the Manichaeans were right, after all."

"Who were they?"

"Heretics. They believed that God and the devil were fighting it out and that God didn't necessarily win."

"What happened to them?"

"They were wiped out, of course—in a spectacularly nasty manner."

"When was all that?"

"Hundreds of years ago. Before our time." She looked at him quizzically and he added, "It's a theory that has always appealed to me."

The footsteps were on the stairs now. Olivia patted her hair nervously. "I can understand why," she said.

Mrs. Staff came in. She looked at Conrad with distaste and said, "The man from the hospital."

"I was just passing."

"Naturally," said Mrs. Staff. "What else?" Around her carefully made-up mouth her face was unnaturally white, and when she poured herself a drink, the bottle rattled against the glass. "This town is falling apart," she announced.

Olivia bent to the dog and did not reply.

"Bombs." Her voice rose slightly but remained under control. "Another maniac with a bomb. I decided to come home by tube—God knows why—and suddenly there was a commotion on the platform. He ran right past me, this man. No, not a man, a youth with pimples. He ran past me and they all came after him, shouting their heads off. I thought he was going to throw the thing at me. I thought I was going to die."

Olivia got up abruptly and crossed the room. She put her arms around her shoulders and held her close, rocking her and making comforting noises.

Mrs. Staff went on, "I caught his eye, you see. That's why I thought he'd kill me."

"Did they get him?" asked Conrad.

"Yes, on the escalator. He actually went up the escalator. Can you imagine?" Olivia held the glass to her mouth and she drank. "He couldn't have been more than seventeen and stupid with it. Of course they were waiting for him."

"What was he?" asked Conrad. "Irish or Palestinian?"

"He didn't stop to say. All that matters is that he was a teenage murderer and I thought he was going to kill me." She shivered suddenly and swallowed more of the drink.

Olivia went on rocking her. "I'm so sorry," she murmured, "I'm so sorry." She stroked the woman's trim gray hair lingeringly, as she had stroked the dog's. Mrs. Staff shifted a little and looked into the girl's face, then she kissed her softly on the mouth. Olivia kissed her back.

They stayed like this for what seemed to Conrad a considerable time. Finally, Mrs. Staff pulled away and smiled at him triumphantly.

"They are like rabid animals," she said. "They should be put down."

Conrad shrugged helplessly. "It's the new life-style."

"What is?" asked Mrs. Staff.

"Terror," said Conrad. "We are preparing for the twenty-first century. Take it or leave it."

"I prefer to leave it," Mrs. Staff answered. "Order not terror. If somebody has to go under, let it be them not us."

"I'll drink to that," said Conrad. "But I wouldn't put money on our chances."

Olivia led the older woman to a chair and knelt by her side. She stroked her hand and peered anxiously into her face. Her mouth was unsteady and Conrad realized that she was frightened. Since Mrs. Staff had entered the room, she had not looked at him once.

"They think they can get away with it, that's why they try. They're common criminals, but when they're caught they call themselves political prisoners and claim special privileges. The authorities should put a stop to it."

"They will," said Conrad. "It's only a matter of time."

"If that dog of yours had rabies, they wouldn't hesitate."

Conrad reached out and patted Kim's head protectively. "Don't you believe it. The English are always keener on dogs than people. It's part of our national charm."

"You're missing the point," said Mrs. Staff icily. "Isn't he, Olivia?"

"I suppose so." The girl laughed nervously.

Mrs. Staff's anger flared again. "The point is, the authorities are like everyone else: they have betrayed their trust, and the rest of us have to suffer for it." She paused and turned to Olivia. "It's a time of betrayal, isn't it, my sweet?"

The girl looked away and repeated, "I suppose so."

Conrad got up wearily. "I'd better be going," he said.

Olivia went downstairs with him. "I'm sorry," she whispered. "It was a nice idea but I can't go away with you. You can see that, can't you?" Her face looked peaked and drawn, as it had in the hospital.

"It's all right," he said reassuringly. "Circumstances beyond your control. Beyond mine too."

She kissed him quickly and opened the door. "You won't just disappear, will you? Call me soon. I mean soon. Let's have another evening or something."

"Or something," echoed Conrad.

I'll take a stroll, he thought, and walked slowly toward the sound of the late-afternoon traffic, the dog running to and fro in front of him, leaving its signature on every lamppost. When he reached the corner he paused and glanced back. The man with ginger hair was sauntering along behind him, his hands in his pockets, an evening paper tucked under his arm.

"Fuck it," said Conrad.

Ostentatiously, he wrapped the dog's chain lead around his fist and marched back the way he had come. The man stopped short, surprised, leaned against the railings, and opened his paper. When Conrad drew level he squared his shoulders and tensed himself, but the man merely grinned at him lopsidedly. He seemed almost embarrassed.

Conrad walked faster. When he reached his car he glanced back again. The man was strolling lazily toward him, his hands back in his pockets, as if enjoying the evening air. Conrad bundled the dog into the car and roared off into the traffic. The man tipped him an ironic salute as he passed and grinned even more broadly than before.

Soho was jammed with cars and people dawdling in the hot night. He parked in the Blue Star on Brewer Street, then lingered in the shadows inspecting the cars behind him as they moved up the ramp. But the man with ginger hair was not in any of them, nor was he waiting out on the street.

Holding the dog on a tight leash, Conrad wove his way

through the crowd. When he reached Wardour Street he paused, pretending to admire the burnished pots and pans in a shop window.

Nobody.

He walked north quickly, then cut through an alley between darkened windows and a high fence. There was still no one following him when he came out into Dean Street.

He double-locked the flat door behind him, pushed home the bolt, and did not switch on the lights. He felt his way into the kitchen, found a tin of dog food, fumbled with the can opener, spilled biscuit on the floor, then settled himself in the armchair while Kim ate noisily. He sat staring at the dark mass of Centre Point, his mind blank.

When the telephone began to ring he did not stir. It rang on and on, on and on, plangently: dear-dear, dear-dear, dear-dear. He remained motionless, listening, staring at the night sky. In the silence that followed he began to comprehend the measure of his fear.

32 INSPECTOR DAVIES was not impressed. He leaned forward and arranged his face into what was intended to be benign concern. "Am I to understand that you are being harassed"—he raised his eyebrows—"by the police?"

Conrad shook his head sullenly and avoided Davies' accusing stare. "You know I'm not."

The blotter in front of the policeman was covered with intricate geometric doodles: cones, polygons, mandalas. The language of silence, Conrad thought. Davies' pen was poised, waiting for him to continue. He wondered what shape his maunderings would provoke.

"At this point," he admitted, "I'd be relieved if they were the police."

Davies carefully drew a circle on the blotter, then stopped and contemplated the empty space. He shook his head. "They've really put the fear of God into you."

"It's not knowing who they are or what they want." Conrad watched the inspector slowly inscribe a pentagram within the circle. "When this started you said *you* knew. Why won't you tell me?"

"As I explained at the time," said Davies patiently, "I am not at liberty to."

"I'm not a suspect anymore, I'm a witness. It's your duty

to protect me." Conrad heard his voice rising, slightly out of control, and this made him blush.

Davies patted the air soothingly above his blotter. "Of course. If that's what you want, it can be arranged."

"I wish I knew what I wanted."

The policeman began to shade in the areas between the circumference of the circle and the sides of the pentagram. When he had filled in one corner he asked, "For starters, do you want to make a complaint?"

"Is there any point?"

"Not really. But it would make it official and some people like things that way—all neat and tidy and in duplicate."

"But not you?"

Davies suddenly grinned raffishly, like a naughty schoolboy. "I can take it or leave it," he said. "But don't let me influence you."

Conrad felt overawed. He had never imagined the policeman's grim, blue-shadowed presence was capable of such transformations.

"I've let things slide. Earlier there were real causes for complaint. But now . . ." He brooded a moment. "The trouble is, I feel more threatened now than I did before."

"But this man, this fellow with ginger hair, offered no violence?"

"Offered no violence," Conrad echoed. "I told you, didn't I, that you remind me of my headmaster?"

Davies nodded pleasantly and said nothing.

"He didn't lay a finger on me. I just got the impression that he was . . . well, gloating."

"No doubt he enjoys putting the frighteners on people. That's the mentality that tends to go with the work."

"No doubt, as you say. But it was something else, too. I felt he was holding back because it wasn't necessary for him to threaten me anymore. Things have gone beyond that and he knows it."

He tapped the desk petulantly in order to draw Davies' attention away from his blotter. "He's like everyone else." His voice rose again accusingly. "You all know something I don't and you won't tell me. Yet I'm the one it concerns most of all." He stood up and leaned on the desk, pushing his face into Davies'. "Tell me what the secret is. I demand to know. I'm the one who has to take all the shit."

His mouth was trembling and he was afraid he was going to weep. He sat down again abruptly.

"I'm the one who's going to be hurt."

"Nobody's going to be hurt," said Davies soothingly, "and everything's under control. There's no secret at all." His voice became earnest, almost pious. "I give you my word. Certain people are being kept under observation, that's all. We all have to be very discreet. It would never do to provoke an incident. I'm sure you appreciate that. In a delicate situation like this all any of us can do is watch and wait. We know what they're about, Mr. Jessup, we have their number, I promise you. But until such time as they do something illegal the motto is, watch and wait." He leaned back in his chair and crossed his arms gravely.

"Thank you." Conrad looked into the policeman's solemn face and felt again as he had felt as a child in the headmaster's study: overwhelmed by the gravity of it all.

"Why me?" he asked.

"I think they think," Davies spoke slowly, choosing his words, "that you are what you're not."

Conrad smiled at last. "Meaning?"

"They think you're after something." Davies, in his turn, smiled encouragingly. "Are you?"

"Only the girl. They must know that by now."

Davies made a prim mouth. "That young lady seems to be a continual source of trouble to you. Wouldn't it be wiser to keep away? Not that it's any of my business."

"You're the second person to tell me that."

"Well, then, why do you go on bothering?"

Conrad shrugged. "Maybe I'm not very bright," he answered. "Also my wife chucked me out, remember? I'm lonely."

"There are other girls, Mr. Jessup. Lots of them, I'm sure."

"So everyone tells me. But the fact is, she's the one I like. Also my life seems to have become involved with hers, willy-nilly."

Elsewhere in the building a typewriter was rattling away and two telephones were ringing. They reminded Conrad of the office. Of another world, more boring but saner. They reminded him of Horace and the tit magazines he had forgotten to send him.

He cleared his throat noisily. "There's something else. You say she's trouble. Everybody says so and it's true. True but not relevant. But she is also *in* trouble. I think . . ." He cleared his throat again. "I think I feel sorry for her."

Davies nodded understandingly. "I'm afraid I have to agree with you, Mr. Jessup. In certain areas you're not very bright."

He studied Conrad's face as though seeking confirmation of this insight. Then he went on, "You see, being sorry for her isn't, as you would say, relevant. If Miss Pelham is in trouble, it's because she's done something she shouldn't have done —just as you initially got into trouble with us by *not* doing something you should have done. This is an entirely practical matter. The emotions don't come into it."

Conrad shook his head: "For me it's the other way around. I don't know about the practical details. I just feel sorry for her."

Davies shrugged and bent again to the blotter. "Then I'm afraid that you, too, are in trouble." Meticulously he shaded in another corner of his drawing. Then he looked up and grinned. "If I wanted to be inconsistent, I'd say I was sorry for you."

"Think nothing of it." Conrad got up and held out his hand. "It's time I went. This conversation is about to become philosophical."

Davies pumped his hand as he walked him to the door. "A pleasure to see you again. You'd be surprised how rarely in this job is it possible to talk intelligently with anyone."

Conrad disengaged his hand from the policeman's and opened the door. "I suspect," he said ruefully, "our conversation contains certain existential ironies that I've missed."

Davies clapped him on the back. "You see," he exclaimed jubilantly, "you see! Existential ironies, indeed. I like it! I like it!"

He shook Conrad's hand again vigorously and closed the door.

Through the pale oak panels Conrad heard him chuckling. "Existential ironies! Existential ironies!"

The duty sergeant behind the front desk smiled at him as he went out, just as if he were an old friend.

33 CONRAD SAT AT HIS WINDOW and listened to the noises of London drifting to him over the roofs. Two cats were playing in the grimy well which separated his building from the backs of the houses in Frith Street. They were stalking each other between the dustbins, as though through deep jungle. Whenever one of them pounced, they sparred amiably, cuffing one another with sheathed claws. Suddenly the smaller of the cats arched its body into a crescent moon and danced sideways until its curved ribcage bumped the other cat's nose. Then it shot off into the narrow space between the dustbins and the wall. The other cat sat down and cleaned its whiskers, then followed slowly.

Conrad wondered if they were about to mate. He felt left out.

"I am leading an unhealthy life," he told the dog solemnly. "I sleep at the wrong hours, I drink too much coffee and eat ethnic junk, I smoke immoderately and fornicate infrequently. This is no way to begin middle age."

The dog groaned sympathetically.

Davies had said there were lots of girls. Abe said the same, though more poetically: "The beaches of the world are strewn with pebbles." Even Betsy had accused him of having girls at the office. He leafed disconsolately through his address book, looking for names and trying to remember faces. But when he tried a couple of numbers the people who answered were not helpful.

"Dinah? No Dinah here."

"Penny who? You've got the wrong number."

Vanished, like the London of his youth, like Ur of the Chaldees. Not that he would have known what to say to them after all these years.

He made one last attempt, though more out of loyalty than conviction, certainly no longer out of desire.

The telephone rang for a long time. Just as he was about to put down the receiver, a harassed voice barked, "Yes?" Children were shouting in the background.

"Is Jenny there?" Conrad asked, though he no longer wanted to know.

"This is Jenny." The voice was harsh and matter-of-fact. The tumult of children's voices grew louder and one of them began to cry. Jenny moved her mouth fractionally from the receiver and shouted, "For God's sake, shut up," then turned again to the telephone and said impatiently, "Sorry. Who's that?"

Conrad rang off.

Jenny with the red hair and white skin. Jenny with the soft voice.

He addressed himself indignantly to the dog. "It's not fair," he said.

But the dog, for once, took no notice.

That night he played again at Herb's, but the game no longer held him. He won a little, lost a little, won again. When the game broke up at half-past three he was twenty pounds ahead and dissatisfied.

Out on the street it was still dark, although there was a vague rim of gray edging the roofs at the end of the road. He leaned against Herb's garden gate while Abe fumbled for his car keys and the dog relieved itself busily up and down the street.

"I'm bored," he announced.

"What have you got to complain about?" Abe replied. "I'm a tenner down."

"That's it, a tenner. Big deal. We've played for six hours and you're ten down, I'm twenty up. That's how my life is going, Abe. I'm frittering it away in fivers and tenners."

"You won, didn't you?"

"Pissing around like this, you lose even when you win."

"That's how it is, mostly." Abe paused to light a cigarette. The tiny flickering light filled his eye sockets with sepulchral shadows. "The trouble with you, pal, is you're a romantic. As I've remarked before."

"Maybe. But I haven't the time left to waste."

"Come off it, Conrad. Don't give me the it-tolls-for-thee routine. Not at three-thirty in the morning."

"I just meant, in four days I'll be back at work."

"What are you planning to do about it?"

"I want some action. Maybe I'll go and play in that big game before it's too late."

"It's never too late." Abe cocked his head first to one side, then to the other. "If you're ready, you're ready," he said.

"What about you? Do you fancy it?"

Abe nodded. "I just might, at that." He climbed ponderously into his car. "There's something else we've got to talk about. I'll meet you for lunch at Harper's."

Harper's had dark booths and greenish light. The waitresses wore white aprons and little hats which were supposed to make them look American. Rock music thundered from the jukebox so loudly that it demolished all other sounds. People ate and drank and showed their teeth in utter silence, like underwater creatures.

Conrad ordered a beer and scanned the menu. The only choice was between the size of the steaks and the ways the hamburgers were dressed. The beer was pale and tasteless but very cold. He told the waitress he would wait to order. She shrugged without interest and bustled off, while he admired her curls and trim backside nostalgically, as though from far off.

The other customers were mostly young and short-haired, which made it hard to tell the boys from the girls. They wore denim, fancy suede, and imaginative dark glasses. Conrad wondered what smoked glass did to the submarine light and vibrating air. Darkness on darkness, noise on noise. It was like one of those experiments in sensory deprivation. Perhaps that was why they all looked so listless.

When Abe arrived, fifteen minutes late, he did not come directly to the booth where Conrad waited. Instead, he went to the bar and began talking to the sallow-faced young man behind it. Two of the waitresses joined them, then a young man in jeans and a florid shirt who seemed to be the manager. From the way they stretched their mouths and flashed their teeth Conrad assumed they were laughing a good deal, but the jukebox swallowed up the sound.

"You're a man of parts," he said when Abe finally settled himself in the booth with him.

"I try to keep up. You never know what friends you're going to need and when you're going to need them. Anyway, at my age the young have their own special charms."

"That sounds to me like a strictly one-way street."

"Don't you believe it. It's amazing the allure I sometimes acquire in the innocent eye. Amazing grace, like they say." He smiled sweetly at the waitress who brought him a whiskey, then added, "Anyway, every time they look at me they think of my charming, muscular son. He spent last summer behind the bar before he went back to college and they all fell for him."

"A son too? Somehow I wouldn't have thought it."

Abe spread his hands expansively. "I have all the advantages: ex-wives, children, friends in low places. Sometimes I even surprise myself." He picked up the menu and glanced at it briefly. "Stick to hamburgers," he said. "The steaks are like leather, but for some reason they don't recycle the leftovers into the mince."

When the waitress came back she seemed anxious to help and smiled understandingly when Abe patted her neat rump in a not altogether fatherly manner.

Conrad watched her hungrily as she hurried off with the order. "I bet she's more edible than the hamburgers."

"I can fix that too."

"I don't doubt you."

Abe sipped his drink. They were leaning their heads together like conspirators in order to hear each other over the music.

"Maybe I should. It might solve your problems."

"If I had problems that could be solved that easily, I wouldn't have problems."

When the hamburgers came Abe lathered his in ketchup and relish, mustard and tabasco, piled on onions and added the lettuce which came to pretty up the plate. Then he picked up the unsteady tower of food, squeezed judiciously until the juices started over the edges of the bun, and began to eat. His mouth seemed to be hinged wider than Conrad believed possible. He ate ferociously and with dedication, without speaking. Conrad nibbled and watched, overwhelmed by the energy, the appetite, the sweat. He began to wonder in a dull way if Abe, too, was part of his troubles. But the implications of that were more than he could handle. He ordered another beer and applied himself gloomily to his hamburger.

Abe mopped the last of the juices from his plate with a corner of bread he had kept back for that purpose. "That chick you fancy"—he wiped his mouth daintily with a napkin—"the smart one, Miss Way Out . . ."

Conrad waited.

"You keep in touch?"

Conrad attempted a little British indifference. "To a certain extent."

"To a certain extent. For Chrissake, pal, what do you think I'm asking you, the intimate details? When I say in touch I mean like touch—metaphorical, not physical."

"What do you want to know?"

"Have you seen her of late?"

"Of late?" Conrad smiled across his beer mug. "You're an old-fashioned lad at heart, Abe. Who would have guessed it?"

"The last of the traditionalists, and you'd better believe me. Meanwhile, I asked you a question."

"Yes."

"And how was she?"

"Distant," said Conrad, "which is par for the course, and worried, which is not. Then the unspeakable Mrs. Staff turned up and that seemed to worry her even more."

Abe nodded. "That figures."

"Why should it figure?"

"A friend of a friend tells me the young lady has deep trouble."

Conrad set down his beer. "You and your friends' friends. You do not know how weary this double-talk makes me. Remember me? I'm just the poor sod in the middle. You don't have to be so sophisticated. Any old clue will do. I don't know anything, anyway."

Abe leaned his large body forward sympathetically. "I'm sorry, pal, no offense meant. Like I told you, I'm a middle-man in all this. I don't have any say so. It's just that we have a tricky problem here. This is a young lady who almost got herself killed once already and now the clouds seem to be rolling in around her again, right? So these people I know are worried. They don't want to see her get hurt a second time."

"I'm glad their hearts are in the right place. Why can't you tell me who they are?"

"I can't, that's all. You'll have to trust me these are kosher people, very sincere kosher people." Abe gave him a pleading, helpless look. "Even a middleman has a position to keep up."

"You know who you remind me of, Abe? That fucking policeman, Inspector Davies. Only he puts it more formally. He says"—Conrad did an accent—"'I am not a liberty to say.' I don't believe either of you. I think it's all shit."

"O.K., O.K." Abe patted the air between them. "But you still don't want to see the girl hurt, do you?"

"In the circumstances, that's neither one way or another."

Abe shook his head sadly. "Don't give me a hard time, pal." He sat silent a moment while the rock music thundered around their heads. Finally he said, "O.K. I'll put it another way. I did you a favor once with that horse, so now I want a favor in return. I'm calling in my bets."

Conrad leaned back wearily against the booth. "How can I refuse?"

Abe soothed the air between them again. 'Don't be so gloomy. Just keep in touch with the girl. Be around, be available. If she wants a shoulder to cry on, offer yours. If she asks a favor, oblige her. If she wants help, be helpful."

"Inspector Davies warned me to keep away."

"Forget the good inspector."

"And?"

"And keep me in the picture."

"Sounds painless." Conrad signaled to the waitress. "Why all the buildup?"

"No buildup. It's just that you're very touchy these days. I have the impression you think even I'm against you."

"It's the not knowing that gets me down. I feel like some kind of idiot."

"Believe me, I empathize. It's not what anyone would call a satisfactory situation. And I'll tell you something else: maybe there's nothing much to know. I hope there isn't. But that's a risk not worth taking."

When the waitress arrived Abe took the bill. "My treat," he said, "I'm the one who's asking the favor."

Outside in the street the traffic seemed scarcely audible after the din of the restaurant. While they were waiting for a taxi, Abe asked, "Are you still interested in that big game?"

"Of course."

"Then you should reserve a seat. I'll do it for the both of us, if you like. When do you want to play?"

"When's the next game?"

"The day after tomorrow."

"Fine by me."

Abe opened the taxi door. "Drop you off?"

"I need the air. My head is full of noise."

"Whatever you say, boss."

Abe waved regally as the taxi drove away.

34 THAT NIGHT, the spider was back, squatting in the far corner of the attic where the roof met the floor. Conrad came up the aluminum steps, lifted the trapdoor, fumbled for the light switch, and inhaled deeply, waiting for the rousing smell of oil paint and thinners and turpentine, the odor of his secret life.

But there was no light switch and the air was closed and stale, smelling of dust. He moved another step up the ladder and gradually his eyes became accustomed to the dim light which filtered through the encrusted skylight. The studio had disappeared. There was no sign of the floorboards he had laid, the strip lighting, workbench, easel, and rows of canvases. Only a cramped area of darkness and dirt, with bare joists and a few scraps of lumber left behind by the Victorian builders.

On a plank in the corner farthest from the skylight was a black shape twice the size of his fist. It seemed so much part of the surrounding darkness that it was some moments before Conrad could make out the taut, hairy body, slung between sharply angled legs. It seemed to vibrate very faintly, as if all the shadows and dust of the house were concentrated in this one small knot of energy. Conrad tried to move back down the ladder quietly, so as not to attract its attention, but his limbs would not stir. Despite his fear, he recognized that the buzz of power the creature gave out was in some way admirable, a quality to be desired and one to which he and his paintings would never attain. He understood that without it he remained a paltry man with paltry ambitions.

Although its legs did not move, the creature seemed to lean a little toward him, as though preparing to attack. Conrad made an enormous effort, moved one step back down the ladder and woke.

The sun was beginning to rise, edging the roofs with lemony light. He could hear the traffic already on the move in Charing Cross Road and Oxford Street. He kept his eyes open and listened intently, afraid of what would happen if he fell asleep again.

When he next woke the telephone was ringing.

"Cancer," said Margy, "of the bowel." Her voice was hushed almost to a whisper. She seemed unable to cope with the enormity of the occasion.

Conrad groped about for an appropriate response, but his head was still full of sleep. "Poor bastard," he mumbled. He sat up in bed and fumbled for his watch: nine-thirty. Margy was breathing noisily, as though trying to make up her mind whether or not to weep. Behind her he could hear the familiar rattle of massed typewriters. It sounded curiously reassuring.

"Take it easy," he told her.

Margy made a throaty noise and did not answer.

"Can I go and see him?"

"No visitors. They only operated yesterday."

"I'll write. I'll send him those tit-and-bum magazines."

"You ought to. You really ought."

He waited for her to start crying. Instead, she said in a loud voice, "I've got to go now," and rang off abruptly.

Conrad drank coffee while he shaved, then went out into Soho, followed by the dog. He bought a Snoopy get-well card, half a dozen nudie magazines, and a large padded envelope. As he walked to the Charing Cross post office, he was astounded that so many people could be going about their business unworried by growths in the bowels or spiders in the attic.

Back at the flat, he swept and dusted vigorously, but his uneasiness would not go away. It seemed unjust that Horace, whom he had known even longer than Betsy, had now joined her in his mind as a topic to be avoided at all cost. He drank more coffee and sat staring at the telephone, wondering who, apart from the dog, was left.

Olivia answered before the first ring was finished. She sounded tense and breathless, but she relaxed slightly when she heard his voice. He asked her to have dinner with him.

"Evenings aren't good at the moment. Let's make it lunch."

"This lunch or tomorrow's?"

"Seize the day," she answered.

"Anywhere in particular?"

"Somewhere with lots of people. Wheeler's, Old Compton Street."

"On my doorstep," he replied. "See you at one."

He was about to put down the receiver when she said in a tentative voice, "Conrad."

"Yes."

"I'm glad you phoned."

"Why should you think I wouldn't?"

"I didn't think anything. I just said I'm glad."

"Me too."

He phoned the restaurant to book a table, then strolled lazily to Soho Square, where he read his newspaper while the dog busied itself with the morning scents and rolled on the grass. At half-past twelve, when the square began to fill with young people carrying paperbacks and packets of sandwiches, he went back to the flat, washed, put on a tie, and then walked over to the restaurant.

It was a hot, idle summer's day, he had a great deal of money in his pocket and was about to have lunch with a girl he fancied considerably. Later, if things went well, he would make love to her in the tiny apartment belonging to someone else. A few months ago he would have sweated out the crapulous office afternoon imagining scenes like that and relegating them to the never-never land of drink advertisements. Now it was happening to him and his heart wasn't in it. Beware of what you want: you may get it.

Things did go well enough. Olivia followed him back to the flat willingly, docilely, almost gratefully. By the time he had drawn the blinds she had taken off her clothes and got into bed. She made love with great concentration, as though she needed reassurance. He held her gently, all kindness and tact, more surprised than excited by the sudden change in her bedside manner. He realized, as he came, that he felt sorry for her and wondered if this emotion, too, would turn out to be a disadvantage to him.

When she began to cry—noisily, helplessly, as though she had been bottling it up for a lifetime—he stroked her hair and her back, soothing her as he would have soothed a small child, knowing that every move he made was dragging him deeper into a mess not of his own devising.

Her sobs ebbed gradually. She sniffed, wiped her eyes with the back of her hand, then blew her nose on the sheet and immediately said, "Sorry."

He got out of bed, poured some whiskey, then sat down beside her and held the glass to her mouth. She swallowed some, grimacing, then leaned her head against his chest. He began to stroke her again in long slow movements from the crown of her head to the small of her back.

Finally he asked, "What was all that about?"

She took the glass from him, drank again and shuddered again. "Everything. This time I've really cocked it up." She sniffed and tried to laugh. "That charmed life I told you about: suddenly it no longer seems so charming."

He shifted his hand and began stroking her shoulder and arm, then upwards over her breast. The perfume she wore mingled with the musky smell of their exertions, stirring him in a vague, far-off way that seemed to deepen his satisfaction instead of exciting him.

"It's to do with your Mrs. Staff, isn't it?"

She nodded, her head against his chest. "With Elizabeth, with Tim, and also with others less lovable."

He waited, listening to the street noises filtering with the sunlight through the curtains. The outer world seemed at a great distance and unable to encroach on his calm.

Olivia lay back on the bed and closed her eyes. "I'm exhausted."

He leaned above her and shook her gently by the shoulder. "Go on."

She opened her eyes and made an effort to focus on him. "You got a joint?"

He shook his head and handed her a cigarette. "You'll have to make do with this." When she made no move to take it he lit it himself. "Go on," he repeated.

She closed her eyes again wearily and seemed about to drift off.

"There's more whiskey, if you want it," he said encouragingly.

She sat up, leaning on one elbow, and sipped the glass he held for her. "It's no substitute." She took the cigarette from him.

"Go on about Elizabeth and Tim."

"He tells her things."

"What kind of things?"

She shrugged dismissively. "I don't ask. It seemed better not to know. Things connected with his job, I suppose."

"Isn't that a bit rash?"

She flipped her hair back angrily. "For God's sake, he doesn't do it because he *wants* to."

"There must be something he wants, to put his head on the block like that."

She moved away from him irritably so that her back was against the newly painted wall. "Christ, you're stupid. He needs the money, of course. What other reason is there?"

"There could be others."

"Tell me them."

"The nuns did a grand job on you."

"Leave the nuns out of it." She closed her eyes and was silent for a while, as though trying to control her annoyance. When she opened them again she looked at Conrad with distaste. "Don't sit in judgment on me. I've got enough crap in my life without you adding to it."

"No judgment. I'm just trying to keep up, and that's not easy."

"Then try harder. For a big swinger and a gambling man you're pretty slow on the uptake."

"All that's my new incarnation. Give me time to get used to it." He took her hand. "I'm on your side, remember?"

She sat still for a moment, then took her hand away and pushed back her hair. "I'm not used to being scared."

"I'm sorry."

"Not half as sorry as I am." She smiled at last, which made her seem wearier than ever. "You can't believe how simple it is to get in over your head when you weren't even intending to swim."

"I can."

Olivia leaned forwards slightly and began talking quickly in a low voice, as if she was afraid of being overheard. "Tim took this terrible beating playing chemmy. I mentioned it to Elizabeth, then he talked to her and she said she'd see what she could do. She knows everybody. But everybody. We thought that maybe she would come up with Father Christmas."

"As she had done before?"

"As she had done before. Then the club started leaning on him. They were very polite, of course, but they made it clear that the time would come pretty damn soon when the politeness would have to stop. They muttered something about handing the debt over to a collection agency. Charming. They pretended to be sorry and that was even more frightening. Then Elizabeth came up with some people who agreed to do a deal of some kind. She and Tim worked it all out. I kept well clear because it seemed better not to know. But when I asked Tim he said the whole thing was ridiculous. He reckoned there was nothing he could tell them they didn't already know. But if they were willing to shell out good money, that was their lookout."

"If it was just between Tim and Elizabeth and these other people, how did you get into the act?"

"Elizabeth set it up, but it was important for her not to seem to be involved. So she asked me to do the delivering and collecting."

"Why not Tim?"

"The Man from the Ministry? Don't make me laugh."

Conrad nodded sagely. He felt overwhelmed by the triviality of it all. "Whereas you were a representative of classless, swinging London, and all that stuff."

"That's right. I know all sorts of unknowable people. Pop stars, photographers, movie folk, smarties from the rag trade—all the quick-money artists."

"In the old days, they used to call it slumming. Now it's being democratic."

Olivia smiled, finally, as if she meant it. "All in all, I've done a lot of slumming in my short life."

"I believe you." He studied her delicate face carefully and wondered how many people she had slept with in that short life of hers.

"Tell me," he asked, "one of these men you had to contact, was he a big fellow with ginger hair?"

She looked away. "Maybe."

"Then I know why you're frightened."

Instead of replying, she stretched out her hand and began to examine her nails.

"All for the love of old Timothy," said Conrad. "I wouldn't have believed it."

"Don't," she answered brusquely. "I did it because I needed the bloody money."

"You mean, they paid you, too, each time?"

"Naturally."

"That's different." He smiled at her fondly. "Then what happened?"

"Things changed. I don't know if Tim told someone at the ministry, or if they just found out from their own sources. Maybe a bit of both. Anyway, suddenly they all knew. It was arranged that every time I went to meet one of these people I had to telephone a number and say when and where."

"Why didn't you get out of it then, when the getting was good?"

"I was stuck between them, wasn't I, two people I'm fond of." Her voice trailed off for a moment, then she added impatiently, "Anyway, I've told you already, I needed the money. I always need the money. It's the one thing in my life there's never enough of."

"You mean the ministry people paid you as well?"

Her eyes widened incredulously. "Of course they did."

"No wonder the others tried to kill you that night."

"Not kill, frighten." She shrugged dismissively. "I'm glad you've worked that one out at last."

Conrad felt suddenly cold. He edged closer to her on the bed. "So the police knew it wasn't me from the word go." He slid an arm around her waist and pressed against her for comfort, not desire.

She sat still, neither responding nor resisting. "More or less, I suppose."

"So none of this was necessary."

"It depends what you call necessary. You must have contributed your share. You must have wanted it too, in some way."

"It didn't seem like that at the time."

She gave him a wan smile. "It never does. I didn't want it either, but I've got it now, right up to here." She drew her forefinger slowly across her throat. "How about a little more of that whiskey, in lieu of anything better?"

He put his head between her breasts and inhaled the mingled smell of skin and sex and perfume. "I can think of something better," he said.

She shrugged and slid back down onto the bed. "We might as well enjoy it while we can," she answered.

They slept after that and Conrad was woken by the whistling of the kettle. The light through the curtains was deeper, more golden, and the noise of the traffic louder. Another day lost.

Olivia came out of the bathroom wrapped in a towel. She waved at him on her way to the kitchen. The noise of the kettle ceased.

"Where do you keep your coffee?" she called.

He showered while she tinkered in the kitchen, then dabbed his face with cologne. Sex, sleep, and hot water made him lazy and mindless, like a sated animal.

When he came back into the main room Olivia was dressed and sitting in the armchair, sipping coffee. She had made the bed and opened the curtains on another beautiful evening.

He poured himself a coffee and sat down on the edge of the bed. "Domesticity." He smiled at her. "I'd have never suspected you of it. Or dreamed it could be pleasurable, for that matter."

She dipped her head as though curtsying. "I'm full of surprises, kind sir. Or so people tell me. Meanwhile, make the most of it."

He leaned forward and touched her knee. "Why don't we go away together? Just clear the hell out of the whole sordid mess and leave them to get on with it. I've got my gambling money and I'm just beginning to understand how much blood it's cost me. If we used it to screw them, that's what I'd call justice."

"You don't ever screw those people. They screw you. And that's what they call justice. Anyway, I'm not that sort of a girl."

He looked at her derisively. "You mean, to walk out on your pals?"

"No. To walk off into the sunset hand in hand. Happy endings aren't my style, Conrad. Likewise happy beginnings and middles."

"You never know till you try."

She gave him her wan, elderly smile again. "You have no conception of what I've tried in my time."

"I'm beginning to."

"I doubt it." She shook her head sadly. "Tim, Elizabeth, and I, we make a perfect trio. Three characters in search of a sensation."

Conrad straightened his spine, trying to gather around him what was left of his dignity. "Correct me if I'm wrong, but I thought you and I were finally beginning to do all right."

Olivia leaned forward in her turn and patted his thigh affectionately. "You know what we have in common, sweetheart? We're both nonentities. Nonentities in reckless pursuit of non-entity."

He bridled again, then saw how gravely she was watching him. He realized that she was asking him something. He smiled encouragingly. "It looks like we're going to find it soon enough."

She was silent for a moment and her expression did not change. Finally she whispered, "Help me."

Her greenish eyes were wide and deep, and he was afraid she was going to cry again.

"Tell me how."

"I've got to do it again." She spoke quickly, still whispering. "Elizabeth swears it's the last time and the other people say not to worry, there'll be someone following me, nothing can go wrong." She stopped, then said loudly, "I'm scared stiff."

"Stands to reason. Why not refuse?"

She shook her head and did not reply.

"Look," he went on, "if it's the money, forget it. I've got my winnings. Don't go and I'll give you what they were going to pay you."

She shook her head again. "I'm in too far. I can't back out now."

"You're a free agent."

She went on shaking her head. "Not an agent and not free. Just a nonentity." She ran her hand around his face and rested her fingers against his mouth. "Come with me."

He closed his hand over hers and kissed it lightly. "I don't seem to have an alternative. It looks like I just joined the club, Nonentities Anonymous."

She leaned back in the chair and sighed deeply. "I knew you'd help."

"That's one way of putting it," he answered. "When's it to be?"

"I don't know yet, but soon. Within a day or two."

He brought his hand up in the ghost of a salute. "*Ave Caesar, morituri te salutant*," he said. "Which is Latin for 'If you can't beat 'em, join 'em.'"

35

THE NEGRO on the rickety platform was denouncing do-gooders. "We don't want your charity. You know what you can do with it?"

A woman shouted cheerfully from the crowd.

"That's right, lady, got it in one." He was a big man with a carefully trimmed beard and shining blue-black skin. He wore sweeping yellow robes and his eyes were fierce, but he was clearly enjoying himself. "We don't want it, we don't need it. You know why? Because we know what good work's all about. We got your number. You hate our guts. Correction: it's the color of our skins you hate. It kinda confuses you, doesn't it? Seems all wrong somehow, kinda unnatural. In other words, it scares the holy shit outta you. But that's not how it should be, that's not how you're supposed to feel. And so you're guilty as hell. So you come on with your good deeds and your donations and your concern and your social-work jive. For why? For us? Hell, no. To make you feel better. Well, let me tell you something." He leaned forward across the lectern and glared at the audience. "We don't want it, we don't need it. We got troubles enough without yours. Keep us out of it. We got our dignity too."

At the back of the crowd a young man with a raw face shouted, "I'm not guilty. I just don't like you, or the way you behave, or the way you sponge off our taxes."

"That's the way," the speaker shouted back. "Sock it to me, man. Let's have a little truth for once."

The crowd laughed uneasily. Off in the distance a military band was playing: pom-pom pompity, pom, pompity-pom.

The young man looked discomfited. He stuck his hands in his pockets, hunched his shoulders, and glowered.

"Go on," shouted the speaker. "Let it all hang out. Let's hear it for hatred. Whatta we got you don't have and don't like?"

"You're inferior," the youth shouted back. "The scientists have proved it. You just swung down from the trees."

The speaker straightened his back and stuck out his chest. In the evening light he loomed enormous, heroic. He spread his arms and smiled at the audience. "I ask you, friends. Judge for yourselves. Do I look inferior?"

The crowd laughed, more freely this time.

"Got the message, friends?" The speaker showed his beautiful teeth again and looked around. As he turned his head to where Conrad was standing, a stone hit him on the side of the face.

The group of black men on either side of the wooden platform leaped forward, barging furiously through the crowd toward the youth at the back. Other youths closed in around him. There seemed to be half a dozen of them, all short-haired and booted, as well as three or four older men. As though by a conjuring trick, two of the older men produced a National Front banner saying, "Niggers and Wogs Out. Britain for the British."

A woman began to scream. Everyone seemed to be struggling with everyone else to get away. The woman went on screaming, high-pitched and eerie, out of control. Kim barked excitedly at Conrad's side.

Then a whistle blew and there were policemen everywhere.

The speaker spread his robed arms ecstatically. "Right on," he shouted. "It's a battle, baby. Always was, always will be. Show them nigger-lovin' liberal peace creeps what the real score is. Let's have a little reality back in this land." He lifted his arms with their wings of yellow cotton as though in benediction, while the blood streamed from the cut in his cheek.

As the police closed purposefully in, Conrad turned and walked quickly in the direction of the Serpentine. A policeman hurried angrily toward him. Conrad raised his open hand in salute and said, "Good evening, officer."

Automatically, the policeman replied, "Good evening, sir," then bustled intently past.

Conrad walked on, his grinning face lifted to the evening sky. Despite the heat, despite the uproar, he felt cool and alert. The noise and violence stimulated him, gave him back his youth. Maybe the spade is right, he thought. True hate is as rare as true love. Take it where you find it and be grateful.

The park was still full of people strolling in the darkening air, digesting their dinners. Couples lay absorbedly in each other's arms, dogs ran to and fro. Gloomy London, with its chills and rain, had been transformed into a foreign city, indolent in the heat, unbuttoned, vaguely seedy. A place to be young in. It seemed as if the summer would never end.

When he reached the Serpentine Conrad sat down on a bench and watched the reflections move on the water. The dog bustled about, delightedly following its nose. The light was fading, orange and gold into green. He studied it, half-heartedly wondering how he could translate the shifting, deepening tones into paint.

When he looked around he saw that the man with ginger hair was sitting at the other end of the bench, placidly smoking a cigarette. His hands were clasped peacefully on his stomach, his long thick legs stretched straight out in front of him, and he seemed, like Conrad, to be admiring the patterns on the darkening water.

Conrad stared at him. He felt neither fear, nor anger, nor even indignation. What he felt was wonder. "You've got to be kidding," he said.

The man looked at him calmly, as though the serenity of the summer evening had affected his mood too.

"Something bothering you, mister?"

Conrad saw that the man had not understood him. "This is a public park," he explained.

"That's right, mister. Likewise the bench. All public. You got any objections to me sitting 'ere?"

Conrad tried to muster some of his old heat. "I could call the police."

The man shrugged his shoulders and grinned. "Now, why would you want to do that, mister? Am I troubling you? More like you're troubling me."

The dog got up, trotted to the edge of the lake, and drank a little. Then it surveyed the lawns hopefully. But finding nothing of interest, it settled itself in front of Conrad and watched him with large eyes.

Conrad tried another tack. "Why are you following me?"

"What makes you . . ." the man began. Then he grinned even more broadly. "Search me. I just do what I'm told."

"And they haven't told you?"

"Why should they? And even if they had, I wouldn't be likely to go telling you, would I now?"

"I suppose not," Conrad admitted.

Even in repose, the muscles and tendons of the man's forearms stood out as though cast in bronze. The skin was freckled, like his face, and covered with wiry ginger hair. Conrad understood the foolishness of trying to face up to that sort of power. In a properly ordered world, all he might hope to do would be to outwit it or charm it or, in the last resort, paint it. But he no longer inhabited a properly ordered world.

"What's the point?" he asked. "I mean, why should anyone want to know about my lousy life?"

"Buggered if I know," the man answered cheerfully. "*Why* ain't my business."

"What is, then?"

The man lifted his massive arms, then let them drop. He laughed. "Guess," he said.

"It would be nice to know what I'm supposed to have done. Or even what makes me so interesting."

"There's no accounting for tastes," said the man good-humoredly. "I gave up asking questions years ago. It don't pay." He offered this information with the air of someone giving advice.

"But you see my point?"

The man stirred uneasily, ran his fingers through his curly hair, and licked his lips.

"There's been a mistake," Conrad went on, "some sort of misunderstanding."

"I doubt that, sir. They don't make mistakes."

He calls me "sir," thought Conrad, just like the police. All the people you can't reason with call you "sir." That's England.

"Tell 'em anyway," he said. "I'm just an ordinary fellow, trying to live my ordinary, crummy life. There's nothing I know that could interest anyone."

"That's not for me to judge."

"I'm not asking you to judge. I'm asking you to tell this to the people who do."

The man shook his head. "It won't do any good." He sounded sympathetic.

"You never know till you try."

Conrad got up wearily and at once the dog was on its feet barking excitedly. He swung at it with the lead, but it arched away out of reach and went on barking.

"To save you trouble, I'm going straight home now. Of course you know my address?"

The man grinned loosely and told him his address, then

added the telephone number. Conrad decided it was better to ignore the implications of this.

"I'm going to bed," he went on, "and I'll be sleeping late. Tomorrow afternoon I'll take the dog for a walk and in the evening I'm playing cards at Knights' Club. Got it?"

"Got it," said the man. "Big deal."

"That's what I mean. Big fucking deal. So why waste your time?"

The man got slowly to his feet. "I'll say this for you, sir. You're a real trier."

An aluminum object the size of a small cigar case protruded from the pocket of his floral shirt. On its top were switches and a knurled knob. Conrad's sense of wonder increased.

"You're even wired for sound," he said. "I never dreamed I was so important."

The man looked sheepish. "It's just so I don't forget anything."

Conrad shrugged. "I'm going to walk, since it's such a nice night. We could walk together, if you like, and continue our little chat."

"I don't think it'd look right," said the man primly. Then he added, "But I'm glad you're taking it this way."

Conrad smiled in the darkness. "It's like everything else these days. I don't have any alternative."

He whistled to the dog and set off in the direction of Park Lane, the man with ginger hair solemnly following twenty yards behind. When he reached Dean Street he turned and waved. The man touched his finger to his forehead in a faintly military salute. Conrad wondered where he would spend the night.

36

"USUAL RULES, gentlemen," said the dealer. "Five-card stud, table stakes, pot limit, five pounds to open. Check and raise is permitted."

In his fantasies the game in the high-ceilinged room at Knights' had become exotic and mysterious. The deferential flunkies in their brown tuxedos, the sweeping velvet curtains and paneled doors which kept out the common world, the large faintly glittering chips were all elements of an arcane ritual. Brooding on it beforehand, he came to see it as the inner secret, the game by which all other games were measured. Solemn, subtle, demanding.

Yet when it came down to it, it was just another poker game like the rest, merely more expensive. Just as the owner of the face he had once painted had proved, in her turn, to be just like all the rest. More or less. Give or take a few quirks, a few details. And considerably more expensive in her own curious way.

There were eight of them at the table, including the dealer. Abe sat mournfully next to Conrad, shoes off, collar open. On his other side was a small man with simian lines around his mouth and beautifully manicured hands, whom Abe introduced as Charlie, "another refugee from the property disaster."

"Between the hammer and the anvil," Conrad said as he took his seat.

Charlie fluttered his hands and replied, "Tell that to my bank manager."

Lou was there, smiling benignly, also the young man with disheveled hair who had lost heavily the evening Conrad watched the game. The other two were strangers. A tall American with pale eyes, pale hair, and a skeleton's face, all teeth and cheekbones, who introduced himself as Chuck and insisted on shaking hands all around. The other was a sad, dumpy little man with a dark complexion who spoke with a French accent and came from Lebanon. The dealer, in his brown tuxedo, was Chinese.

"Like the United Nations," Conrad murmured to Abe.

"Except that here it's for real."

The chips were larger and heavier than Conrad had handled before and the smallest of them was stamped £5. The fifties, hundreds, and two hundreds were solemn and oblong, like envelopes. The little plastic chips he usually played with had no relationship to real money; they were simply colored counters in a game. These, however, were expensive and important in themselves. Piling them neatly according to their values made him understand the seriousness of the occasion. He felt not so much nervous as over-awed.

He played carefully, anteing when he had to and folding almost everything. Like everyone else. Even the young man with disheveled hair was holding himself back, trying to sound out the new players. For the first half-hour no hand was contested to the end. The atmosphere was businesslike, vaguely depressed. Lou, Abe, and Charlie sat hunched forward dourly, as though laboring at a not particularly pleasant job. The night shift. Conrad wondered if they had an understanding and racked that up as another possible danger. The other two strangers also watched and waited, although the Arab grimaced irritably whenever he folded his cards.

After about forty minutes Conrad was dealt an open king. He bet five pounds automatically, because he had to, then cupped his hands around his hole card and raised one corner with his thumb: an ace.

Next to him Charlie folded but the American pushed in a chip, showing a seven of hearts. The young man with disheveled hair snapped his fingers impatiently and turned over his card, Lou called the bet with a queen, the other two folded.

"Jack to the queen," said the dealer, "four to the king, ten to the seven, flushing. King bets."

When Conrad bet twenty pounds the American gave a death's-head grin and raised forty.

Ace of hearts in the hole, thought Conrad.

Lou leaned back briefly, then bent forward again. "See the sixty," he said quietly, "and raise another hundred."

Two queens, thought Conrad. Now's my chance. His throat was dry and his heart bumped heavily in his chest. He pushed a hundred and forty pounds into the center and said, "Raise the pot." He was relieved that his voice came out quietly and without expression. He was also relieved that he had followed Abe's advice and drawn a thousand pounds' worth of chips, "so you can bet 'em if you get 'em."

"Three hundred and eighty pounds," said the dealer.

Nothing moved in the room except the smoke curling gently around the edges of the light over the table.

The American eased his shoulders against the back of his chair and grinned broadly. "Like they say in the movies, your blood's too rich for mine." He turned over his cards.

Conrad stared at the green baize in front of him, but when he looked up Lou was studying him intently. He glanced at him demurely, then concentrated on the baize again. He was afraid the thumping of his heart was audible all around the table.

The silence continued. Lou peered at the pile of chips in front of Conrad, then at the pot. Finally he shrugged and turned over his cards.

It was as though an overstrung wire had snapped. Suddenly everyone was stirring and muttering. Conrad kept his head down and piled the chips which the dealer pushed over to him, saying nothing. But when Abe bent inquiringly toward him he lifted the corner of his hole card. Abe smiled like a proud father and said, "Nice."

Lou fumbled in his jacket pocket and brought out a large handful of oblong chips which he slipped beside the stack already in front of him. He caught Conrad's eye and nodded in friendly acknowledgment.

Conrad realized with surprise that what he felt was neither triumph nor elation, but pleasure. He was doing something he loved, and doing it well with others who also did it well. An equal among equals. For a moment he was perfectly happy. It had been worth waiting for.

The ice was broken and the cards began to flow. For half an hour Conrad continued his run and was about five hundred ahead. Then the lanky American hit a streak, while Conrad folded steadily and nursed his winnings. The players seemed to be taking their turns, playing tight, working the percentages, making their moves carefully.

Only the young man, his dark hair bristling, stayed in regularly and chased cards. He raised on a dead ace into Abe's queen, called when he was raised back, then was outraged when Abe contemptuously flipped over his second queen. He sat around expensively, betting into cinch hands and waiting for miracle cards which never arrived. At each new disaster he shook his bushy head and muttered, "Diabolical luck," peering around the table for sympathy, which the others duly gave while they waited to take their turn at him. Conrad wondered briefly where someone so young could find so much money to throw away. But he did not linger over the problem, knowing that sympathy would only spoil his own edge.

By midnight the young man had lost two and a half thousand. He threw his last losing hand histrionically into the center of the table and got up.

"Have you ever seen such luck?" he asked no one in particular.

As usual, the others murmured sympathetically.

"Diabolical, unbelievable, unspeakable." His voice was plaintive and unsteady. He seemed near to tears. He ran his hand through his hair and pulled on his jacket. "I'll be back," he announced from the door. "Next time it's my turn."

"Must be," said Charlie in a soothing voice. But when the door closed the little man spread his arms and raised his eyes and open palms to the ceiling. "With schmucks like that," he asked, "who needs cards?"

The dealer cleared his throat discreetly, the players settled in their chairs, and the cards went around again.

I really am happy, Conrad was thinking. He felt free, almost weightless. No more problems, no more responsibilities, no more fears. Just silence and concentration. The intricate ebb and flow of the game purged his head of its confusions, leaving him lucid. For the time being, the world seemed simple and full of light.

But the cards had gone cold for him. He turned over hand after hand, waiting for his chance, but it did not come. The three regulars, Abe, Lou, and Charlie, began to take charge. They chatted together comfortably between hands, as though they were playing in a small social game.

"Dan's marrying again," said Charlie. "Did you hear?"

"What's up with that guy?" Abe replied. "He's already got a great collection of Ming wives."

"It's the heat," said Lou. "Everybody's doing it. Only

the other evening my girlfriend said to me. 'Lou, why don't we get married?' So I said to her. 'Sure, honey, but who'd have us?' "

Conrad laughed along with the others, thinking: They're trying to soften us up. They're trying to break our concentration. I know you, he thought. Don't think I don't.

But the Lebanese businessman was relaxing in the seemingly easy atmosphere. The irritation he had shown earlier now impelled him to call on questionable hands. He began to lose, though not spectacularly, while the long-legged American continued to play by the book and stay even.

About one o'clock Conrad got up and said, "Deal me out for a couple of hands."

Nobody looked up. They seemed oblivious to anything not actually taking place on the green baize in front of them.

He went down to the palatial lavatories in the basement, relieved himself, washed his hands and face in cold water, then stood for a moment peering dully into the mirror. The ornate toilet with its marble walls and basins made him look shabby.

On his way back upstairs he went outside to sniff the night. A soft wind had got up, cooling the air and making the leaves of the plane trees whisper together secretively. Two uniformed chauffeurs were leaning against Rolls Royces, chatting quietly. One of them was polishing his car's radiator while he talked. Nothing else moved in the street, except the shadows thrown by the trees. He knew the man with ginger hair was out there somewhere, but there was no sign of him.

Before he went back into the poker room he paused to watch the roulette. The noise and bustle struck him as faintly distasteful. He realized that the busy pursuit of luck was an illusion which no longer interested him. It seemed an odd moment to discover that he had ceased to be a gambler.

A tubby woman with a pronounced shadow along her upper lip jostled him in the doorway and did not apologize. Her eyes were shining and she was chattering loudly. Her companion had frizzled gray hair and the face of a woebegone sheep. She marched up to the cashier's desk and upended her handbag on the counter. Lipstick, keys, comb, and compact poured out with the colored chips; fragments of paper floated slowly to the ground.

"My night," she told the cashier, who smiled politely and began to sort the chips. She turned to her companion and ordered him to cheer up.

"When *I* win I make good your losses," he complained.

"That's different." She laughed expansively and started to put her makeup back in her bag. Her fingers were heavy with rings. "What's yours is mine and what's mine's my own." She laughed again even more riotously, but the cashier took no notice.

"So I see," said Sheepface bitterly.

The cashier went on counting the chips. He piled them according to color, checked them again, then began to count out banknotes. They were crisp and clean, not like real money at all. He arranged them in a fan on the counter, as though preparing to do a card trick. The woman with the mustache swept them up and stuffed them jubilantly into her handbag. Her companion's face grew more woeful; the corners of his mouth sagged.

Conrad watched them as though from far off and wondered what he was after. Not luck, like those clowns. Something which began when discipline and skill were taken for granted: talent, insight, the natural gift expressing itself in the natural way.

Art.

Which was what he had always been waiting for, in one way or another, to redeem his shuffling existence.

"Nonentities in reckless pursuit of non-entity," Olivia had

called them. Maybe there was an alternative in the decorous, shadowy room across the corridor.

Go with the flow, he told himself.

He went up to the cashier's desk, pulled out his wad of gambling money, and counted out fifty dog-eared twenty-pound notes. "Poker chips," he said.

The cashier counted the money impassively. "How do you want it, sir?"

Conrad smiled and said, "Fast." But the man's blank expression did not change, so he added, "In hundreds."

When Conrad opened the door of the poker room the supervisor of the game raised an admonishing finger to his lips and closed the door softly behind him. Conrad nodded and waited where he was.

The room was hushed, the figures around the table motionless. Then Lou said gently, "Your two hundred, and raise five."

A car started up outside but the noise, muffled by the curtains, seemed to come from a great distance. The ecclesiastical silence descended again.

Finally Abe sighed and leaned back in his chair. "I gotta believe you." He sounded relieved.

"*Moi aussi*," said the Lebanese businessman.

Conrad took his seat, and while the dealer was shuffling he slipped the new pile of chips next to the stack already in his place. He saw Charlie cock his head and look across at Lou. They exchanged glances briefly.

"Got to be prepared," Conrad explained in a mild and reasonable voice. He was unwilling to let the moment pass unremarked. Neither of the men replied.

The game went on as before, restrained, formal, expensive, and predictable, like a diplomatic reception. Six skillful men watching each card that fell, calculating the odds, subtly varying their tactics. But there were no revelations.

The Lebanese began a streak, taking each of the three

regulars in turn, though not for big money. Conrad wondered if this was part of their strategy or something less easily controlled: a Jew's stubborn unwillingness to be beaten by an Arab. The Lebanese began to smile a great deal, showing a mouthful of gold-capped teeth, and the others smiled with him as if they too were pleased he was having his turn. Strategy, Conrad decided; they have softened him up and now they are waiting their chance.

His own cards were poor, but he was still well ahead and no longer bothered by the high stakes, so he played along occasionally on hunches and, when he was beaten, looked rueful and smiled with the rest. If they want strategy, he thought, they can have it.

But underneath he was disappointed. He had expected more of the game. Then it occurred to him that he always expected more of everything; his childish optimism was unplumbable. And this thought depressed him. Maybe it was the revelation he had been waiting for. He had also, of course, expected more of revelation.

He stretched, yawned, and looked at his watch. Two-forty-two. Time to go home.

The dealer sent around the cards again, smoothly and without pause, as if his hands were controlled by some precise and intricate machine. "Ace, six, eight," he announced, "another ace, five, nine."

The second open ace was Conrad's. As usual, he cupped his hands around his hole card, raised one corner with his thumb, and leaned back. The third ace in the pack stared up at him.

Lou had the first open ace and bet the mandatory five pounds quickly but without enthusiasm. The American folded. Abe called on the eight, then Conrad called, feigning caution. Behind him Charlie folded but the Lebanese leaned forward, flashed his gold-topped smile, and raised twenty pounds on his nine.

Lou hesitated a moment, then pushed his money in with even less enthusiasm than before. Abe also paused, then called the bet slowly.

Not two eights, thought Conrad, but something high in the hole. He too called the bet, trying to appear unwilling.

The cards went around again. "Seven to the ace, ten to the eight, nine to the second ace, four to the nine," the dealer intoned. "Ace-nine bets."

"Check," said Conrad immediately.

The Arab showed his gold teeth again and bet fifty pounds.

Lou studied the other cards and nodded. "O.K.," he said at last, "I'll see that."

Abe shifted his great bulk in his chair. "Come on, boys," he said. "We're here to gamble, so let's gamble. See the fifty and raise a hundred."

Tens, thought Conrad, a nice pair of tens. He grinned amiably at Abe. "What the hell. One loose call."

The Arab glared at Abe's ten for a long time, then finally pushed in a large glittering chip. "Vairy vell," he muttered, but this time he did not smile.

Lou also studied the pot at length before putting in his money. He can't have the last ace, Conrad told himself, or he'd have reraised. He's got a king in the hole, a king or a queen.

The dealer waited impassively until the money was in, then slid out the cards again. "Eight to the ace-seven, three to the eight-ten, seven to the ace-nine, another three to the nine-four. Still ace-nine to bet."

"Check," said Conrad quickly, and the Arab echoed, "Check."

Lou nodded. "I'll check to the raiser."

"Two hundred," said Abe. His voice and hands were steady, but his face ran with sweat.

Conrad counted slowly to ten and pretended to study the

other hands. Nothing could beat him so far. "I'll call that," he said quietly. He was at peace, floating free at last. This is what it's about, he told himself.

The Arab blew air from his cheeks, then tossed his cards disgustedly into the middle. " 'Eero I am not," he said. "*Jouez sans moi.*" He took out a gold toothpick and began to prod angrily at his gold teeth.

His outburst created a ripple of disapproval around the table. Lou waited until it died away, sitting hunched forward and gazing impassively at the cards. Finally, and with great reluctance, he pushed in two large chips. "Call."

The dealer sent around the cards for the last time: a king to Lou, a jack to Abe, a queen to Conrad. "Ace-king bets," he announced.

"Check," said Lou without hesitation.

"Check," repeated Abe.

Conrad waited, staring at Lou's hand. There was only one ace left in the pack. If Lou had it, the king made him unbeatable. But he had checked all along, just as Conrad had, and now was checking again. It's not possible, he decided. He has a pair of kings.

There were two stacks of hundred-pound chips in front of him, ten to a stack. With great deliberation, Conrad picked up one of the piles and counted it out into the middle. "Bet a thousand," he said.

He heard Abe sigh deeply at his side, but kept his eyes on Lou. Nobody moved, nobody spoke. Conrad could hear his heart thumping outrageously in his chest.

For a long minute Lou stared thoughtfully at Conrad's cards and the pile of chips beside them. Finally he looked Conrad straight in the eye and smiled almost tenderly.

"Your thousand"—his voice was soft and careful—"and raise a thousand."

"Wow," said the pale American.

Abe mopped his streaming face with a handkerchief. His

eyes shifted from Conrad's cards to Lou's, then back again.

"Holy shit," he murmured, and seemed to collapse in his chair as if he had been punctured. "You two can have each other." He turned over his cards.

Conrad had been poised on a peak of calm and clarity, now he was falling. Until his raise he had played his cards flawlessly. Better than ever before, better than ever again. Then he had made one move that laid him open and Lou had stepped in.

The voice of sanity said: These things don't happen. It's not possible that you both had aces wired from the start and both checked all through. It could not be. Either he is trying to buy the pot or he has a pair of kings and reads you as queens.

And the voice of the artist answered: Your gift against his. You did it, so why shouldn't he? Maybe you've been out-classed, friend.

But the other voice replied: You and your artistic intui-tions. See where they've got you in this world. If you fold this, you might as well fold everything. It's your last chance to be blessed.

"O.K.," he said wearily, "I call." And he pushed in his last stack of chips.

Lou watched them go into the center, then straightened his back and turned over his hole card. It was the fourth ace.

Conrad nodded sagely. "You had 'em all along. Of course." He nodded again and flipped over his own ace in the hole.

There was, in the end, an order in things. It was as well he should know his place.

Lou nodded back at him in recognition. "So did you."

"For Christ's sake," Abe erupted at Conrad's side, his great bulk quivering. "You both had 'em all along." He mopped his face vigorously. "Out of my class, baby."

Conrad turned to him and shrugged. "Sometimes you get the elevator, sometimes you get the shaft. Isn't that what you say?"

"Some elevator," Abe replied, "some fucking shaft."

The lanky American leaned forwards admiringly. "Who said you English are finished? That hand was the Battle of Agincourt, the Khyber Pass, and the Charge of the Light Brigade rolled into one."

"Forget the Light Brigade," said Charlie. "They got outdrawn."

Conrad pushed back his chair and got up. "That'll do me for one night," he said. "Thank you, gentlemen." He nodded around the table, then said to Lou, "A pleasure to meet a real artist. An expensive pleasure, God knows, but a pleasure nevertheless."

Lou smiled back at him. "It takes one to know one," he said.

Abe followed Conrad out into the night. Thick orange clouds were driving across the sky and the wind was blowing strongly. The street was full of threshing shadows.

"That was some hand," he said. "I couldn't read you for aces, him neither. None of the pictures had shown, so I thought you'd both outdrawn me on the last card."

"That's what I tried to tell myself: that he'd made a pair of kings. But somewhere I didn't believe it. He's too canny for that." Conrad was silent a moment, listening to their footsteps echoing hollowly in the darkness. "You know what made me bet and then see him?" he asked. "Vanity. I was boxing so clever I fooled myself. I couldn't believe anyone could be that inspired. So when he raised, my pride was hurt. That's why I saw him." He paused at his car door, key in hand. "He must have reckoned on that."

"Think of it this way," Abe said consolingly, "poker is all he does. That's his profession. But you, you have other things on the ball, right?"

"Like what?"

"Like your paintings, your job." He hesitated, then added almost apologetically, "I mean, like this interesting life you've got yourself these days."

"Come off it, Abe my friend. Class is class. You have it or you don't have it. Why should I fool myself, particularly considering that interesting life I've made for myself?"

"Have it your way, boss. At least you got your action."

Conrad thought about this for a moment. "I suppose you could call it that," he said.

Abe shrugged and spread his hands, palms upwards to the blowy summer night. "What else?"

As he drove away, Conrad could see the fat man standing, rather forlornly, in the middle of the road. He was waving. He waved back, wondering if the gesture was visible against the moving shadows of the trees.

37

THE DOG WOKE HIM at ten by licking his hand. He half-opened his eyes, then closed them again and drifted between sleep and waking, fondling the dog's head and listening to the city noises which filtered across the roofs. They seemed somehow different, farther off, muffled by a faint tapping and muttering. When he opened his eyes again he saw it was raining at last. The drops slid down the windowpanes, leaving little runnels in the dust. The air felt cooler, easier. Something was finished.

Well, he thought, I'm still a couple of thousand ahead. It's not the end of the world.

He made himself some coffee, then settled into the armchair with yesterday's paper. Although his hands were steady, his arms and legs seemed to be trembling invisibly and the edges of his perception were blurred from lack of sleep.

He stared at the newspaper with its daily installment of doom, but could take nothing in. He too was going to pieces, just like old England. Nevertheless, the sound of the rain was soothing after all the endless, sweltering weeks, and in a couple of days he would be back at the office. For the first time in his life, the office seemed something to look forward to. He wasn't cut out for the free-lance, opportunist's life. He wondered how Betsy and the children were managing their freedom, and tried to pretend he did not already know.

He stood under the shower a long time, soaking the staleness from his hairy body, then put on clean clothes and deposited everything he had been wearing the previous night in the laundry basket. Nursing a fresh cup of coffee, he sat down again in the armchair facing the courtyard filled with rain and the grimy windows of the houses opposite. He picked up the telephone.

Betsy answered almost at once. "Oh, it's you." Her voice hardened. "I was wondering where you'd got to."

"I've found somewhere to live. I want to pick up my stuff sometime. And maybe see the kids."

"Not this evening. I'm busy."

She has a life of her own, see. He was supposed to react to this.

"How about tomorrow afternoon?" he asked pleasantly. "If I come between five and six, the boys'll be home from school."

"That's all right. I won't be in. And leave your keys when you're done, please."

"Betsy . . ." Conrad began, then changed his mind. "What have you told the boys?"

"The truth, of course. I said we were separating. I said these things happen."

"How did they react?"

"They took it in their stride." Her voice rose slightly. "What do you expect? It's not like they ever saw you when you were here."

"You've told me that before and I'm not arguing." There was a bristling silence, then Conrad added placatingly, "Look, I'm sorry."

"It's a bit late in the day for that."

Another silence. Conrad could hear pop music playing in the background. He supposed it was the kitchen radio. It was too early for that sort of television.

Betsy said, "I want a divorce, you know."

"I know."

"How do you know?" Immediately, her voice was tense and defensive. "Have you been prying?"

"I know because I feel that way too. It's all over."

"Yes, it's all over."

"So long as I can see the kids from time to time."

"I've told you, haven't I? Stop getting at me."

She rang off.

There was something he wanted to ask her and had forgotten. Something had been nagging at him since he woke, but he couldn't think what.

He sipped his coffee and listened to the rain against the window.

> *The toil of all that be*
> *Helps not the primal fault;*
> *It rains into the sea,*
> *And still the sea is salt.*

The painting. He had forgotten to ask her about the painting. After what had happened last night, he had a great longing to have it with him. He needed evidence that he had done one thing well in this life.

Beyond the pattering of the rain was the larger, uneasy sound of London, humming ceaselessly like a generator. Millions of people were milling around out there with one thing in common: they were going to die and leave nothing behind. Their bits and bobs would be divided up, and maybe, if they were lucky, their families and friends would remember them for a year or two. Then nothing, as if they had never been.

Is that what they meant by the terror of death? Not the pain, not the indignity of aging, but the anonymity of it. A lifetime on the run and nothing to show for it at the end. That's why they invented heaven: not as a reward, but to give life a point.

A painting, however. It had your name on it and lasted longer than you, maybe longer than your children. And unlike your children, who also had your name, it did not change.

Conrad addressed the dog out loud, "If I'd known the amount of shit I was going to eat in this life, I'd have handed back my ticket before I began."

The dog stared soulfully into his eyes and wagged its tail.

"You see things differently," said Conrad. "You like shit, don't you, old boy?"

The dog went on wagging its tail dubiously.

He picked up the telephone again and this time the voice at the other end was welcoming. "Thank God you phoned."

As usual, he found it difficult to fit Olivia's young, fresh voice with her languid manner. It made him feel old.

"I couldn't find your number. I was going to come around and leave you a note or something."

"Come around anyway. Or something."

She took no notice. "That meeting I mentioned. It's tonight."

Conrad waited a moment, then said, "A bit sudden, isn't it?"

"Oh, I knew it was coming soon."

"This soon?"

"Will you come with me?"

"What about the Honorable Tim?"

"Tim's not here. Tim's been sent away somewhere. Tim's always sent away somewhere when you need him."

Conrad said nothing.

"You promised." She sounded younger than ever. Just like a child.

"Why's he been sent away? It sounds like an excuse. It sounds like someone's fucked up and he wants out."

"He'd have told me."

"Would he?" He waited a moment, listening to the rain. "Meanwhile, what about your lady friend?"

271

"Awfully tense. Tense and distant. You know, steely."

"I know," said Conrad. "It hurts her more than it hurts you. You don't have to tell me."

"You promised," Olivia repeated.

What else is there? Conrad was thinking. You've made your choice without knowing it. Now ride it till it falls. Maybe this is what they mean by love.

As usual, it was less than he had expected.

"I feel awful," said Olivia.

Conrad scratched the dog's shaggy chest. The sound of the rain intensified.

"Of course I'll come with you. A promise is a promise."

He heard her sigh into the phone. "Thank God."

"You worry too much. When's it to be?"

"Late-ish. Around eleven."

"Let's eat beforehand."

"No. I've got to stick around here. I don't want to give Elizabeth ideas."

He wondered what ideas she could get that she did not have already.

When he did not reply, Olivia added, "Afterwards we'll have all the time in the world."

"I bet you say that to all the boys."

"Not anymore I don't."

"Then come away with me when it's over."

It was Olivia's turn to be silent. Finally she said, "Maybe. When it's all over maybe I will." She was silent again, then said hurriedly, "I've got to go now. I'll see you at ten-thirty at the Whitestone Pond."

"That's where I came in," said Conrad. But she had already hung up.

Finally, thought Conrad, I'm going to see what it's all about. He sat still for a time to attend to this while the rain shushed down outside. His heart was beating quickly, the skin around his eyes felt tight. He realized that he was scared and this irritated him. It had to come, he told himself. Sooner or later. Just because you've led a cowardly life doesn't mean you're a coward. But he was not convinced.

The dog was still watching, sitting with paws crossed, eyes bright with expectation, waiting for him to move.

"I'm going to have my action at last," Conrad informed it.

Which reminded him of Abe. He picked up the telephone again.

"I dreamt about that hand"—Abe's voice was loud and cheerful, slightly fawning—"and now I'm awake I'm still dreaming about it. A classic, man, a pure classic."

"No postmortems. I'm calling about something else. You asked me a favor in return for the favors you've done me, remember?"

Abe grunted.

"So here it is." He paused. It didn't seem like much when he came down to it.

"Go on."

"Tonight's the night. The girl's making a collection and I'm going with her."

There was a sudden, complete silence at the other end, as if Abe had stopped breathing. Then he boomed, "Where?"

"The Whitestone Pond, ten-thirty. Her date is for eleven."

"Fine. Just fine." Abe's cheerfulness increased.

"Is that all?"

"What more is there?"

"You tell me."

The act Abe was putting on for his benefit was curiously exhausting. He began to feel sleepy.

"Not a thing, old buddy. Don't get uptight. There's nothing to worry about. It'll all be taken care of. You just gotta trust me a little."

Conrad yawned. "I don't have any alternative, do I?"

"Don't take it like that. Haven't I looked after you so far?"

He stretched his legs and yawned again. "After your fashion, I suppose."

"Who better? And tonight there's nothing to it. She meets her friends, they exchange mementos, you both walk away. I wish everything was so simple."

"So do I," said Conrad with feeling.

But after he put down the telephone he realized that he still understood nothing. An ordinary little man with ordinary little desires. He wasn't up to it. The idea filled him with sorrow.

He went downstairs with the dog and for half an hour walked the wet streets with the lunchtime crowd, enjoying the soft rain and the freshness. He did not see the man with ginger hair.

Then he went back to the flat and slept like a baby. When he woke, the gray light was already thickening into evening. He felt calm and refreshed and ravenously hungry, like a young man full of energy and with nothing to lose.

38 THE RAIN HAD CEASED by the time he got to the Whitestone Pond and the air was heavy again. He left his car in the park behind Jack Straw's Castle, then lingered in the shadows to see if he was being followed. But nobody came, nobody went. In the pub a woman was singing "If you were the only girl in the world." Her fruity contralto swelled effortlessly above the talk and laughter. When she finished there were shouts of applause.

With Kim straining on the lead, Conrad crossed the road. There was no sign of Olivia. He unclipped the dog and leaned against the railing while it rooted about among the bushes on the slope below him. The lights of London were blurred in the damp air and thick, orange-bellied clouds moved slowly over the City. There was a distant rumble of thunder but the rain held off.

A young man and his girl came out of the pub, crossed the road to where Conrad lingered, then disappeared purposefully down the slope toward the Vale of Health. The girl was giggling shrilly. "It's too wet," she was saying. "We'll catch our deffs."

"Nah," said the boy, "I've gotta mac, ain't I? We'll be dry as two old biscuits."

"Thanks," said the girl. "Thanks very much." She went on giggling until they were out of earshot.

The thunder rolled again beyond the City, over the Surrey hills, more faintly than before. When Conrad turned finally to the pond he saw the clouds were breaking up in the north and the moon was coming and going between them. It was a half-moon, lying on its side, and it seemed to be performing a complicated balancing act on the hurrying cloud wrack.

The dog emerged from the bushes and came bouncing up importantly. In its mouth it held something black and vaguely shiny, like a patent leather boot. It stood wagging its tail, delighted with its own cleverness.

"Sit," said Conrad.

The dog sat.

"Give it here."

He bent and took the object gently from the dog's mouth. It was a dead crow. It lay on Conrad's palm, damp and soft, its head flung back as if in ecstasy, its beak primly closed. A patch of feathers had gone from its throat and the gray skin was smeared with blood. Nevertheless it shone under the lamplight like a pool of ink. Even in death it retained a black-coated, Fred Astaire chic, a debonair survivor whose time had finally come. Conrad had a brief image of himself as a child, peering through the bars of the banisters at his parents dancing together in the sitting room while a scratchy record played "They Can't Take That Away from Me."

How wrong can you be?

They can take whatever they want.

He ducked under the railing and laid the dead bird under a bush. The dog started forward to it again.

"Let it be," he said sharply.

When he clambered back under the railing he saw Olivia getting out of a taxi. He waited in the shadows where a hawthorn tree overhung the pavement until the taxi drove off, then stepped forward and raised his arm in salute.

She ran to him, hugged him, kissed him on the mouth.

She smelled strongly of patchouli. He put his arms around her waist and kissed her back.

"We drove right around the pond and I couldn't see you. I thought you'd let me down."

"I said I'd be here."

"I was scared."

"Don't be. That'll make things worse. Just play it cool and everything'll be fine."

"It's gone on too long."

He took her hand and they began to walk toward the Spaniards Inn. The smell of patchouli was very strong. It made Conrad suddenly angry. Fear he could understand, fear was appropriate. Frivolity wasn't.

"Are you high?"

She shook her head. "No more than is strictly necessary."

After a few yards, she pulled him to the right. "This way." They went along the broad graveled path that led above the Vale of Health, Kim running to and fro in front of them.

"Where are we meeting them?"

"At the corner of Ken Wood."

The dog came lolloping up to Conrad in the hope of a stick, then disappeared again into the bushes.

"Why on earth did you bring him?" It was Olivia's turn to sound exasperated.

"He's our alibi. What could be more natural than walking the dog? Anyway, he needs the exercise. There's not much going for him in Soho."

Where the graveled path bent off to the right Olivia went straight on downhill under the heavily leafed oaks and chestnuts. The clouds were clearing fast and the moon dispensed a bland and equal light. She held his hand tightly and kept so close that her thigh brushed his as they walked.

"Why so frightened?" asked Conrad. "You've done this before."

"That's just the point."

"This time you're not alone."

"Yes." She sounded doubtful. Then she added, "I could use a joint."

"Enough is enough. First we see this thing through, then you get stoned."

"Sometimes," she said mildly, "you can be a real pain in the arse. I wish you'd all stop getting at me."

"Who else?"

"Elizabeth. She's been packing for some business trip and marching around with a face like thunder, as if it was all my fault."

"Isn't it?"

"You see. Everybody's getting at me. It gives me the creeps."

They went down into the dip and labored up the slope on the other side, their feet slipping in the fresh mud. Beyond that was a grove of oak trees. The moon filtered palely between them and the air smelled rich and summery, as though the rain had finally released all the scents the ground had secreted during the long parched weeks. Conrad clicked his tongue at the dog to bring him to heel and the three of them walked on in silence.

When they came out into the open again they stopped and listened. Nothing stirred. Off to the left the great white facade of Ken Wood House glimmered faintly in the moonlight. In front of them were the woods, black on black.

"Here?" Conrad whispered.

"A bit farther."

It was dark at the entrance to the wood, although the open ground beyond was full of moonlight. They stood hand in hand waiting, the dog beside them.

Suddenly Kim growled, then began to bark.

Two figures stepped out from the shadow of a large holly tree.

Even in the darkness Conrad could recognize the man with ginger hair. He tugged Olivia's arm and moved back into the open where they could see better.

The dog went on barking.

The man with ginger hair swung at it vaguely with his boot. "Shut that fucking brute up."

"Sit," hissed Conrad. When the dog backed toward him he grabbed it by its collar and pulled it back onto its haunches. Surreptitiously he wound the chain leash around his knuckles.

The man with ginger hair said, "Oh, it's you, Mr. Jessup." Then he turned to his companion. "This 'ere is Mr. Jessup."

"I know that," said the other man. He was broad and short and was wearing a stylish suede jacket. Just as Conrad had expected. He had been driving the car on the night when the man with ginger hair entered his life.

"I have his number," said the other man. His accent was educated but careful, the vowels faintly blurred, as though with some far-off memory of another language. "We've spoken on the telephone."

"So you're the hypothesis," said Conrad.

"And now I'm a fact. Satisfied?"

The man with the ginger hair turned back to Conrad. "You didn't ought to 'ave come, sir. You didn't ought to interfere." He sounded genuinely sorry.

The dog growled again. Conrad reached down and touched its head with the tips of his fingers.

"Not interfering. Chaperoning. This is no place for a young lady to be at this time of night on her own. As must be obvious."

Olivia giggled briefly, but the man with ginger hair appeared not to have heard. "I warned you, sir," he said sorrowfully.

Conrad took it as a bad sign that he was calling him "sir" again. He could feel Olivia trembling slightly, though whether from fear or excitement he was not sure. What a time to be high. He tightened his grip on her hand.

The short man said, "Why did you bring him, Olivia? You know the arrangement."

279

"For company, of course. And the name is Miss Pelham."
She sounded bored and a little contemptuous, as though she
were addressing an impertinent servant. "Have you forgotten what happened last time?"

So now I know who I've got with me, thought Conrad. It
occurred to him that maybe she was worth it after all.

The short man was not impressed. "That's very rash of
him. Rash of you both."

Olivia squeezed Conrad's hand as though for reassurance.
But when she answered her voice was as arrogant as before.
"Nobody pays you to pass judgment, Mr. Miller. I have
what you want. Just give me my envelope and we'll be on
our way."

"You seem to be missing the point," said Mr. Miller.
"There are too many people involved already. You can't say
you haven't been warned."

He stepped forward and the dog growled ominously. Conrad shifted slightly so that he was between Olivia and Mr.
Miller.

"I don't know what this is all about," he said to Olivia,
"but I think we should go."

Mr. Miller turned to his companion. "The man's a hu-
morist. He thinks Olivia's going to go without what she
came for."

The dog growled louder.

"You really didn't ought to interfere," repeated the man
with ginger hair in the same melancholy voice. "It ain't none
of your business."

"My business is to take care of this young lady," Conrad
replied pompously.

This seemed to enrage Mr. Miller. "Listen to the cock-
sucker," he said incredulously. "A knight in shining armor."

Conrad turned his back to him. "Let's go," he said to
Olivia. Holding her firmly by the hand, he began to walk
away.

Mr. Miller lunged forwards to stop him, and as he did so,

the dog began to bark furiously and snap at his ankles.

Conrad let go of Olivia's hand and pushed her in the small of the back. "Run," he said. Still moving backwards, he turned toward the two men.

Kim had his teeth fastened in Mr. Miller's ankle. The man was thrashing his leg around and trying ineffectually to pull something from his tight-fitting suede jacket. "Get this fucking brute off me," he shouted.

The man with ginger hair was standing stock-still a few yards behind him. His hands hung loosely at his sides and he seemed puzzled.

Mr. Miller went on shouting and kicking.

Finally the man with ginger hair reached into his belt and pulled out a tire lever, raised it, blundered forwards, and brought it down heavily on the dog's back.

It let go of Mr. Miller's leg and let out an eerie, yelping scream. It writhed on the ground, its legs twitching in tiny, frantic movements, as if it were running in its dreams.

The sound tore something in Conrad's head. "No," he yelled. He careered toward the man with ginger hair, ducked under the descending tire lever, and landed, with all his unaired weight and rage behind him, headfirst in his solar plexus.

Olivia began to scream.

The man with ginger hair gasped and doubled up on the ground with Conrad on top, flailing at him with his chainbound fist.

"Shitbag. Bastard." He was sobbing with rage and frustration. "I'll teach you." He pounded his fist into the man's face and the chain seared his knuckles.

Olivia screamed louder.

Off to the right, a voice yelled, "Over here."

Conrad struggled to his feet. He was out of breath and tears were streaming down his face. Behind him he could hear the dog yelping pitifully. He paused a moment to take aim, then kicked the man with ginger hair hard in the

281

crotch. The man doubled up again, made a sharp creaking noise with his mouth, and began to thrash his legs around like the dog.

As Conrad straightened up to kick him again, Mr. Miller jumped at him. Something metal grazed Conrad's left ear and smashed into his shoulder. His arm went dead. Then he was on the ground with Mr. Miller on top of him. He saw a raised fist holding a gun and made a grab at it with his good arm as it was about to descend.

They hung there a moment, straining together, their faces close as lovers. Conrad could smell the garlic on Mr. Miller's breath and his heavy violet aftershave. He was surprised how strong the man was. It was like trying to bend back an iron bar.

Then an arm locked around Mr. Miller's throat, pulling him back, and someone else grabbed at his gun. Conrad could see the fair-haired detective's face looming in the darkness, lips pulled back, eyes staring with the strain.

The revolver went off with a hollow, tinny noise and the struggling group seemed to disintegrate with the shock of it. Conrad was left lying on the wet ground while three shadowy figures heaved and grunted above him.

The gun went off again. He heard a bullet tear into the bushes behind him, then lay listening to the outraged colony of rooks shouting their grievances above Ken Wood.

He sat up, nursing his aching arm. There were people all around. A little way off he could hear Olivia sobbing, and a vaguely familiar voice murmuring to her consolingly.

He felt dizzy and slightly sick. He peered about in the confused gloom until he could make out patches of white on the ground. The dog was lying where it had dropped, a few yards from him. He poled himself over to it on his one good arm.

Its legs had stopped their frantic twitching, but it was shivering and panting noisily. There was foam mixed with blood at the corner of its mouth and its eyes were moving to and fro restlessly. Conrad pulled out his handkerchief and gently wiped its mouth. He brought his face down close to its face and fondled its ears. It looked at him reproachfully and made a rusty groaning noise deep in its throat. Conrad groaned back in answer and rubbed his cheek against the dog's. But when he moved his hand softly along its back the creature yelped shrilly and snapped at him.

"Its spine is broken," said Inspector Davies. "We should put it out of its misery." He was standing above Conrad and looking down at him quite kindly.

Conrad studied the policeman's cavalry twill trousers and desert boots. "Fuck you," he said.

Kim's breathing was shallower now and the foam had reappeared on its mouth. Conrad went on stroking its head.

Off to his left near the entrance to the wood, he could hear muffled groans and gasps. He turned and peered through the darkness. Evans was standing above Mr. Miller, kicking him rhythmically and contentedly—stomach, face, stomach—while Mr. Miller's plump body curved and straightened like a clockwork toy. Near him a policeman was kneeling on the back of the man with ginger hair, trying to force his arms together, while another policeman struggled with a pair of handcuffs.

"Who are these comedians?" he asked, but Davies walked off without replying.

Conrad went on murmuring to the dog and stroking its soft smooth face. Its breathing became steadily noiser and quicker, then suddenly seemed to stop. It made an effort to lift its head and looked at Conrad with great sadness. Then its head dropped back, it made a gargling noise and a stream of bright red blood poured from its mouth. It quivered violently, then was still.

Conrad got unsteadily to his feet. His shoulder ached, his

arm was numb, and he was crying like a child. There were people everywhere: policemen in uniform and burly, purposeful men in parkas and jeans. A siren whined in the distance, coming closer. Off in the open he could see Olivia standing with someone tall and bulky. She was leaning against him, her face into his shoulder, sobbing and giggling. The man's back was toward Conrad, but he recognized him immediately and was not surprised.

As Conrad came near, Abe took hold of Olivia's shoulders and shook her roughly. "That's enough," he said sharply. "Knock it off." Then he saw Conrad and grinned. "Hi there." He seemed embarrassed. "Sorry about the pooch," he said.

"Bullshit," Conrad replied.

The noise of the siren grew louder and weird bluish shadows began to appear among the trees. A police car came over the rise and stopped a little way from them, headlights glaring, its blue light whirling feverishly. Timothy got out of the back of the car and hurried over to them. He hesitated a moment, hands fluttering nervously, then put his arm tentatively around Olivia's shoulders. She began to sob and giggle again. He too seemed embarrassed.

Inspector Davies went up to the car and leaned into the front window. The radio squawked incoherently. He took the microphone from the driver and talked into it in a low voice for what seemed a long time. The radio squawked back briefly.

When he had finished, he walked briskly up to Abe and said, "Everything's under control, sir." He stood very stiff and straight, as if at attention. "They've detained Mrs. Staff at Heathrow. She had a ticket for Copenhagen."

Olivia went on sobbing weakly.

"That figures," said Abe.

Conrad turned on him angrily. "What's all this 'sir' crap?"

"A manner of speaking," Abe replied.

"Every time I hear the word 'sir' I reach for my paranoia."

"Don't take it so hard, old buddy."

Conrad shook his head wearily. "Mr. Middleman," he said, "what kind of a shitty life do you lead?"

"That's poker, friend. A guy's gotta make a living."

"Poker, my arse. And that's the trouble. I still don't know what game I've been playing in."

"Don't blame me. You insisted on being dealt in."

"All I asked was to live my miserable little life."

"Come now, Mr. Jessup," Davies said in his schoolmasterly voice. "You must admit I warned you continually to be careful about the company you keep."

Conrad looked at him with loathing. He longed to say something scathing and witty but it wouldn't come, so he fell back on his old faithful. "Fuck you," he said with feeling. It seemed, in the end, a perfectly satisfactory reply.

"Have you got the envelope from Miller?" Abe asked.

"Of course." Davies removed it carefully from his pocket and handed it to the American.

Olivia jerked suddenly away from Timothy and tried to snatch it. "That's mine," she said indignantly.

"No way." Abe fended her off with one hand and slipped the envelope into an inner pocket. "That's evidence."

"But you *promised*," she wailed.

"First you stand up in court against your girlfriend, then I'll see you right. Haven't I always?"

"What about tonight? You swore nothing would go wrong. You said everything was under control."

"Well, I was right. They didn't lay a finger on you."

"Thanks to him." She nodded at Conrad. "No thanks to you."

"We had to provoke 'em a little."

"They killed my dog," said Conrad.

"Yeah," Abe replied, "I'm real sorry about that."

"You could have pulled in those two thugs any time you wanted. Mrs. Staff too."

"For what? This time we've got a case."

"Some fucking case. A dead dog, a toy pistol, and a couple of envelopes."

"Every little bit helps."

"They're small fry. They're nothings."

Abe pushed his face angrily into Conrad's. "Don't give me a hard time again, pal. What did you expect? Ché Guevara? SMERSH? Baader-Meinhof? This is a fifth-rate operation like all the other operations. They were making a nuisance of themselves and we didn't have an excuse, we didn't have a case. Now we have. Of sorts."

"Of sorts," Conrad echoed. "What'll you shop them for, GBH or dogslaughter?"

Abe shook his head. "You and the big time. Come on down into the real world, man, before it's too late."

"Tell that to the poor bloody dog."

Conrad turned and began to walk away, back toward Jack Straw's Castle. In the boot of his car was his passport and an overnight case he had packed for his fantasy elopement with Olivia. What was left of his gambling money was in his wallet.

"Just one moment, Mr. Jessup."

Davies started after him, but Abe put a hand on the policeman's arm and murmured, "Take it easy. He's upset." Then he raised his voice and called after Conrad, "Where're you going to go?"

Conrad paused, already in the shadows of the trees. "Anywhere. Now I don't have the dog there's nothing to keep me."

"Where's anywhere?"

"I dunno," Conrad called back. "The Pacific, Tahiti, Gauguin. Hula-hula and *la vie de Bohème*. What've I got to lose?"

"You'll have to stay for the trial," Davies shouted sternly. "You're a material witness."

"What'll you use for money?" called Abe.

"I've still got a couple of thousand. Thanks to you."

It was amazing how dark it was outside the glare of the headlights. The figures of the people who had been running his life for months seemed flat and without detail, like shadow puppets, against the light.

"Two gee won't get you far."

"It's a start. Maybe I'll stop over in Vegas on the way."

Abe let out a roar of laughter. "They'll skin you alive. You think Lou's good. Those boys are real pros."

Conrad moved quietly back from tree to tree.

"When you get to your tropical island," Abe shouted, "what'll you do?"

"Take up backgammon and paint dogs," Conrad called back. "What else?"

Abe laughed again. "You'd make more money doing that in England."

"There are other things than money."

"Name 'em."

Olivia suddenly started toward the trees. Among the hulking shapes moving so busily in the clearing she seemed small and forlorn. The headlights threw a faint halo around her blond head. She stopped at the edge of the light and called, "What about me?"

"Abe'll pay you," Conrad shouted.

Then he turned and began to run, his numb arm hanging awkwardly at his side. As he ran, he threw away the dog's lead.

Abe bellowed with laughter.

Inspector Davies looked at him with distaste. "Shall we go after him, sir?"

The American shook his head. He was laughing so much that tears ran down his sweating face. "Where can he go," he managed, "that we can't pick him up when we want him? Let the poor schmuck have his day."

He cupped his hands around his mouth and roared into the darkness, "Go, man, go."

Conrad ran on.

ABOUT THE AUTHOR

A. ALVAREZ was born in London in 1929 and educated at
Oundle School and Corpus Christi College, Oxford. He has
lectured at Princeton University and has been both Poetry
Editor and a contributing editor to the *Observer*, as well as
drama critic for *The New Statesman*. He received the Vachel
Lindsay Prize for poetry and is the author of four volumes of
poetry, including *Autumn to Autumn*, recently published in
England.

Mr. Alvarez is also the author of *Beyond All This Fiddle*,
a collection of literary criticism; the highly praised *The
Savage God: A Study of Suicide;* and *Hers*, his first novel.
He lives in London with his wife and children.